JÓGVAN ISAKSEN (born 1950) is a leading author of contemporary Faroese crime fiction. His novels – eleven so far – feature the resilient detective Hannis Martinsson, who persists in his dogged investigations when wiser counsel might suggest a tactical retreat. The conflict is played out against the wild and beautiful, but harsh and unforgiving backdrop of the Faroe Islands, a remote community used to relying on its own resources and solving its own dilemmas.

As well as writing detective fiction, Isaksen teaches Faroese language and literature at the University of Copenhagen, and is the prize-winning author of several books on Faroese literature and writers, among them William Heinesen and Jørgen-Franz Jacobsen.

JOHN KEITHSSON is a Teaching Fellow in Scandinavian Studies at UCL, where he teaches Faroese, Swedish and Scandinavian Linguistics. John lived on the Faroe Islands for a time while completing his PhD on Faroese use of the Danish language.

Some other books from Norvik Press

Jørgen-Frantz Jacobsen: *Barbara* (translated by George Johnston)

Klaus Rifbjerg: *Terminal Innocence* (translated by Paul Larkin)

Kirsten Thorup: *The God of Chance* (translated by Janet Garton)

Jens Bjørneboe: *Moment of Freedom* (translated by Esther Greenleaf Mürer)
Jens Bjørneboe: *Powderhouse* (translated by Esther Greenleaf Mürer)
Jens Bjørneboe: *The Silence* (translated by Esther Greenleaf Mürer)

Johan Borgen: *The Scapegoat* (translated by Elizabeth Rokkan)

Arne Garborg: *The Making of Daniel Braut* (translated by Marie Wells)

Svava Jakobsdóttir: *Gunnlöth's Tale* (translated by Oliver Watts)

Viivi Luik: *The Beauty of History* (translated by Hildi Hawkins)

Henry Parland: *To Pieces* (translated by Dinah Cannell)

Amalie Skram: *Lucie* (translated by Katherine Hanson and Judith Messick)
Amalie Skram: *Fru Inés* (translated by Katherine Hanson and Judith Messick)
Amalie and Erik Skram: *Caught in the Enchanter's Net: Selected Letters* (edited and translated by Janet Garton)

Walpurgis Tide

by

Jógvan Isaksen

Translated from the Faroese and with a Translator's Note
by John Keithsson

Foreword by Dominic Hinde and Author's Note
by Jógvan Isaksen

Norvik Press
2016

Norvik Press Series B: English Translations of Scandinavian Literature,
no. 66

A catalogue record for this book is available from the British Library.

ISBN: 978-1-909408-24-1

Norvik Press gratefully acknowledges the generous support of the
Mentanargrunni Landsins towards the publication of this translation.

Norvik Press
Department of Scandinavian Studies
University College London
Gower Street
London WC1E 6BT
United Kingdom
Website: www.norvikpress.com
E-mail address: norvik.press@ucl.ac.uk

Managing editors: Elettra Carbone, Sarah Death, Janet Garton,
C. Claire Thomson.

Cover design and layout: Marita Fraser
Cover photographs by Schnuffel2002 and Vincent van Zeijst.

Contents

Walpurgis Tide

Foreword

Death on the Beaches

The Faroe Islands are a contradiction in terms. A tiny cluster of standing stones on the plain of the North Atlantic, they embody a romantic ideal of traditional society supposedly long lost on the European mainland, yet the archipelago is also modern in the extreme, with a higher quality of life than most of the rest of the continent. On a sunny day, walking the razor ridges that bisect each of its long islands and watching crystal water tumble hundreds of metres over basalt cliffs into the flat sea, the Faroes present themselves as a pastoral utopia where the violence of industrial society is barely visible and where the benefits of global development and local tradition harmoniously co-exist. The green hillsides, crystal waters and black cliffs are alluringly filmic, and onto their canvas people project many different things.

The islands have been hailed as a model to follow by Scottish nationalists, as a Germanic Christian Eden by members of the far right, and most famously as the last bastion of a barbaric primitive practice by the international environmental movement. The yearly *grindadráp*, or whale hunt, is synonymous with the international identity of the Faroese and is a regular fixture in the annual global news cycle.

Early on in *Walpurgis Tide*, its narrator and reluctant detective Hannes Martinsson is challenged by a British activist to help find the killer behind two deaths related to the hunt, or the country will be 'shut down.' The international environmentalists in Jógvan Isaksen's novel verge on caricatures, but then this is, perhaps, merely the logical corollary of the novel's approach to the Faroes themselves. What the international environmentalists share with the Lutheran churchgoers of the Faroes is a moral certainty in tandem with their identity. If Lutheranism is the Faroese national religion, environmentalism is the global post-national religion.

One of the uncomfortable truths of international campaigning, be it aid, environmental work or human rights, is that it often has unintended consequences or can come across as culturally ham-fisted. What has taken place in the Faroes with whaling is also threatening to engulf the wider North, as international mineral and fossil extraction companies face off against the assembled forces of the green movement from Alaska to Scandinavia. Though different in many ways, there are parallels in this respect between the Faroes and Denmark's other overseas territory, Greenland, where prospectors and environmental organisations alike are engaged in a constant struggle to implement their different visions of the future, more often than not without the local population at its centre.

Like whaling in the Faroes, Greenland has had to contend with opposition to its traditional marine mammal hunts. Ultimately, though, it is environmental change that may prove to be the nail in the coffin for these age-old rituals. Applying a moral lens to whaling obscures its systematic disruption of the shared global environment. Global warming, ocean acidification, oil spills and air pollution can all be quantified by their impact on the international situation. Their effects can be rendered in numbers, but how do you apply value to the life of a whale if the whales are not endangered?

What is it that makes the annual harvest of whale meat in the Faroes worse than venison from Scottish shooting estates? Is it the sight of blood in the water, or is it the knowledge that this is a community activity? For crime fiction there is something strangely captivating to the outside world about the consensus of a closed community, and this is the premise on which *Walpurgis Tide* rests. Whether it be an island, a village or a social set, there is always mystery in tacit agreement. It reminds us that morality is a group activity.

This intrigue is exactly what will have made many people buy this book – reading foreign fiction does not merely give readers a different story with a new set of names, it gives them access to another world and its rules in a way that mere ethnographic description cannot do. Exoticism sells, but the whole point of translation is to normalise what might otherwise remain a mystery.

Widely translated from Faroese into Danish, and in Denmark as often as the Faroes, Isaksen is a liminal writer in the same way that an author like Alasdair Campbell mediates between the Hebrides and mainland Britain and between Gaelic and English. The largest of the Western Isles, Harris and Lewis, are not entirely unlike the Faroes, both physically with their Atlantic storms, dramatic hills and abandoned whaling stations, and culturally with their impenetrable language and sense of difference. They also possess their own version of the *grindadráp* in the yearly Guga hunt for young gannets to the skerry of Sula Sgeir.

When I made a journalistic inquiry about covering the Guga hunt, a member of this annual pilgrimage from Ness at Lewis' northern tip told me he was afraid of how the world outside might judge the ritual. Each year a boat of men set sail into the North Atlantic to harvest Guga for consumption back on Lewis. An old tradition that once supplied the community with food is now a tradition only, the need cultural rather than material. The participant I spoke to admitted that people might think their method of execution (hitting the birds on the head with a stick) was 'not politically correct.'

Perhaps the Guga men of Ness have intruded less into the emotions of the mainstream because they have not yet been boarded by Sea Shepherd or drawn the attention of Greenpeace, though there have been several armchair petitions to stop the practice. Most people would likely agree that the life of a gannet is worth less than that of a whale, but rarely are we challenged to articulate and justify that hierarchy. Asked why, we would likely grapple with it awhile, before admitting that the ethics of the community tell us that it is true. Modern, civilised people do not kill whales; everybody knows that.

The American anthropologist Kay Milton has described a process called the 'Myth of the Primitive' in European and American environmentalism that attempts to locate a pristine natural order in undeveloped societies. Based on the idea of the non-European living in harmony with nature, cultures from American First Peoples to Australian indigenous groups and the Arctic fringes of the North Atlantic live in cooperation (and closer contact) with nature, or so goes the trope. Is the crime of the Faroese to be too recognisably modern to indulge in such practices? Does having cable TV to watch Champions League football mean that a threshold of modernity has been passed?

In 2015 the Faroe Islands did the unthinkable and beat former champions Greece in qualifying for the European football championships. The media portrayed the victory as a brave group of fishermen from the very edge of the continent overcoming the cradle of European civilisation, but as Isaksen makes clear, the Faroes have a cultural heritage to rival the maritime states of the Mediterreanean as well as their football teams. As the Faroese football team celebrated in the dressing room in Piraeus, it was a victory for one of the few things apart from the whale hunt that gives the tiny nation any sort of international profile in its own right and a reminder that the Faroes are not merely a far-flung part of Denmark. The international protestors holding 'Shame on Denmark' banners to protest against whale slaughter mis-read the situation – to call the Faroe Islands Danish is akin to calling the Hebrides English. A 2015 Reuters agency report on the hunt carried the picture caption 'Whales being slaughtered on a beach in Denmark.' It was technically correct but culturally blind.

The Danish government is as averse to the whale hunt as the international environmental movement. But just as in Greenland, where 'Danification' has had its social consequences, the legacy of Denmark's North Atlantic empire still looms large over local politics in the Faroes. In any country that has been under the control of a distant government, attempts to influence from the outside and 'civilise' are likely to be met with resistance.

This is not to say that the Faroe Islands are immune to environmental problems – the territory recently flirted with becoming an oil-rich micro state, only to be defeated at the final hurdle when reserves were found just outside of its territorial waters. Much of the whale meat harvested with each *grindadráp* is unfit for consumption due to the presence of toxins and heavy metals, and the rising temperature of the North Atlantic will seriously alter the vital fishing grounds around the islands. These are not problems the Faroese can solve by themselves, any more than the outside world can stop Faroese whaling.

This friction between the inside and the outside is the crux of *Walpurgis Tide*. Isaksen's reluctant hero is tasked with being the international community's inside man in a complex balancing act, asking questions of both his employers and his countrymen. A crime has been committed, but as Isaksen makes clear, understanding how and why is a two-way street.

Dominic Hinde

Dominic Hinde is a writer, academic and journalist focusing on Northern Europe and the environment.

Author's Note

For many years the Faroe Islands have come under intense pressure from international environmental organisations that have threatened to boycott Faroese exports unless the Faroese abandon the killing of pilot whales. The vast majority of Faroese consider these attacks to be unfair as they don't see themselves to be doing anything not done in slaughterhouses the world over: mammals are killed in order to be eaten. The pilot whale is not an endangered species and the Faroese 'harvest' up to a maximum of 2 percent of the whale stock a year. When the Faroese ask the environmental organisations why it is not acceptable to kill whales, but the killing of sheep, pigs and cows is fine, the response more often than not is: 'You just can't.'

The Faroese whale hunt has a long history. How long, we don't know, but since 1584 all whales killed have been recorded. We have, therefore, exceptional statistical material which shows that the number of whales killed today corresponds with that from over 400 years ago. The whale hunt on the Faroe Islands has never been about money, but about food and gaining the necessary vitamins from the whale blubber above all. Once the hunt is over, the meat and blubber are divided according to time-honoured rules among those who took part and the inhabitants of local villages. Throughout history the hunt has been of immeasurable importance in sustaining the lives of those on these remote islands.

A whale hunt is violent to observe and traditionally women, children and priests were not allowed to witness the hunt itself as it is not something for sensitive souls.

Most whale hunts are over within a few minutes, but that short time period is grim and brutal. The sea turns red and the whales often fight desperately to escape. Practically all Faroese accepted this barbarism as a necessary condition of life on the Faroe Islands and a God-given gift. The twenty-first century, however, is unlike those that preceded it and many Faroese have begun to question the necessity of the whale hunt. Today we can survive without the meat and blubber, the hunts are damaging our fish exports (by far the most important source of income for the Faroese) and the whales are highly contaminated by heavy metals.

Doctors on the Faroe Islands generally recommend that whale meat is not eaten too often as there is a considerable risk of mercury poisoning. For several decades they have discouraged pregnant women from eating any meat or blubber at all. There is a fateful irony in the fact that, by and large, the environmentalists come from the very countries that have polluted the world's oceans to the extent that whales, which are at the end of the food chain, are no longer safe to eat. Many on the Faroe Islands think, therefore, that the whale hunt will eventually come to an end because whale meat will actually become poisonous.

While this fact has been accepted by parts of the Faroese population, there is no great appetite for being threatened by militant environmental organisations who seek to stop whaling. There is a common view that perhaps efforts should be directed towards halting the pollution of the oceans, which if not stopped will eventually kill all whales.

It is in the midst of this conflict between an ancient Faroese tradition and a modern world that doesn't care for that tradition that the novel *Walpurgis Tide* came to be written. I wanted to present Faroese attitudes as well as the counter-arguments of the environmentalists. The Faroe Islands is a little country with only 48,000 inhabitants, who feel as if the whole world is against them. Several leading voices from the Faroese business community think that the hunt should be stopped as it is no longer necessary for most Faroese. Others argue that the country should never give in to pressure from animal welfare fighters who have a tendency to put the rights of plants and animals above those of humankind. The opposing sides have difficulty communicating and so yell at each other.

All of this could have been detailed in a non-fiction book, but not by someone who is a man of letters rather than a historian. On the other hand, I had already written several crime novels and I thought that the subject was perfect for that treatment. I undertook thorough research into the whale hunt and then I incorporated the Faroese fish farms. These are becoming the Faroes' chief source of income, but there is a constant risk that disease could destroy the whole thing. The Faroese economy is far from diverse: everything is connected to fish. If the fish farms could be developed and kept disease-free, the country's economy would be somewhat more secure. The search for oil in Faroese waters, which is also discussed in the book, is another hope for the future. Both of these sources of income remain uncertain and therefore opponents of the whale hunt can easily put pressure on the Faroe Islands.

The dual intention of this book has from the beginning been to tell an exciting story, while at the same time detailing the Faroe Islands' conflict with the outside world as regards the whale hunt. Whether or not I have succeeded in this is for the reader to decide.

Jógvan Isaksen
September 2015

Translated by John Keithsson

Prologue

The Faroese are aggressive and kill pilot whales because they have so much mercury in their blood.

American doctor at a conference in 2003

The whale hunt was over within ten minutes. Although the pod of pilot whales wasn't large, it had been difficult to steer it in towards the bay at Sandagerði. But once it was on course, the whales were beached without any problems. A large team of hunters waded out to cut their throats. The waters gradually became red. The fleet of boats was so large that they got in each other's way; the air turned blue with shouting and swearing.

The hillside and the slope up to the road that led to the hospital were teeming with spectators. These were somewhat fewer in number on the Argir side of the bay. It was the middle of April, so there weren't many tourists about, but the call to the whale hunt still tugged at the hearts of the Faroese. Even though these days that call was only whispered, there were always swarms of people whenever a hunt took place.

Down at the foreshore a woman and a man in their twenties were taking photographs of a whale pup which had gone astray among the rocks. The interest they showed in the poor thing revealed that they were foreigners. As did their clothes. Both were dressed in dark blue anoraks, jeans and white lace-up wellington boots.

The pup squealed and people called for one of the men on the sand to put him out of his misery. The man, who was soaked up to his waist, ran along the stones with a bloodstained knife in his hand. When he got to the pair with the camera he roughly pushed them aside and cut the pup's throat. Then he briskly returned to the beach.

The woman in the dark anorak sat down on a rock and cried, while the man alternately photographed the pup and the hunter's back as he walked away.

Suppertime was approaching. There was nothing left to look at and the spectators began to make their way to their cars. The majority of the boats sailed off towards Tórshavn to register their participation in the hunt with the sheriff. Some of the cars were heading that way too. A few boats remained which had already started to haul the dead whales towards the quay at Vestara Bryggja. After being marked the whales would wait there until the all-important slips of paper came back from the sheriff. Only then could they be divided up among all those who had taken part.

At nine o'clock the slips appeared and people rushed down to the quayside. Some had had more than a sip to drink and were chattering loudly. Laughter and cursing rolled into the darkness, as men sought out the whale meat they owned. The area around the quay was poorly lit, which complicated the dividing process. Washing-up bowls and buckets were lying everywhere, making it difficult to get about. Nevertheless the work was quickly underway and after a short time the blubber had been cut away, revealing the reddish-brown meat.

The poor street-lighting and the light drizzle combined to give a sinister atmosphere to the picture of bloodied men and partly cut whales down at the quayside.

Suddenly a voice cried out.

At the furthermost edge of the quay, where the lighting was poorer still, were two whales that had not yet been divided. Their insides were halfway-out, creating a grey-blue mass on the ground between them. The man who had yelled pointed at the bundle of intestines, beneath which two pairs of white lace-up wellington boots were protruding.

Part One

It would be better if the Faroese ate each other rather than whales.

Member of the British Labour Party

One

The smell of turpentine was overwhelming.

Every window was open, but it made very little difference. At regular intervals I was still forced to stick my head out to get some fresh air.

The weather was beautiful, as was the view down to the glassy harbour and the boats – and behind that the shipyard and the Bacalao fish factory. Calm and still were the order of the day on that Saturday afternoon in April. People were pottering about on a couple of the boats, but the area around the quay was otherwise completely deserted. The world seemed clean and pure.

I was painting my new office, but the smell hadn't come from my painting. An artist had had a studio in this space before me and, judging by the stench, he had lived on turpentine. He had now moved to the other side of the bay, and the large attic had been offered to me for an absurdly low price. The state owned the building on úti í Bakka, but because they did not intend, or perhaps could not afford, to do anything with it, they were very happy to see people in it and hoped that whoever occupied it would keep it in good nick.

The building was in such a bad state that it would have been impossible to ask for any further rent. The roof leaked, the doors were so crooked that it was almost impossible to close them, let alone lock them, and the steps up to my office on the top floor were unsteady and dangerous. One of these days I was going to fall through and wake up in the cellar – if I ever woke again. The cellar, which had previously been a mechanic's workshop, was some four metres deep and had a concrete floor.

Nevertheless, I was very satisfied with both the building and my office. They were in an excellent location, cost next to nothing and had a splendid view. I had found my desk and chair in the classifieds in the *Dimmalætting* newspaper, as well as both white fold-up chairs. On the table was my new, navy-blue phone. Otherwise there was nothing else in the room, apart from the tins of paint on newspapers on the floor. But in my mind I could see bookcases, a sofa for the occasional nap, and pictures on the wall. Maybe I would be able to convince the artist who had been here before to sell me a painting or two for a reasonable price?

A Faroese home or a Faroese office without paintings is nigh on unthinkable. You're not really Faroese if you don't have some canvasses on the wall depicting aspects of the Faroese landscape. The quality is less important. Oil paintings ideally. When you buy yourself some furniture, you automatically buy yourself some paintings. Full stop.

With the paint roller I painted the walls as white as snow to cover up what had been there before and whistled and hummed 'Surfin' in the USA' as best I could.

Of course it's true that the Beach Boys and I are hardly from the same background, and I've certainly never been on a surfboard, but I have grown up with so much American culture that I consider myself to be partially resident over there. Donald Duck, Illustrated Classics, Davy Crockett, Captain Micky, Elvis Presley, John Wayne, Humphrey Bogart; these were my spiritual bread and butter when I was growing up . I felt just as at home with American rock as I did with the Faroese chain dance. Sometimes more so. In a different way in any case.

Maybe I'm not really a proper Faroeman? Or maybe that's what being a proper Faroeman is?

Nevertheless, it's strange that although I've travelled so much in the big wide world, I've never been to America. Perhaps it's my subconscious and I just don't want to spoil the dreams of my youth? Or maybe just chance, which seems to govern most things in life.

After many years abroad – most of these in Copenhagen and Rome – I had returned home to work a good ten years or so ago. I had got a job as a journalist, found myself a girlfriend and bought half a house on Jóannes Paturssonargøta in Tórshavn. But when the economic crisis of the nineties hit and continued for several years, and my girlfriend didn't find me fun any longer, I left the country like so many others. My house was rented out, most of my belongings were stored down in the basement or up in the attic , and the rest I either threw out or took with me to Denmark. But once we'd come into not only a new century, but a new millennium, the Faroese economy had picked up and was running quite nicely. Fish prices were higher than they usually were, the sea-farming industry had been developed and an oil industry seemed to be in prospect. Many in this superstitious little country had no doubt that they were soon to be living in the Promised Land. Others were more doubtful and felt that the economy had become stagnant and that a recession was on the cards.

Whatever the case, I had moved back home, but only had a faint idea of what I should do; maybe some writing for foreign newspapers and magazines – I had made a living from this before – and perhaps some consultancy on the side. Consultants were all the rage. As an old journalist I knew what to do to get to the bottom of something or if someone just wanted to know all the details about something as soon as possible. I thought I might – with the little thought I had given to it – be able to combine two worlds. If there was no consultancy work to be had for a time, I could write my articles, and if jobs came along, my articles could be put on the backburner. The articles I wrote about the Faroe Islands and Faroese affairs were rarely urgent.

There was a frosted pane of glass in the door to the office. I had considered getting my name and occupation painted on it, but things aren't generally done that way any more. It costs too much. At the place where I ordered the plastic sign which I would have to glue to the door, I said that my name was Sam Spade. When I was asked how to spell Spade, I gave my real name. A joke that the other person doesn't get is not particularly funny.

The sign for the door said: *Hannis Martinsson. Consultant.* The sign for the front door downstairs said the same, but with the appendix: *Top Floor.*

An hour later, I put the roller down and looked at the finished job. My conclusion was the same as that other great workman many moons ago: I saw that it was good. Happy with myself, I took out a cigarette, lit it and leaned out of the window to smoke.

It was just after four and the sun continued to warm the land and the people. I looked left to the south and saw that there were a few boats fishing out on the Argir coast. It wouldn't have been a bad idea to have gone out myself to catch some fish for a dinner or two, but it was too late to go out now. And anyway I didn't know whether the friend I usually went out fishing with would have the time or the inclination to come out with me.

I could hear noise from the shipyard. A badly rusted fishing boat that still had a little yellow paint on it was in the dry dock for repair. Now and then there was a blue light from the deck. They were welding.

I looked up to the Kirkjubøreyn mountain range, and then along the Velbastaðhálsur over the Steinafall and Húsareyn ridges to Hotel Føroyar, which also enjoyed a beautiful view over the town.

By the quay just below my window and all along the quayside there was a fleet of boats so large that it could be compared with the Greek fleet at Salamis in its day. If you included the boats in the other bay, it was perhaps even on a par with the Persian fleet. And just as the Greek ships during that ancient battle were moored side by side, it was also rare for these boats to be freed from the land. They were more like grazing sheep, tied up in the field.

I had finished my cigarette and now all that was left to do was to clean the roller and paintbrushes before I was done for the day.

Then I heard a noise on the steps. A dark shadow stopped on the other side of the glass pane.

For a moment there was complete silence.

Who could it be? Few people knew about my office, and those that did would not have stopped outside the door.

A job? Unlikely. I hadn't advertised in the newspapers and although I had applied to be included in the yellow pages of the telephone book – under both Consultants and Information Services – it hadn't yet come out. Without a doubt it was someone who wanted a painting as a wedding gift and who didn't know that the artist had moved.

There was a knock at the door.

Two

'Come in!' I called loudly. In my mind I was already pointing across the bay: 'On the top floor of that concrete block over there is where your Faroese landscapes now come to life.' I was suddenly stopped in my tracks as a tall, dark-haired man came through the door. He asked me in English:

'Is this Hannis Martinsson's office?'

'It is,' I answered in English. 'Or rather,' I added with a smile, 'it will be an office once I've finished putting it together.'

The serious expression on his face didn't change.

'And are you Hannis Martinsson?'

'Yes,' I answered, wondering who on earth might have sent him my way.

'You're in the business of finding things out?' he continued.

The foreigner was about my age – well into his forties, that is. His facial features were sharp and he had dark brown eyes. I'm somewhat taller than average and this guy was considerably taller than I was. At least six foot three, I reckoned. But it was his clothes that really marked him out as unusual. They couldn't be bought in just any shop, neither here nor elsewhere. The navy-blue suit was without a doubt tailored, the black turtleneck was made from the most expensive wool and the shoes had Gucci buckles. He had a dark blue woollen coat around his shoulders, Italian style. He was as unlike the man in the street as the Danish High Commissioner in gala uniform at Ólav's Wake, the Faroese national celebration.

'Yes, that was the idea,' I answered, suddenly conscious of my own attire: a white vest, torn jeans, replete with paint stains, and badly worn boat shoes. For some reason I felt inferior – God knows why.

'I want you to carry out an assignment for me.' His tone was decisive; there was no indication that he was asking me whether I'd like to take this on. I was just to say 'yes' and 'amen'.

The foreigner looked around the office. Although his face remained expressionless, it probably wasn't because he was so blown away by what he saw.

'I don't really know,' I responded cautiously, trying to dry my hands on a piece of cloth. 'It's going to take some time before this place is ready and I wasn't planning to get going for at least a month yet…'

'Does it matter what the office looks like?' the man interrupted. 'I see you have a telephone, a desk and a chair. What else do you need in an office? In any case, at least some of the investigative work I'll need you to do for me will require you to work elsewhere.'

'Hang on, hang on,' I lifted up my hands to stop the well-dressed man. 'Before you get too carried away, there are a few things I'd like to know. OK?'

The foreigner looked at me coldly, but nodded all the same.

'How did you find me? I've only just moved back to the Faroes, and suddenly you come here with a job for me to do.' I knew I was getting agitated, but I tried to control myself. It doesn't take much to make you defensive when you feel like the lesser man.

'The Greenpeace membership list.'

'What?' Now I was stumped.

'I needed a man as soon as possible to do some investigative work for me in the Faroe Islands and you were on the Danish membership list. And you're a journalist who does odd jobs.'

He said this as though it were completely natural that he should have access to this information. As far as I was aware, no one knew – and I had almost forgotten it myself – that for a short time back in the eighties I had been a member of Greenpeace. I wasn't proud of it, but I wasn't exactly ashamed of it either. We're all allowed to make mistakes. The French were carrying out nuclear tests in the Pacific, so I joined. But once I'd had enough of Brigitte Bardot, seal pups and whales, I cancelled my membership. Evidently they'd never actually removed my name.

'How do you have access to old Greenpeace membership lists? I mean, they're not in the public domain.'

'Different environmental agencies work together,' he said matter-of-factly. 'And I found your address on the internet. It also said that you lived on Jóannes Paturssonargøta. It was obviously just luck that I found you here.'

The telephone company had evidently added me to their website very quickly. But what did he mean when he said that environmental agencies worked together? Where was he going with this?

'Were there other things you needed to know?' He looked mockingly at me.

'You bet there are. Firstly, I want to know who you are, and secondly, what it is you want me to do. And why.'

'Who I am is hardly important, but if it helps, I can tell you my name. Mark Robbins. I'm from Britain and I work for Guardians of the Sea, or GOS. That's the important bit.'

'Right, but…,' I tried to keep my thoughts together in my surprise, but in vain. The foreigner, who now had a name, carried on coolly.

'No doubt you've heard about the two Brits that were found dead among the whales two weeks ago. Their throats were cut.'

There was fire in Mark Robbins' eyes. He wasn't completely unaffected by this.

'They also worked for Guardians of the Sea.' He stopped and looked down. 'They were just 25 and 26 years old when they were killed. Jenny McEwan and Stewart Peters.' He looked me straight in the eye. 'I'm the one who sent them to the Faroe Islands to observe the whale hunt and get material for us.'

So that's what it was about, I thought. His conscience is troubling him.

As if he could read my thoughts, Mark Robbins added, 'It's not that I have a guilty conscience. They died doing their duty for GOS.' In true English style he pronounced each letter of the acronym separately. 'But we would like to get our hands on the bastards who took their lives and maybe get the whale hunt banned that way.'

Wouldn't you know it, I mumbled to myself. I had heard about the dead pair among the whales down at the quayside. The story had made headline news not just in the Faroe Islands, but elsewhere too. Unfortunately for the Faroe Islands, other environmentalists had also been there while the whales were being divided and had filmed both the human bodies and the whales. The pictures went global. When you saw them on the BBC or CNN, you could see why you should be against the whale hunt. The dead whales and the dead environmentalists lay side-by-side, so the viewer got the impression that the Faroese weren't really bothered whether they cut the throats of whales or people.

We didn't need to wait long for a response from the rest of the world. The environmental agencies, led by Guardians of the Sea, called for a boycott of the Faroe Islands. If the Faroese would not stop killing whales immediately, other countries were to block them from all international cooperation. In those cases where the Faroe Islands were represented by Denmark, Denmark would be boycotted, unless it put pressure on the islands over the whaling question. Such little time had passed that no international bodies had put anything into motion yet, but extremist groups such as the Environmental Investigation Agency, EIA, and Sea Shepherd, led by the extremist, Paul Watson, had organised protests in Britain, Germany and the USA. For now.

And now one of these people, who hardly bore the Faroe Islands any good will, was standing in my office, wanting me to work for him.

'Isn't it a little cheeky to come here and ask for my help to make life difficult for my own country? You Brits don't need to be so hard on the Faroese in your attempts to stop the whale hunt. Your polluting of the seas will soon make the meat and blubber inedible. So at some point the Faroese will have to stop killing whales.'

29

I was becoming agitated again. Mark Robbins stared at me, completely unmoved. Once I'd stopped talking, he asked me coldly:

'Are you finished?'

I shrugged my shoulders and nodded.

'We can talk about what you said another time. We might not actually disagree as much as you think. But for now we have common interests.'

Three

'How could we have common interests?' I asked, surprised.

'War and love make strange bedfellows, eh?' Mark Robbins smiled before continuing: 'You need to find the ones who killed Jenny and Stewart. And when you've found them, you'll give us their names. If this isn't done within…,' he stopped for a moment, 'shall we say a week? That should be long enough. If we don't get the names within a week, those of us in GOS, together with other international environmental agencies, will see to it that in the future it will be extremely difficult to live in this country. And believe me, it won't be hard, even if things seem to be going reasonably well for you at the moment. Don't forget you're pretty small.'

The well-dressed man was so definite in what he said that I was inclined to believe him. Nevertheless I wasn't happy about it, and protested:

'I'm sure you could make life difficult for us, but after a while everything will be forgotten.'

'Not this time. Two members of GOS have been killed in connection with one of your whale hunts. Think hard and no doubt you'll remember what we did to France when they sank one of our ships in New Zealand and a photographer died. Just imagine what we could do to the Faroe Islands.'

I remembered that the boat, *Rainbow Warrior*, had been sunk in the harbour at either Auckland or Wellington in New Zealand and that there had been a huge scandal when it came out that the French intelligence service had been behind it. The French had been forced to exile one or two members of their intelligence service to a Pacific Island for a number of years. The two were let off eventually, but the scandal caused a lot of problems for France.

'Yeah?' I asked hesitantly.

'Within a few days we'd be able to see to it that not a single Faroese fish would reach the shores of either Europe or the USA. Similarly, just like that, we could make the oil companies lose interest in the Faroe Islands. And if Denmark tries to help the Faroes, we'll go after them too. Denmark is also a rather small country, and there's nothing to say they'd want to sacrifice themselves for the Faroe Islands.'

No, I thought. The way that things between the two countries had been over the past few years meant that the Danes were very unlikely to put their heads on the block for the Faroese. But although I was now starting to believe the man, I still wanted to get everything straight.

'How are you planning to get other countries to boycott the Faroe Islands? You've been after us for so many years, but it's never really bothered us.'

'The difference is that now two people have died. And there are those pictures of them between the whales,' he added. 'The pictures have already been shown on television screens the world over, although no real connection has yet been made with Faroese exports. Dead bodies on the television won't cause much of a commotion. Maybe a bit of a fuss here and there. Like the protests we've seen over the last couple of days.'

Now Mark Robbins was smiling, and a shiver ran down my spine.

'I'll give you an example of what we can do. And this is just small time.' He put his hand into the inside pocket of his jacket and took out a silver cigarette case. He opened the case, took out a cigarette and put it in his mouth. The case went back into the pocket, and with a gold lighter he lit it. He didn't offer me one. It probably didn't even occur to him.

Once he had inhaled and breathed out the smoke, he continued: 'There are increasing numbers of private broadcasters these days that compete for advertisers by airing more and more infotainment, news designed to entertain. No one has the opportunity – or can be bothered

– to check whether these news items are true or not. If you don't broadcast it, your competitor will. The result is that these stations transmit all kinds of crap. More often than not, it's complete lies from beginning to end. So we can make up whatever we want to about the Faroe Islands and thereby get people across the world to demand that all the terrible things that take place here come to an end.'

The thought of what GOS could potentially do to these islands in the middle of the Atlantic if they wanted to seemed to make Mark Robbins happy. I was beginning to think that I probably didn't care for this man.

'And if you want an example of what these television stations can come up with, I'll give you one.' He exhaled a cloud of smoke which floated up to the ceiling.

I said nothing and waited.

'In Germany one TV producer made up a load of false reports that were broadcast by well-known stations. One programme accused Ikea, among others, of exploiting poor Indian children in their production process. You saw the poor kids on film. It was a total lie. They had paid some children from Central Europe to pretend to be Indian kids that worked for Ikea. All of the accusations had been made up, but they caused Ikea big problems. And Ikea is more powerful than the Faroes.'

I remained silent, but was now sure that there was something in what Mark Robbins was saying. I remembered the scandal with Ikea and the children, but hadn't realised, I'm ashamed to say, that the whole thing had been made up. With their fragile economy and the discovery of oil still a dream, it wasn't going to be hard to bleed the Faroe Islands dry. I could always just keep myself to myself – I was hardly a crusader – but on the other hand, getting hold of information was my line of business. Part of it, in any case.

'I think you understand the situation.' Mark Robbins' voice interrupted my thoughts. 'Find out who killed Jenny McEwan and Stewart Peters, and we'll go back to how things were before the murders. More or less.'

'Oh, really?' Now it was my turn to be sarcastic. The

brown eyes flashed with anger, but I continued: 'There's still something I don't get. Why do you want me to investigate the murders? The police are working on the case.'

'That's true. They've been looking into it for a fortnight and haven't got anywhere. A journalist isn't restricted in the same way as the police are. He can dig where they can't.'

'That's as may be. But if the police haven't been able to get to the bottom of this yet, it's obviously much more easily said than done. They have so many resources at their disposal, while I on the other hand have next to nothing.'

'Whatever,' answered Mark Robbins, brushing aside my protestations with a simple wave of the hand. 'I don't care how you manage to find the murderers, just that you do find them.'

'How do you know that several people were involved in killing your members? Why not just one?'

'Who says I think that there are several of them?' he asked, answering my question with one of his own.

'You just said that as long as I find the *murderers*, everything will be fine. And before, you called them "the bastards".'

'I see.' He looked at me from top to toe. I thought I could detect a glimpse of acknowledgement in his expression. But I was probably wrong.

'So far we do know from your police that Jenny and Stewart weren't killed among the whales down at the quayside. No traces of their blood have been found there, so they must have been moved from somewhere else. They weren't dragged there, but carried, which leads us to believe that there must have been two people involved in any case. Possibly more.'

He put one hand in his coat pocket, took out a white envelope and placed it on the table.

'Here's an advance of one thousand pounds and all you need to know. Find out sufficient information for us and you'll get a further five grand. I don't reckon that's bad for a week's work.'

I didn't pick up the envelope. I could hardly have wanted this job less. And I had no idea how I would even go about starting with this one. On the other hand, I was practically broke after the move and needed the money.

'If – and I repeat – *if* I find anything out, how do I get hold of you?'

'Don't you worry about that,' Mark Robbins replied. 'I'm flying back to England tonight and I have your number. So don't call us, we'll call you,' he added mockingly.

With that he disappeared through the door and I heard him walk down the stairs.

Four

'Well, there's a rock and a hard place', I said to myself. If I helped Guardians of the Sea I'd destroy my reputation, or worse. And if I didn't help them, we'd all lose out. A dichotomy, you might say. Or maybe even a true dilemma, something my logics teacher used to talk about back in the day.

Yes, like so many I studied philosophy at university for a few months. Like most of the others planning on taking that course, I also went to a private tutor whose job it was to bang the basics into us. When he was going through dilemmas with us, he used a picture where there was a drop of several hundred metres on one side and a raging bull on the other. This was evidently a dilemma you couldn't come out of alive. Jump off and you die. Head for the bull and it kills you. You have to do one or the other, but in both cases the ending is the same. But the teacher said that there was a way, and that was to grab the bull by the horns, as it were, or to try to slip between the two.

How I could get out of this one was hard to say. How could I grab the bull's horns, and what would I do once I had? Would I creep up between the horns or would I do a somersault, like on those ancient paintings from Crete? None of this seemed particularly useful to me, but maybe that was because the premise and the conclusion were wrong?

What did I know?

I sat there for a while staring into space. It was no laughing matter. Being forced to work for an organisation that had never wished the Faroes anything other than ill. But if I turned the job down, the Faroes would become an international scapegoat, and things were bad enough as they were.

No, I'd have to try to find out who killed those two youngsters. I sighed, longing for a glass of schnapps, but my office hadn't become so civilised that there was a bottle of the good stuff in the bottom drawer of the desk. It was easy enough for Mark Robbins to use me as an errand boy. By this evening he would probably be sitting in some cosy pub in London. Or in his nightclub.

The envelope was still on the desk, glaring at me. Let it glare.

After some bad experiences environmental organisations weren't rated highly among the Faroese, although you could get people to admit that they did some good. They just didn't do it here. Most people could support their attempts to stop the Sellafield nuclear power station in England polluting the seas with radioactive waste. That these very organisations also interfered in the whale hunt in the North Atlantic was another story altogether and, for us, just a source of trouble.

I sat back in my chair and put my feet up on the desk. I lit a Prince with my sky-blue plastic lighter and gave my thoughts free rein.

How was it possible that all animals had become so cuddly in recent years? Walt Disney could hardly take all the blame, although he had certainly played his part. Fairy stories about animals and people had always existed, but they had never been as syrupy sweet as they were now.

For animals to be worthy of our attempts to ensure their survival, we try to make them human and doll-like. No one says that they should survive even though it's in their nature to be ruthless meat-eaters. No, we try to make them suitable for the drawing room by describing them as nice, fun and friendly. Instead of saying that we should value them for what they are, we know no bounds when trying to show how good they are.

I laughed to myself.

From a Faroese perspective this army of sweet teddy bears and talking whales was completely absurd. A sign of alienation. A sign that we have lost our connection with nature. To forget how bad people are, we do all we can to make sure everyone knows how good animals are. The actions of these organisations could really be seen as a hidden crusade against humanity.

I sighed and brushed the foolishness of the world to the back of my mind, a place deep in my brain where there was already a hint of doubt.

I picked up the white envelope and opened it. There were twenty fifty pound notes and a folded piece of paper inside. I left the notes where they were and opened up the piece of paper.

Five

It was a normal A4 sheet without a letterhead. The text was in English and filled half the page. It said no more than was necessary. Jenny Mary McEwan was 25 years old, born and bred in Newcastle and had studied biology at the Institute of Freshwater Ecology at the Windermere Laboratory and at the Institute of Aquaculture at the University of Stirling. Stewart Andrew Peters came from York, was also a biologist and a year older than his friend. He had studied at the Department of Zoology at the University of Aberdeen and the Institute of Aquaculture at the University of Stirling.

This told me that they had probably met during their studies at the University of Stirling. Wherever that was! Aberdeen I knew, and Windermere was in the north-west of England. But Stirling? I'd have to ask someone about that.

The two young Brits had written their dissertations on the farming of salmon and herring, and this was the reason for their trip to the Faroes. Supposedly. As Mark Robbins had said, they were both working for Guardians of the Sea, and it was this group that had sent them to the Faroes three months previously. But they knew full well what the Faroese thought of environmental activists, so they saw to it that the students were attached to the Sound Salmon fish farm in Sund.

The latest information was that the two youngsters had been staying at the Heljareyga Guest House on Dr Jakobsensgøta in central Tórshavn.

You certainly couldn't accuse Mark Robbins of saying more than was necessary.

I put the paper down and tried to get my head around it all. It didn't go well. My thoughts were going around in circles and I had no idea where to start. The police? Sound Salmon? The guest house?

I wasn't keen on the first possibility. Apart from one friend in the criminal department, I wasn't particularly popular at the police station. And there was a woman there I'd had some history with and I didn't feel like getting her mixed up in all of this. The police could wait until tomorrow, when I was actually going to have dinner at my policeman friend's house anyway. And they probably knew next to nothing, otherwise Mark Robbins would have known about it. He seemed to have good sources.

What about Sound Salmon? I found them in the telephone book, and although I didn't expect anyone to be at work on a Saturday afternoon, for all I knew the salmon were being fed.

The phone rang three times, before the call was picked up by an answering machine:

'Sound Salmon, Faroese fishing in Faroese hands. I'm afraid there's no one available to take your call at the moment, but you can leave a message after…'

I hung up. I couldn't stand talking to an answering machine, so I didn't do it often. Sound Salmon would have to wait until another time.

That left me with the Heljareyga Guest House. But I couldn't imagine that they'd be able to tell me anything. Nevertheless, I gave them a call. No answer. A mobile phone number had also been given in the phone book, but I didn't try it. There was no certainty that anyone at the guest house would know anything about the departed. And if there had been someone who had stayed there a little longer and maybe had something worth passing on, it would be much better to meet them personally, rather than catch some random worker on a mobile while they were out in their car or standing in a shop.

I finished my cigarette and tried to pull myself together to finish clearing up. But now my head was full of whales and foreigners. A truly terrible combination.

Because I had lived abroad for so many years, I was out of the habit of taking part in the whale hunt. I didn't really feel

I could put myself up for it. And these days, people hardly dared whisper the word 'Grindaboð!', the call to the hunt. The environmental organisations were so aggressive in their treatment of the Faroes that the whale hunts were carried out almost secretly. In most cases you didn't hear about the whales until quite a long time after they had been killed.

And there was the fact that I wasn't particularly eager to take part in a whale hunt. It's not because I necessarily have anything against it, it's just that I didn't run down to the beach as fast as I could unless someone was pushing me.

When I was at primary school we were *given* time off when there was a whale hunt taking place down at Kongabrúgvin. Well, to say that we were given time off is perhaps a little misleading; as soon as the call of 'Grindaboð!' was heard in the classroom, there was simply a mad rush for the door. It didn't occur to anyone that the teachers should be asked about this – not even to the teachers.

Later, at senior school and at the sixth-form college at Hoydalar, things were different. The school was somewhat removed from civilisation, on a plain down towards the Hoydalar Stream – the old buildings had been a sanatorium for tuberculosis sufferers – and here, which we considered to be very far away from the town, the call to the hunt couldn't be heard. Other than those students that boarded there and a few teachers, no one lived in the area around the school, so for the students to find out about the hunt, someone from Tórshavn would need to phone one of the teachers. Therefore the direct contact had already been cut. It was almost as though the teachers and students in Hoydalar would need to have an invitation to take part in the hunt. The headmaster decided to adapt to these modern times and forbade anyone from going to the hunt.

Whenever we found out about a hunt taking place in Tórshavn – and this was not often – someone always went down there (including one or two of the teachers on occasion), but otherwise we soon became accustomed to these changes. The whale hunt had nothing to do with us any longer. I've no doubt that my gradual alienation from the hunt began at this point. I had nothing against it, but neither did I have anything to do with it.

At home we ate whale and blubber for dinner at least once a week – generally on a Saturday – but I hardly ever saw a living whale and only saw dead ones around the boarding house. They had an agreement that whenever there had been a hunt – not just in Tórshavn, but in other places too – they would receive a whale. This would be carried to the school by a crane and placed in the area between the kitchen and the storehouse. In their break times, students could stroll around here in their shirt sleeves with their hands in their pockets and observe the beast.

Some of the older students who came from smaller villages where they had learned to divide the whale meat helped the boarding teachers with this once the school day was done. For their efforts they'd receive a schnapps, even though alcohol was strictly forbidden on school grounds. At parties too. But this only applied to a selected and special few.

The rest of us had nothing to do with that side of life in our country. We declined foreign nouns and learned mathematics, so that we would be able to go abroad to study further. Faroese matters we concerned ourselves with very rarely – it just didn't happen.

Calls from oystercatchers came in through the open window, but the natural idyll aside, I felt all alone in the world.

Once again the telephone came to the rescue.

It was an old friend asking whether we should meet at Eyskarið at about 9.30pm for a game of cards, before the place got too busy.

I gave an immediate yes and felt that my life once again had some purpose. My friend had a great many whale hunts under his belt, so maybe he'd be able to give me a hand in this hopeless farce.

Six

From Bøgøta I turned into Dr Jakobsensgøta, where the Heljareyga Guest House was to be found. This consisted of three buildings, the cladding of which had been painted white and the lower half light blue. Two of the buildings were tall and shapeless, while the third was a normal residential house from the sixties. On all three was the word 'Heljareyga' in big letters. On the little square outside the guest house was a statue of two naked women with their arms around each other. Maybe an indication of what took place inside?

I walked between two of the buildings, trying a door marked 'Café Heljareyga'.

Closed. I tried to peer through the glass panel in the door, but it was completely dead inside.

There were some concrete steps around the back of one of the tall houses, so I climbed them. The blue door at the top was unlocked. I opened it and went inside. There was just a small hallway inside with some narrow stairs leading to the first floor. No sound to be heard.

The sun was shining outside and the birds were calling. One or two cars were even out and about on this Saturday afternoon. But the hotel was like a graveyard. I was tempted to call out to see if anyone was around, but couldn't bring myself to break the sacred silence.

The stairs creaked underfoot as I slowly climbed the stairs. I had a strange sense that I was trespassing, but I tried to reassure myself that I had rung in advance and that I had tried the door to the café first. And what was so strange about crossing the threshold of a guest house?

It made no difference. I had the same feeling of uncertainty, and the sense that I was on forbidden territory was by no means diminished.

Upstairs there was a narrow corridor with about five or six doors leading off it. The door furthest down on the right was open, casting light into the corridor.

It was a small, somewhat shabby kitchen with two hotplates, a microwave and a fridge. A narrow kitchen worktop with a stainless steel sink stood beneath a window which was ajar. Through it, sounds from the birds outside broke the silence.

A table stood up against the wall, one that was so small that it had space for at most two plates on it at a time. Nevertheless, most of the floor space was taken up by three chairs.

According to a note on the fridge, each room had a shelf in there. I took a look inside. Two of the shelves were full with cheese, sausages, yoghurt and the like, while three were more or less empty. In the door there was some milk and a couple of bottles of beer.

My powers of deduction told me that there were probably two guests up here. 'Elementary, my dear Watson' – ironic praise from somewhere within my subconscious.

On the wall there were two cupboards and a noticeboard covered with all kinds of papers, including several postcards. One of them, depicting a ship with a multi-coloured stripe on the side and the words 'Rainbow Warrior', immediately caught my attention.

I pulled out the drawing pin and turned the card over. It had been sent from Honolulu in Hawaii to Stewart Peters. The receiver's address said, 'Heljareyga, Faroe Islands'. I couldn't make out the date, but the short message was legible: 'Enjoying the sun and sea. I hope your hush-hush project is coming off. Best wishes, Matthew'.

A hush-hush project? What?

Mark Robbins hadn't said anything about a secret project. If I remembered correctly, he hadn't mentioned anything about a project whatsoever. Just something about observing the whale hunt. I had only understood, or worked out myself, that the two youngsters had come to the Faroes to find out more about the hunt and to take pictures that could be used against us. Of course it was their ultimate aim to ban the killing of whales, but I had no idea about a secret project.

'What are you doing here?' asked a voice in English, but with an indeterminate accent.

I was so startled that I almost dropped the postcard, but was nevertheless quick-witted enough to manage to stick it into a pocket before I turned around.

In the doorway stood a tall man with red hair and freckles. He was in his mid-twenties, in a Faroese jumper with a grey and black pattern, jeans and hiking boots. He was holding a bag from the co-op in his hand. Everything about him screamed 'tourist'.

His blue eyes examined me, but there was no aggression in them. He just wanted an answer.

'I'm looking for someone that might have known Stewart Peters or Jenny McEwan,' I answered in English.

'Aren't they the ones that were killed a couple of weeks ago?'

'Yep'.

'I've only been on the islands a week, so I don't actually know anything about them. The guy who's staying in the attic knew them, I think. In any case, he's been here for a few months. But he's not here right now.'

'Are you from Holland?' I asked the obliging hiker. I thought I could hear something of that in his accent.

'Yes, from Vlissingen. It's a little flatter than here,' he smiled.

'The guy in the attic,' – as things seemed to be going well, I thought I'd carry on – 'where's he from?'

'He's from Scotland. His name is Alan.' The redhead came into the kitchen and set his bag down on the little dining table. 'I haven't spoken to him very much, just a little now and again in the evenings when we've been making dinner.'

'You don't know what he's doing in the Faroes?'

'I think he's working at the Prime Minister's Office, but I'm not sure.' He began to empty the contents of his bag into the fridge.

What on earth was a foreigner doing working there?

I moved into the corridor. 'You don't know when this Alan is coming home?'

'No, I don't. Like I said, I've only been here for a few days, so…'

'And you two are the only ones here?'

'No, there's a woman too, but she leaves before I get up, and she never comes into the kitchen. Not when I've been here, anyway.'

My powers of deduction were obviously not something to boast about. So there were three people living here, not two. Nevertheless, I tried to push for more.

'So how do you know it's a woman?'

He blushed.

'I've seen her come out of the bathroom and go into her room.'

I thanked him and let the young Dutchman be alone with his thoughts about the mysterious woman.

Once I was outside I wondered whether I should try one of the other houses, but a mixture of shrewdness and laziness convinced me to be satisfied with the floor I had already investigated.

I set course for home.

Seven

I hung out of the window smoking a cigarette, while the dark voice of Leonard Cohen sang about Suzanne in the living room. The room was south-facing and the sun was still warming the land and its people. *Vesturkirkjan*, the West Church, the highest building in the Faroes and one aptly described by William Heinesen as a 'giraffosaurus', lay diagonally opposite, and even though there were several boat lengths between here and the church, you still had the feeling that you could reach out and touch its mighty copper roof. The neck of the ancient monster – the architect undoubtedly had a sail and the sea of life in mind – divided the Kirkjubøureyn area into two parts. The southern part ended at Glyvursnes, where several boats were out fishing, while the northern part led out towards Velbastaðhálsur, which I couldn't see for all the houses.

Although several days had passed since I came home, the only thing I had opened was my suitcase. Books, utensils, LPs – everything was still in the same cardboard boxes that much of it had been in for years. Fortunately I'd managed to find my CD player, but once James Joyce's *Finnegan's Wake* turned up in one of the boxes, I quickly closed it again. That book is one of the best sleeping tablets ever put on the market, but I didn't have time for sleeping. I had to try to sort my house out a little.

I let the cigarette fall to the ground below. I didn't exactly have green fingers and the garden was in an awful state. An old bathtub, usually occupied by birds, adorned the gravel. Before I went back to Denmark, I had thought about having it removed, but on the other hand, I was an animal lover. That was my excuse anyway.

The bookcases were still up in the attic, so something that resembled a dining table and four rickety chairs constituted all of my furniture. There wasn't as much as a single painting on any of the walls.

Once I had owned several paintings by Faroese artists, but when my girlfriend and I split up, and I was leaving the islands in any case, I let her keep everything she wanted to have. Some books, the CD player, an old gramophone (I needed to find that!) and a few kitchen bits and bobs were pretty much all that was left. At the time I didn't expect I would ever return to the Faroes and I just could not be bothered to lug a load of freight with me. The reason I hadn't sold the house was because the prices were too low. It simply would not have been worth it. But perhaps right at the back of my mind there was a thought that one day I would be convinced not to give up on my home country forever. And now I was sitting here in the mess, while the dust danced in the rays of sunlight over the packing cases.

'Come over to the window, my little darling…'

The deep voice filled the living room.

I went into the kitchen to fetch a bottle of gin. At Kastrup Airport in Copenhagen I had bought a bottle of *Bombay Sapphire*, because I found the light blue, square bottle titillating. Moreover, it was 47 per cent, like proper gin should be. Not that 37 per cent dishwater which is sold in most parts of Europe under the label 'gin', because the EU has decided what strength alcohol is allowed to be. They should find something else to interfere in. Why not a big topic, like what our driving licences should look like?

A splash of tonic – Schweppes that I had found in a shop – was also poured into the glass, but I made sure that the concoction wasn't diluted too much. The American author Helene Hanff commented that you know you're dealing with decent people if they're gin drinkers. Ideally neat. And the filmmaker Luis Buñuel said that if you were mixing gin and vermouth, it was enough to let a ray of sunshine pass through the vermouth bottle and into the glass of gin. No more was needed.

I wasn't that extreme, even if I had – on several occasions – sat eating dried fish and drinking neat gin for breakfast after a wild night. But that was in my younger days.

With the glass of gin in my hand I went over to pull down the ladder to the loft, so I could get the bookcases. Sun, gin, Leonard Cohen as an accompaniment to putting books in their place. Who could want for more?

Eight

You still needed a key to get into the Eyskarið beer club, but it was no longer the same club. Now only a few of us old boys still used the term 'beer club'. On the posters it said 'nightclub'. Formally the establishment was called the Eyskarið Recreation Club, a name that we chose half seriously and half in jest years before. For some years the members spent a good deal of their free time at the club, so Eyskarið created both a bridge and a billiards section. When I was at home in the Faroes I was almost part of the furniture. But back then it was housed in another building and had largely other members.

Time had cut down the number of old members, who had mostly either died or become so middle-class that they seldom went into town. A fire had destroyed the building and in its place a new building had been erected, very expensive and in no way better than the one before. On the outside it was nothing to write home about and on the inside it resembled the southern brothels we know from American films.

So the new Eyskarið looked like a whorehouse, but how could it be otherwise? In days gone by we learned what we know from meeting together in the evening and from ballads and folklore. That's where our understanding of the world came from. Today we get most of it from American films, and clearly those who had overseen the decorating of Eyskarið were fans of westerns, where there are ladies of easy virtue on plush sofas. Presumably they saw themselves as John Wayne or Clint Eastwood, mumbling with screwed up eyes, 'This town ain't big enough for the two of us'.

But Eyskarið wasn't in a cowboy film and it looked like what it was: a cheap copy without the least charm. It took more than a schnapps and a beer to get used to the surroundings.

There weren't many people. From upstairs came the sound of billiard balls hitting each other and in one corner two men in overalls were trying to pull themselves together enough to go home. At one of the high tables an older man was standing, leafing through the *Dimmalætting* newspaper.

Haraldur wasn't there.

A young, fair-haired girl in black from top to toe was standing behind the bar, fumbling with a tape-recorder. Once Hermann Jacobsen's voice and Evert Taube's words were coming from the loudspeakers, she turned around and asked me what I wanted.

Her dress was so low-cut that I didn't dare say what I was actually thinking. Instead I asked for a Danish strong beer. With my beer bottle and glass in my hands I went upstairs to see whether I knew anyone up there. But the three billiard players were in their own world and hardly acknowledged me. They were circling the green table in an almost silent ballet, in which the cues formed graphic patterns above the felt and into the air. Occasionally there was an outburst of joy or disappointment, but otherwise they just played.

There was a large television screen on the wall, but there was no football game on a Saturday evening, so it was off.

The windows upstairs looked out over the Old Cemetery and the town, and I stood for a while staring into the clear, silent evening, where the moon shone over the Nólsoy Fjord.

Then I went back downstairs and sat down on one of the plush sofas, thinking about the American author William Faulkner, who said that a brothel was the best place for a writer to work: peace in the day and a party at night. The party hadn't started yet, but in a couple of hours it would be packed. No Faroese person with any respect for themselves would be seen out in the town before midnight.

The atmosphere in the club was muted, as though the eternal peace from the cemetery had gravitated over to this side of the street. It was almost 10 o'clock and now it was just the newspaper reader and me in the bar. The men in overalls had left with an observation that it was about time to go home for dinner.

There was no one behind the bar, but Hermann Jacobsen was still singing Taube, and in the song Fritiof and Carmencita were dancing their hearts out.

'You sitting there dreaming about women?' The caustic voice broke into my humble thoughts.

Haraldur í Sátudali was in his fifties and somewhat larger than most. Both his hair and beard were grey, with the odd dark hair in there. The blue eyes in his red-cheeked face, though, shone like those of a much younger man. He was in a dark blue T-shirt, a black leather jacket and dark trousers. In his Sunday best for once.

'If only it was that,' I answered. 'No, it's whale hunts and foreigners.'

'Crikey. That's a bit of a quagmire for a Saturday night in town. What do you want?'

'Give me a Hof and a Gammel Dansk.' I answered. 'Single,' I called after him. At Eyskarið a schnapps, whatever the brand, was always a double, unless you specified otherwise.

'Two Elefants and two Gammel Dansks', boomed Haraldur in his northern accent.

'Ah, it's you,' said the girl behind the bar with a giggle. 'No Elefants, I'm afraid. That beer was banned ages ago in the Faroes.'

'I know. It's just fun to say it. Give me a Veðrur and a Hof instead. The Hof's for the Dane over there.' He gestured in my direction.

Haraldur had once been a bouncer, but then became a fisherman out in the big, wide world for a while, before coming back two years ago. He lived in an old house in úti á Reyni, a suburb of Tórshavn. He still made most of his money from fishing, but from time to time he'd lend a helping hand elsewhere. Most often at Eyskarið. It was obvious that he was a bachelor, because otherwise he never would have been able to live so casually.

Haraldur placed two beers and two double Gammel Dansks on the table and groaned as he leaned back on the sofa.

'They never should have let them sell alcohol in the Faroes. It was much nicer when it had to be ordered from Denmark.'

He sipped the schnapps and washed it down with the beer.

'The worst thing you can do for people is to allow everything. When stuff's not banned it's not fun. Look at the Danish laws on pornography. They took away all the restrictions on sex and a great deal of the excitement. Now that you can more or less buy alcohol freely in the Faroes, you might just as stay at home or go to some nice restaurant rather than come here.'

He looked around. The place was practically empty.

'In the old days the five o'clock slot after work on a Friday was the best time of the week, because it only happened on that day. Now everything's open all day long and the five o'clock slot has disappeared.'

I didn't disagree with Haraldur, but I thought it probably best to ask him my questions before much more drink had gone down.

I told him about Mark Robbins and GOS, and that they were trying to find out who had killed the two youngsters. Haraldur was a real supporter of the whale hunt and this was one of the reasons why he'd given up fishing out in the big, wide world. While I was explaining everything, various curses rained down on Greenpeace, Sea Shepherd, GOS and other environmental organisations that interfered in Faroese affairs without knowing anything about them.

It was very clear to me that he didn't care for my assignment, and to tell the truth, I was also feeling a little trapped. But after another beer and some schnapps – double – we agreed that there was nothing wrong with me trying to investigate the situation a little. If I discovered anything, then everyone was a winner. And if I didn't manage to get anywhere, at least things wouldn't be any worse than they were now.

We raised a toast to our shrewdness and Haraldur promised to put me in touch with the people who were in charge of the whale hunts at Sandagerður. We also spoke about how in the time after the whales have been marked but before the notes are issued, it's often very quiet down by the beach, so perhaps it wouldn't have been so hard to hide a body or two among the whales.

'We'll leave the rest for another day,' said Haraldur, abruptly bringing the conversation to an end. He looked around the bar, which was now no longer as deserted as at the dawn of time. 'Let's go and find someone to play cards with.'

Nine

It was gone three o'clock when I made my way along Jóannes Paturssonargøta, not entirely steady on my feet. Cars rushed by and the thumping of the deep bass was mixed with laughter and the shouting of the people in them. That night's party was far from over. Cars full of drunk youngsters would drive around until the dawn at the very least.

The air was cool and I felt semi-sober, but years of experience told me that I probably wasn't. On the corner by the joiner's workshop I had to stop and wait for a lull in the traffic. I laid my head back and looked up to the sky, where countless stars were shining, with only a few small clouds obscuring them here and there. I took a deep breath to give me strength against the coldness of the spring air, but filled my lungs instead with exhaust fumes. Oh well, you couldn't have everything. Even on islands in the middle of the ocean, fresh air and a welfare society didn't go particularly well together.

The evening at Eyskarið had been good to begin with, even if the end hadn't gone quite so well.

We had played cards for about two hours – both three-handed and four-handed – and when we stopped the place was heaving. Not only on the ground floor, but also on the first, where there was no longer room for billiard cues, and in the basement, where there was dancing.

I wandered around and from floor to floor – if you can call it wandering when the place is that full – but only knew a few people. Most of them were young enough for me to be their father, and inwardly I was cursing that *my* pub should have undergone such a change that older people no longer came along. It then occurred to me that my friends and I had been younger than most of the people here when we became members. But that didn't comfort me one jot.

The basement under the bar had been excavated and a dance floor installed with an Irish bar. The bar was the same as Irish bars across the globe and was probably now a bigger export for the Irish than whisky. A band was playing so loudly that you couldn't hear what was being said. But you weren't supposed to talk here – if you wanted to do that you could go upstairs. The basement was for dancing – and drinking.

There was drinking on all floors and there were bars on all floors, but in the gloomy darkness down here, the reins were a little slacker than in the light upstairs. It was warmer here, people danced, and men and women got closer to each other and therefore got thirstier.

The music pounded, couples swirled around, men embraced women and women embraced men, smoke billowed around the room, without the fans making any difference, and glasses were emptied. An ancient Dionysian dance was undertaken with heart and soul and there were many who gave the Devil their little fingers. It was the day before the Sabbath, but these souls hadn't planned to better themselves at Sunday school while the Devil counted fingers. In any case, it wasn't certain they should even be allowed in for fear of them corrupting the children.

In one way or another, I felt a pang of jealousy, even though I hardly wanted to admit it. I knew I didn't really have any business to be part of this aspect of life any longer. There were still women in my world – things hadn't got that bad – but I wasn't as eager to chase them as I had been before. Thinking ahead had increasingly become the order of the day, and I no longer threw myself into battle without giving tomorrow a thought. I tried to tell myself that there were other things in life than partying and chasing women, but even in my best moments, I found it hard to believe it.

Well.

You can't return to your youth. I looked around the dark room one more time, but there was no one there to offer me even the slightest of hopes.

I went upstairs and sat next to Haraldur, who didn't seem to be struggling with the same thoughts as me. How had things been going for him in that respect? I knew he'd been engaged once but not married, but I didn't know any more about that side of his life.

We had been friends for many years, but had only lived in the same place as each other for short periods of time. So the ins and outs of his everyday life were something of a mystery to me.

Then I noticed that Haraldur and the woman he was sitting next to were holding hands. I sat there for a moment with an open mouth about to make some sarcastic remark, but fortunately I was sensible enough to swallow the words before they came out.

It wasn't because there was anything wrong with her. At least not as far as I knew. She looked happy. She was somewhat plump, like many women in their early fifties, and had brown hair with a whole range of different shades, suggesting she'd paid a rather long visit to the hairdresser. I knew that her name was Sanna and she was a secretary at the government offices. I seemed to remember hearing that she had got divorced.

The more I looked at her, the more I liked her. She was in a good mood and she laughed a lot, but at the same time there was nothing fake about her. She was entirely natural.

But her and Haraldur… he hadn't said anything.

I left the room to take a leak, and of course at that moment an idiot from Hósvík decided to give me hassle. I couldn't remember his name, but I'd been close to coming to blows with him many years before.

I was standing at the urinal when I heard his irritating voice.

'Come home to sponge off us, have you? You're a bloody traitor to your country.'

I knew immediately who it was, but at that exact point in time I was somewhat unable to do anything other than what I was doing. I would happily have stopped, but a little too much beer had gone down for that, so I just pretended I hadn't heard.

'Answer me!'

The voice became louder, but I had to carry on with the task in hand.

'A Dane-lover like you should never be allowed back into the country.'

I was almost finished.

Just then I received a push to the back which knocked me into the urinal. Water was running, so the front of my trousers was now soaking.

That was it. I turned around as fast as I could and smacked my left forearm up under his chin. He fell back into one of the cubicle doors and a rattle came from his throat. His face was bright red. Before he'd had time to catch his breath, I shoved my right hand into his groin and squeezed his testicles as hard as I could. His eyes almost popped out of his head before he fainted.

I was standing over the grey bundle of clothes breathing heavily when the door opened. Fortunately it was Haraldur.

'What on earth's going on here?' He looked down at the man on the floor and then back at me. He gave a wry smile.

Only then did it dawn on me that a smaller part of my anatomy was hanging out through the wet material. I hurried to put the escapee back inside.

'You can't go exposing yourself to people and making them pass out.'

'Oh, shut up! That arsehole knocked me into the urinal and soaked me.'

'I know him and I know what he's like. Come on, help me get him out into the entrance.'

Once there, we sat him up in a corner against the wall. Haraldur told the bouncer to chuck him out once he'd woken up and to give him a temporary ban for fighting.

Maybe something good had come out of the fight after all? Now I wouldn't run into that arsehole at Eyskarið for the next couple of months.

Outside my half of the yellow concrete box I lived in I took out my keys. I was halfway up the stairs when I suddenly stopped. I was certain that I'd left the light on in the porch. Now it was off.

Ten

I always left the light in the porch on whenever I went out in the evening, because that would allow enough light through the pane in the door for me to find the keyhole.

I carefully climbed up the last few steps and put my hand on the door handle.

The door was locked.

That was a relief. Presumably the bulb had gone, so there was no need for me to panic after all.

I unlocked the door, opened it and flicked the light switch. The light came on.

I turned the light off again, walked over to it, reached up and touched the bulb.

It was warm. The light hadn't been off for long.

Now I was beginning to worry. The bulb hadn't gone and I hadn't forgotten to turn the light on when I left the house to go into town.

Someone had been there.

Or was still there.

I turned the light on again. Then I took two careful steps towards the door to the kitchen and reached my arm in to turn on the light in there.

The white kitchen gleamed before me. There was no-one here, just the gentle buzz of the fridge.

My heart was thumping and most of all I just wanted to get out of there. But where would I go at half-past three in the morning? Down to the police station to tell them that the light was off in the porch, but that the bulb was warm?

They would have thrown me in one of the cells so that I could sleep the drink off.

Neither was it tempting to walk the streets until it got light. I concluded that I would need to try to find out whether there were uninvited guests in the house.

One floor at a time.

Slowly I pushed open the door to the living room. I could see most of the room by the light from the hall, but there were dark shadows behind the piles of cardboard boxes.

A naked bulb was hanging from a fitting in the ceiling – I still hadn't found a lampshade – and when the electricity made it shine like a blinding sun, it revealed that I was alone in the living room.

If someone had been here there was no way of telling with all the mess.

That left the upstairs. And the basement. But I wasn't worried about that as it hadn't been sorted out and was full of rubbish. That was hardly of interest to anyone.

I found a Swedish knife with a red handle in the kitchen and, armed with that, I climbed the stairs step by step. The intention had been for the knife to give me a sense of security. Deep down I knew that the added safety was negligible, because I didn't know how to use a knife. But I felt better all the same.

Upstairs there were three rooms and a bathroom with a toilet at the end of the corridor. The first room was completely empty, without so much as a chair inside. In the next room was my suitcase lying wide open on the floor and there were two bags on the narrow bed. But no visitor.

The third door led into my bedroom, the only one that had been furnished to any extent. Holding the knife ready in my right hand, I pressed the light switch just inside the door with my left.

The unmade double bed filled most of the floor. On either side were bedside tables with books on them. There were also some books lying spread out on the floor.

Before I went in I looked through the gap between the door and the frame to make sure that there was no one there. Then I got down onto my knees to look under the bed. I learned that I needed a vacuum cleaner. There was no one in the wardrobe either.

That left only the bathroom.

Not a soul. I noticed how much easier it was to breathe and felt my muscles relaxing. Ever since I had discovered that the bulb had been switched off the adrenaline had been pumping around my veins and my eyes and ears had been fully strained.

Now that everything had relaxed, I realised I needed to pee. It was as I was in full flow that I heard a sound from the porch downstairs. The front door was opened and I heard someone running down the concrete steps to the house and then disappearing down the road.

For the second time that night I was caught by surprise as I stood peeing. I needed to make sure that didn't become a habit.

I finished off at my leisure. The uninvited guest was long gone by now, so there was nothing else to do, and I wasn't particularly sure that I wanted to meet him. I didn't really feel that I was in the best condition to give him a round if it came to blows.

Once I'd come down the stairs I saw where he had been hiding. The door to the basement was open and while I'd been looking for him, he had presumably been standing on the stairs waiting for an opportunity to get away without being seen. Once he'd heard me go to the toilet shortly afterwards, it was plain sailing.

The door lock was of the old type that you can buy keys for at an ironmonger's. I locked the door and found a skewer in a kitchen drawer. I bent it round the handle and stuck both ends through the hole in the key. At least nobody would be coming in that way now .

It was definitely time for bed. But first I had a snack while I tried to think who might have paid me a visit. I doubted that it was a common thief. They happened here too, of course, break-ins and thefts, but it was almost unheard-of in people's private homes.

And common thieves didn't generally make sure that they had locked the door while they were inside the house. You needed a key both to lock and unlock this door.

Whoever had been here had been after something other than the little bit of money people kept at home. It wasn't too hard to guess what it was about. Undoubtedly it had something to do with Mark Robbins' visit.

I needed to check whether the uninvited guest had also broken into my office. But that would have to wait until later in the day. Now I just wanted to be allowed to sleep.

Eleven

The church bells woke me up for the service just before eleven o'clock, but even though they carried on for some time and became increasingly obtrusive inside my head, I didn't take up their invitation. On this Sunday the church would simply need to get by without me, as it had by and large since I was a little boy.

As I stood under the shower, I started to think about the night at Eyskarið and particularly the man from Hósvík who had called me a traitor to my country because I'd left the Faroes during the economic crisis. It wasn't because it particularly annoyed me, but the stupidity of digging ourselves trenches and chucking mud at each other didn't strike me as particularly pleasant. Those who wanted to declare independence from Denmark right here and right now called those who were less sure traitors without any hesitation, while those who fought determinedly for the policies they believed in were accused of using Nazi methods. A distinct lack of unity has always existed on our islands, but this had never been more evident than during the crisis at the beginning of the nineties.

That the Faroese people should govern themselves was generally agreed, but how this should be done was another story altogether. Iceland was a role model for many, but the Faroese were simply not as united as the Icelanders. When Iceland declared independence in 1944, some 98 per cent of the population were for it, while we were unable to agree on anything. Not even on whether or not there should be a referendum.

On the other hand, the Icelanders were somewhat blinded

by arrogance in those years. Worse than the Norwegians today. In all seriousness they made demands on East Greenland and parts of Norway – and Newfoundland, because Leif the Lucky had been the first white man there.

On my way down the stairs to eat breakfast, it occurred to me that we also have disturbed people like that here. For about fifteen years they had been writing in the newspapers that there was an agreement from the fifteenth century that had never been cancelled – and therefore the south-western part of Norway should actually belong to the Faroes.

It would have been fun to have had Stavanger and all the Norwegian oil while we were waiting for our own. We would all have been oil sheikhs by now.

In the fridge there was some yoghurt left in the carton, a couple of slices of rye bread and some cheese. It would hardly be breakfast for a king, but the house was no palace, so that seemed to fit quite well.

But I did have some coffee and as I sat at the little kitchen table, drinking from my mug and staring through the window at the road as cars occasionally zoomed by, I felt reasonably happy with the world. And the weather wasn't bad either. No sun like there had been yesterday, but it was clear, dry and still.

That the infighting among the average citizens and among the politicians was so merciless was partly due to the fact that no one on the Faroes had taken responsibility for the economic crisis. The upshot was that in 1992 the Faroes basically went bankrupt. Those working in industry and those who had been in charge for years excused themselves from any blame, pointing their fingers at each other instead. Investigations were undertaken, but other than one Danish bank being told that it had acted immorally when it tried to absolve itself of all responsibility for a Faroese daughter bank, most of the blame disappeared like dew before the sun.

Thousands of people were forced to leave the country, as many of them had lost house and home and had large debts to deal with. Everyone felt they had been cheated, but no one was able to say who they had been cheated by. It was no one's fault because the political system had been so wisely put together. But there had to be a scapegoat, and as it was difficult to find one in the Faroes, one would need to be imported from abroad. Denmark was an obvious choice.

Wasn't the bank that had tried to deceive us Danish? Hadn't Denmark oppressed us for centuries? It was all Denmark's fault. One author wrote in a newspaper that after the fall of the Berlin Wall, Denmark had chosen to have the Faroes as an enemy rather than the Soviet Union. The whole crisis was a Danish plot. A dirty conspiracy.

It was the same type of paranoia that ran free in Germany after the First World War. It wasn't the Germans' fault that they had lost the war, no, all along the whole thing had been a Jewish-Bolshevik scheme to take over the world. The German Army had been stabbed in the back and, just like that, this legend became accepted as the truth and, as a result, the Second World War was a direct consequence of the First.

I lit the first cigarette of the day, whilst singing to myself:

Mummy dear, it wasn't me.
It was those nasty boys, you see.
They pushed me into the dirt
And laughed until they hurt.

We should make that our new national anthem. Short and to the point. It was just one verse and most people only knew the first verse anyway. It clearly connected with something in our psyche.

Those in charge on the Faroes had often been careless with public money – and back then there wasn't much public money to be careless with. The strange thing is that the Faroese have always been excellent at coping with bad times as if they were the norm. But we've never really been particularly successful at coping with the good times.

The number of cars on the road outside grew – a clear sign that church services were over. A short while later a large number of people walked by and I sat there looking at them like some living pot plant. Most of the people were older, but there were some of roughly my age. I knew several of them and some of them I had seen at Eyskarið the night before. Evidently Our Lord could be found in many different places.

A jolt went through me. I thought I recognised a dark-haired woman who was coming down the hill on the other side of the road. Wasn't that…? Now that she was just outside the window I could see that I was mistaken. It wasn't Duruta.

Duruta was the woman I had been in a relationship with before I went to Denmark the last time, and I had to confess that the quickening of my pulse implied that there was still something there.

As far as I was concerned.

As far as she was concerned, it was possibly a different story altogether. For all I knew she could be married. I hadn't seen her since I left, but I remember hearing that she had had a daughter a few years back.

On my way into the living room to call Haraldur about the meeting with the people from the whale hunt, I caught sight of the spit that had been bent around the door handle and through the keyhole. I had almost forgotten last night's guest.

But only almost.

Twelve

There was a Yale lock on the door to my office, but over the years the door had become so crooked that there was a strip of light between the door and the frame. It wasn't necessary to pick the lock or force it. If you lifted the handle and pushed at the same time, the door opened, even if it was locked. Nevertheless, I chose to use a key.

In the attic, everything looked just like it had when I went home the previous afternoon. The smell of turpentine was more or less just as strong, even though the windows were ajar. I didn't really know how I would be able to see whether any uninvited guest had paid a visit. There was nothing on the desk and on the floor there were only tins of paint and newspaper. And their appearance was exactly what you would expect from them.

But in the toilet there was something. On the middle of the black toilet seat there was a footprint. The cistern was of the old school – mounted high on the wall with a chain to pull. Someone had tried to see where there was anything up there. There wasn't.

Whoever broke in had presumably come here first and when he had been unable to find anything had then tried my house. But he'd had no success in either place. What he was looking for was here, but it was somewhere else.

I walked out onto the landing, down to the next floor and to the end of the corridor. On the wall there was an old electric meter with large black casing. I removed the casing and took out the envelope I had taped to the inside of it.

Before I had left my office the day before, I had mulled over what I should do with the thousand pounds. It wasn't that it

68

was such a large sum of money, but just leaving it in a drawer in the desk wasn't something I was prepared to do, seeing as it was so easy to get into the office. I had been planning to get a little safe where I could keep some money and important papers, but for now I would need to find something else. Keeping a thousand pounds on me or leaving it somewhere at home didn't seem much better. That was when I remembered the electric meter. Luckily I had hidden the piece of paper along with the money, because it was clear that the paper was what the intruder had been hoping to find.

Someone had seen Mark Robbins pay a visit to my office and undoubtedly knew who he was. But how could he know that I'd been given a piece of paper with various pieces of information on it? I mean, it wasn't particularly hard to see someone go into an office, but how on earth could anyone know exactly what he had done here?

When I came back into the office I noticed that the wind had veered to the west and that it was picking up. The sky had also become darker. I walked over to close one of the windows because the breeze was now blowing right in and the newspaper on the floor had started to flap.

I had just lifted the window latch when the window next to me shattered and I heard a gunshot.

Thirteen

'I'm telling you, if you're up to your old tricks again, I'll smash your face in.'

'That seems an appropriate way of dealing with a member of the public,' I replied.

'Don't you start again! It's been so wonderfully peaceful round here while you've been off overseas. You've been back for two minutes and you're already giving me hassle.'

The angry man was Detective Inspector Piddi í Útistovu, a man I'd had rather a lot to do with in the past. He was from Hvalba, was around sixty, had a long, thin face and an angry temperament. One thing had changed since I last saw him, however: he no longer had a pipe to gesticulate with. He used to be permanently surrounded by a cloud of ash and tobacco. Maybe missing that was what was making him so angry?

As soon as I had heard the shot I had thrown myself to the ground, but after the sound of the glass shattering, it was completely silent. There was just the one shot. After a short pause I plucked up the courage to look out of the window, but there was nothing to see that was out of the ordinary in any way. The boats by the landing stages were bobbing up and down as the wind picked up, but on the other side of the harbour there wasn't a soul to be seen.

There could be no doubt that the shot was a warning shot. If the person who was lying in wait was planning to shoot me, he would hardly have hit the window next to me. Someone wanted to make sure I knew that I should stick to my own business. It was also probable that the same person had been in a position to observe my office through binoculars and would have seen Mark Robbins give me an envelope.

While I was trying to see whether there was anything over on the western side of the harbour – trying all the while to keep myself as covered as possible – there was a sudden and powerful burst of rain, a real downpour which meant that I could only see a few metres before me. So I decided I'd make for the telephone and call a police officer I knew.

Shortly afterwards my old classmate, Karl Olsen, arrived. After I had explained the situation to him, he called forensics and more officers to the scene. While forensics were digging the bullet out of the wall and the additional officers were carrying out investigations on the other side of the harbour, Karl and I headed for the police station on Jónas Broncksgøta.

We sat there for quite some time while I tried to explain what I knew: a representative of an environmental organisation had asked me to investigate the deaths of the two young Brits; there had been a break-in at my office and my home and that someone had fired through the attic window of my premises at úti í Bakka.

It was difficult to get my story out as Piddi broke out in frequent bursts of anger, saying that nothing good ever came of anything whenever I was around.

All the while Karl sat there smiling to himself, looking like a Romanesque carving of a father figure. There wasn't much hair left on his head, so instead he had grown a full, dark beard since I saw him last, with definite hints of red in it.

'I had to make up for what I'd lost on top,' he laughed as I brought up his beard on the way to the station.

'If you're trying to look like the Viking chieftain Tróndur í Gøtu, you don't have enough freckles. And don't they say that he also had unusually coarse features?'

'Some people are now saying that they've read the old manuscripts incorrectly. Apparently it should say that he was handsome. In that case the comparison's bang on,' Karl laughed.

Although he certainly didn't look much like Tróndur í Gøtu, Karl nevertheless had that Viking strength of will. You wouldn't try anything when Karl was around. Many a man had winced when the usually amiable police officer banged his fist on the table and put everybody in their place with just a few well-chosen words.

Piddi had come to the conclusion that I had made the whole thing up. I had invented the break-ins and had broken the windowpane myself just to get some attention. I obviously had some sick desire to get into the newspapers.

'The newspapers?' I asked. 'Who on earth wants to get into the newspapers? You're way off there, my dear Piddi.'

'Don't you "my dear" me!'

But I wasn't about to be stopped.

'And the two that were found dead among the whales? I killed them too just to get into the papers?'

'I wouldn't put it past you.' Piddi snorted in his anger. 'When it comes to you, nothing's impossible.'

'And what about the assignment that Mark Robbins asked me to undertake for GOS? Did I make that up too?'

Piddi and Karl stopped abruptly and stared at me.

'Did you say Mark Robbins?' asked Karl carefully.

'Yes, he came to my office yesterday. He represents the environmental organisation I said I was working for.'

'You didn't say the man's name,' said Karl quietly. 'Mark Robbins is dead. His plane came down last night over Suðuroy.'

Fourteen

'But I spoke to him yesterday, and….' I was more than a little shaken.

'And it was yesterday that his plane went down on the west side of Suðuroy,' interrupted Karl. 'We only found out about it a short time ago. People in Tvøroyri and Hvalba heard a loud crash around sunset, but didn't really pay attention to it, just assuming it to be a stone slide. This morning some people who were walking in the outlying fields came across the wreck.'

Karl looked thoughtfully at me. Fortunately Piddi was now behind me, so I was spared his facial expression.

'At the airport in Vágar they were able to tell us that it was a Cessna 525 from the registration number on the tail. It left at about eight o'clock. On board there was the Englishman, Mark Robbins, the captain and the co-pilot.'

'Why did it come down?' I asked.

'That we don't know, but according to the people who have seen the wreck, it exploded when it hit the ground. It hadn't been in the air for more than fifteen minutes and was full of fuel.'

Karl's expression revealed that his mind was not filled with pretty pictures.

'But how is it possible that the airport didn't report it when the plane disappeared from the radar?'

'The airport chief said that the Cessna was the final flight of the day. They followed it for about fifteen minutes or so and then turned everything off and went home.'

'When will you investigate the wreck?'

'That's a job for the experts. They're coming over from

Denmark tomorrow and we'll go to Suðuroy by helicopter.'

'I could…,' I had only just opened my mouth when Piddi cut in.

'You won't do anything. You need to keep out of this and preferably leave the country again to give us some peace.'

With gritted teeth he left the room.

'He's trying to stop smoking,' said Karl, trying to make excuses for the man.

We sat there in our own thoughts for a time, which as far as I was concerned, had to do with the fact that the guy from Hósvík at Eyskarið the night before had said the same as Piddi. That I had no business being here on the Faroes. And, what's more, I was now unemployed. On the other hand, I had my thousand pounds, and I should probably do something for it, but the appointment that Haraldur had set up with the men from the whale hunt wasn't until Wednesday or Thursday. It was a little unclear which day it would be. So I had two days, and God only knew what…

The telephone interrupted my thoughts.

Karl answered it and for a while all I heard was: 'Yes… hmm… right… hmm… really? … hmm!'

'That was the duty officer', said Karl, once he had replaced the receiver. 'On the top floor of Skeiva Pakkhús there is an attic room with a window that faces your office, and someone has been there. They haven't really found much, because whoever it was cleared up after himself, but there are several signs that someone has been there for several days. And possibly slept in a sleeping-bag. If these half-guesses are correct, then it would seem that somebody out there is particularly interested in what you're up to.'

Deep in thought, Karl looked at me, but I didn't really know what to say, so I said nothing.

'They have also investigated the bullet, which is a rifle bullet of calibre 222 or 223, but with a steel core, which is unusual around these parts. It has been sent to Denmark for further analysis.'

For a moment nothing was said. There were noises elsewhere in the police station, but these were too far away to disturb our thoughts.

Karl broke the silence: 'Piddi's right about one thing. Things do start happening when you're around.'

'But… I haven't done anything.' In one way or another I felt implicated nonetheless. 'I was just painting my office when Mark Robbins came along and blackmailed me into carrying out an investigation for him. Then someone breaks into my office and my home, a bullet is shot through a window in the loft and I find out that my new employer is dead. And the whole time I've done nothing. I spent the whole of last night at Eyskarið playing cards.'

I shrugged my shoulders as if to stress that I was as white as the driven snow. Or something close to that.

'I almost think you'd be better off if you stayed at Eyskarið,' laughed Karl. 'At least there you can only do yourself damage, drinking until you keel over.'

If only he knew, I thought to myself, as the guy from Hósvík came to mind.

'Chin up,' said Karl with a smile. 'Soon Katrin will have finished putting dinner together and you're coming to ours. No ifs, no buts.'

Fifteen

It has always been tradition on the Faroes to eat Sunday dinner at about two o'clock in the afternoon – since the radio's on then anyway – but increasingly people have acquired the continental tradition of having dinner in the evening. On Sundays too.

There were four of us around the table. In addition to myself and Karl, there was Karl's wife, Katrin, and one of their two grown-up daughters. The other one was studying something or other to do with oil administration in Aberdeen, I seemed to recall, while the one at the table was training to become a nurse at the National Hospital. Or *sjúkrarøktarfrøðingur*, 'one-who-studies-caring-for-the-sick', to use one of the new Faroese words that we were now supposed to use, but no one there that evening made use of the clunky term. That word should enter a competition as one of the greatest monstrosities ever forced into the Faroese language. But there was a lot of competition. There had been a lot of these ridiculous words over the past thirty years and it was far from certain that this one would win.

Katrin had cooked a leg of lamb with roast potatoes, and as we ate it, along with its usual accompaniments, we spoke about this and that.

Their daughter – her name was Elin – talked in great detail about the hospital: how the students were given far too many jobs to do because there were never enough staff members and how some dropped out for that very reason; how this doctor and that chief nurse were really good, while others were completely intolerable. Katrin had worked as a laboratory worker at the National Hospital until a few years

76

before, but had since moved over to the Faroese Food, Veterinary and Environmental Agency in Debesartrøð. She asked about employees she knew from her time there, and mother and daughter laughed out loud at this one or that one who had done this or that.

I sat and smiled obligingly, enjoying the food and the wine. Particularly the latter, as I hadn't tasted proper wine since I arrived in the Faroes, and this was first-class Argentinian wine. It was strong and a little spicy, but at the same time pleasantly smooth, as a wine connoisseur might say. I was no connoisseur, but I knew what I liked and what I didn't like. And I liked this.

I was lost in my thoughts, envisioning *gauchos* on an endless *pampas*, when Katrin interrupted my summer dream.

'We're completely ignoring you, Hannis, but it's not every day that we see Elin. She lives out at the hospital, so it's much too far for her to come *all* the way up here to Stoffalág to visit her poor old parents.'

'Mum, that's not true! I was here on Wednesday.'

'Yes, but you're never here for long and it's rare for you and your father to be here at the same time.'

'I was here for Dad's birthday.'

'Yes, darling, but that was over a month ago.'

'Now, now.' Karl lifted his hands paternally. 'Don't argue when we finally have Hannis here with us. It's ages since he was last sat here.' He looked over to me. 'Why did you come home again? Didn't you have a good job in Denmark? Or was there something drawing you back home?'

A gentle smile crossed his lips and I knew exactly whom he was referring to, but I wasn't planning to play his game.

'I don't really know, but there's an awful lot going on in Faroese society at the moment, in various ways. There have been huge economic and political changes. And anyway, I had had the same job at Ritzau for six years and that's more than enough.'

Both Karl and Katrin smiled, as though they knew more than I did, so I thought it was best to brush it all aside with humour.

'And then there's the oil. If I was planning to become an oil sheikh then I knew it was high time to head this way again before there was a barrier set up to prohibit Faroese people living abroad from coming home.'

Karl took the bait.

'Yep, they do say that if we find an elephant, as it's called, we'll all be able to fly our private jets to Copenhagen, Edinburgh or Reykjavik for the weekend. Then it will be great to be Faroese, so you did the right thing in coming back to us.'

He winked. Katrin and Elin laughed, as did I. We raised our glasses.

'It will be heaven for the Faroese if they're able to buy more technology than they have today. Last night I was over at the station and read in one of those coloured scientific magazines that astronomers reckon the planet will have burned out in four billion years. According to a French philosopher this knowledge is hidden deep with our subconscious and is the driving force behind our efforts when it comes to technology. He reckons we're secretly working on leaving the planet while we still have time.'

Karl sipped the red wine.

'It's common knowledge that there are no people in this world that value technology more than the Faroese. The conclusion therefore has to be that we're the ones most desperate to get into outer space.'

Karl was clearly well pleased with his reasoning. He was no longer completely sober.

I was happy that my private life was no longer on the programme for the evening and so joined in the ponderings about the Faroese and technology. It was a subject that had often been discussed at great length by Karl and me, so we were not really saying anything new. But we were having fun talking in turns about men who stood waiting outside the builders' yards whenever a new machine came out. The longing for tools that could do people's work for them undoubtedly stemmed from a time when all work was physical graft: on the land, the seas, the mountainside. Life was a struggle and laziness was the greatest sin there was, so when tractors, diggers and boat engines came along, it was as though God himself had sent them.

Katrin and her daughter cleared the table, while Karl and I stayed where we were. Karl was usually the one who did all the cooking, so as far as he was concerned, that was acceptable. Less so for me, as I felt that I should probably help out, but I stayed there all the same and emptied the second bottle of wine with Karl. A picture of the eternal struggle between laziness and morality.

Karl got up, went over to the CD player and turned the music on. After a short time the voice of the folksinger Hanus Johansen came through the speakers:

Beautiful, peaceful homeland fair,
Resplendently dressed in winter's wear.

We sat in silence for a time as we listened, and I remembered how much Karl liked Poul F's poetry, especially when it was sung by Hanus' powerful voice.

'Yep, tomorrow I'll be on Suðuroy, the poet's home island,' said Karl thoughtfully in a brief pause between the songs. 'We'll see whether we can find anything out.'

'It has to be said that it's lucky the plane came down over land, when you think about how little of that there is between the Faroes and Great Britain.'

I pictured a map of the North Atlantic in my mind, where the Faroes were just a number of dots surrounded by vast amounts of water.

Deep in thought, Karl looked over at me. 'Maybe the plane crash wasn't an accident. I mean, after you were visited by the Englishman, you get broken into twice and today someone fires a gun into your office. Someone is definitely making an effort to scare you away from the dead environmental activists. From where I'm sitting it doesn't look like a coincidence.'

I didn't really have anything to add to Karl's musings, as I was completely in agreement with him. With a little reformulation, I felt like making Hamlet's words my own: 'There's something rotten in the state of the Faroe Islands'.

Sixteen

For the first hour of the ferry journey south to Suðuroy the weather wasn't much to write home about. The sea was calm, but it was cloudy and misty, so that we could hardly make out the Skálhøvdi promontory as we passed it. But once we had come south of Sandoy Island it cleared up, and shortly afterwards the islands of Stóra Dímun, Lítla Dímun and Suðuroy were lying in the most beautiful sunshine.

The word 'Dímun' is said to be Celtic and to mean 'twin peaks', and just like two mountain tops the two Dímun islands rise vertically from the sea, green on top and in gorges and ravines and black around the base. Usually the current or waves would create a foaming roar between rocks and the sea, but today it was dead calm. In the swarming bird cliffs there was a screeching noise of guillemot and puffin cries and on the water there was fluttering and diving to get away from us, but the weather was so still that the birds found it hard to take to their wings.

I was on board *Smyril* on the way to Suðuroy. It wasn't because I had any clear plan of what I wanted to achieve on this journey. It was more because I didn't know what else I should do. I wouldn't hear from Mark Robbins again, so I could have left it to the police to solve the murders of the two young environmental activists. But I had received money from GOS and the only morality I knew was personal. So even though no one was putting any pressure on me with this, I was putting it on myself. I didn't know whether I thought I was going to discover something, but I had decided that I wanted to see the wreck with my own eyes. How I thought I'd be able to see something that the experts wouldn't see, I didn't know, but I wasn't bothered about that. I really wanted to see the wreck. And I felt a need to make Mr Micawber's words my own: 'Something will turn up'. Moreover, many years had passed since I had been to Suðuroy and it was certainly no bad thing to go back. Many people considered the place to be the most beautiful island in the Faroes.

At Karl's house I had said that I was considering heading down south, but Karl maintained that it was a bad idea and that Piddi would tear my head off if he caught sight of me. But I'd caught *Smyril* anyway at around ten o'clock and we were due to arrive at the ferry port at Drelnes at half past twelve.

Karl and I had carried on until about midnight, when Katrin said that it was time for Karl to go to bed if he was planning to get the helicopter the next morning. We had spoken at length and perhaps drunk more than we should have, and when Hanus Johansen – we were listening to the same CD – started singing 'I miss you so, my darling' once again, Karl remarked sarcastically that it was a song for me. I let the sarcastic comment go – I didn't feel like going down that road again.

As we drew close to Stóra Dímun the farm came into view. In the past up to thirty people had lived on the island, even though it had never been particularly easy to get service people out to this outpost in the sea. The authorities helped by forcing people to live there and now and then the island was also used as a prison. Instead of being sent down to Bremerholm in Denmark, you could be sentenced to living and working out on Stóra Dímun. Although the island was cut off in the winter and the steep terrain meant it was always easy to put a foot wrong and end up leaving this earthly plane, it was nevertheless preferable to bolt and chain in Copenhagen. Many Faroese people had met that fate over several centuries. They were condemned to hard labour for the Royal Navy and never came home again.

As we approached Suðuroy, the vertical cliffs near Froðba were visible on the starboard side and shortly afterwards *Smyril* turned into the Trongisvágur Fjord, where the basalt columns on the northern side bade us welcome. In my mind I could see black and white photographs from olden days when there had been a whole fleet of boats at anchor in winter inside the fjord. That was in the days when Tvøroyri had been the engine of the Faroese economy, as the country changed from a farming society to one based on fishing. Everything had been possible here. The large ship owners and shops had been here, here was where the work was, and it was here that life could unfold in a completely different way to elsewhere in Faroese society. Whenever something happened that wasn't to everyone's taste, people used to say 'That kind of thing might go on in Tvøroyri, but not here'. Tvøroyri led the way into the future before the rest of the Faroes and it was here that the workers' movement first drew attention to itself.

Today the Faroes had been following the course that Tvøroyri had set for many years, but the pioneer village was eventually left behind. The whole of Suðuroy was left behind. While the country as a whole managed to rise up from the economic crisis, the southernmost island seemed to be in a permanent state of crisis. And while the other islands were being drawn closer and closer to each other with bridges and tunnels, Suðuroy was out there all by itself, some two hours from Tórshavn by boat. While the population was rising on all the other larger islands, it was falling on Suðuroy. It was hard to identify any sort of solution for the once so proud island.

A short time later we docked by the massive and odd-looking salt silo at Drelnes. This resembled no other building in the entire country. It was like an overgrown hut with a collection of sheds on the roof, finishing in something that resembled a clock tower. From a distance you might think it was a medieval cathedral, but as you got closer you could see that the tin roof was perforated by rusty holes and that the building was in decay. That it was about to collapse. Maybe that was an appropriate symbol for Suðuroy?

For a while I stood by the railings up on deck, smoking a cigarette and thinking about Tvøroyri then and now. As I disembarked there was no bus or taxi to be seen. The freight lorries had also gone, so I was more or less alone at the quayside. Most of the village was on the other side of the fjord, but it was a walk of about three kilometres to the head of the fjord and then out to Tvøroyri. Even though I only had a little shoulder bag and was wearing walking shoes, I didn't feel massively tempted to walk so far to get a car to take me to the tunnel.

So I went back on board *Smyril* to see if I could find someone who could help me get hold of a taxi.

Seventeen

The driver dropped me off where the road turned northwards to the Hvalba tunnel. A farm road led westwards, but the taxi was an American Chrysler that was so low you couldn't have put a matchbox under it. A car built for freeways in the US, rather than Faroese mountain roads.

I put my bag – which was now a little heavier than before – on my shoulder. We had made a stop at a grocer's and I had bought myself two plastic bottles of Hawaii Dream and some packs of dried fish. And a Yankie bar for dessert. I felt well-equipped to last until dinner time.

In the three-quarters of an hour that had passed between me getting into the taxi at Drelnes and getting out again I had almost drowned in a sea of words.

The driver was short and round, wearing a chequered peaked cap and with a home-rolled cigarette in the corner of his mouth.

'So, northerner, you're going to the circus?' was the first thing he had said when I had asked him to drive me as far west as possible.

'The circus?' I asked, surprised.

'Yeah, the police and several helicopters full of people are out there having fun near the Telescope. First came the helicopter with police officers and Danish experts, and then came one helicopter after another full of tourists from the north.'

'Tourists?' I asked.

'Yeah, people just coming here to see the wrecked plane. It's not because there's loads to see. Pretty much everything was blown to smithereens. I haven't had a chance to go out there myself yet, but I've been carting people over to the tunnel all morning so that they can stroll westwards in the beautiful weather and look at burned bodies. God only knows what the smell must be like.'

He took a brief pause midstream to draw smoke into his lungs, but the pause was short.

'Nope, I told them that this was nothing. During the war, in 1942, an English plane hit the mountainside over Mýridalur. Now that was a crash that could be heard, the old people say. I wasn't born then, you understand. Four men died, just one made it. He was the rear gunner, so I always sit at the back whenever I fly. That was what you might call an accident. The itty-bitty plane that crashed here, so they say, only had three people on it.'

And so he carried on the whole way from Drelnes, only interrupted by a short pause when I went into the shop to buy my provisions. It was a real relief to walk westwards for a while hearing only birdsong.

But it didn't last long. After a ten-minute walk in the open, sun-drenched landscape I heard voices and then saw the wreck. It had been eaten up by the flames and all that was left was a black skeleton on the ground. Around a radius of about twenty metres all the grass had been burnt, so I found it hard to believe that there was much left of the three men. The wreck was surrounded by red and white plastic tape.

I couldn't see anyone from the authorities, neither police nor anyone from the hospital, so from that angle I had nothing to worry about. But there were about fifty people standing around, talking and pointing in various directions, trying to get as close to the deathly plane as the cordon would let them. I had little doubt that if they had dared to in front of all the other people present they would have taken a souvenir. For those that weren't heading up north again there would be another day for them to get hold of a memento from the wreck in which three men had died.

Now I could see that further up on the grassy hillside, about one hundred metres away, was the tail of the plane, which was also cordoned off. But the fire didn't seem to have ravaged this part, so it wasn't as interesting for the crowds. A few smaller boys chased each other around the lost tail, while the adults were gathered around the place where the really unpleasant drama had unfolded. Where three men had been burned to death.

Out on the edge of the cliff there was a telescope surrounded by a low railing, and several people were using the opportunity to look at the bird cliffs to the north and south, seeing as they had taken the trouble to come out this far anyway. I walked northwards for a bit, where I could find respite from the curious crowds, and sat down on the sloping grass, where a few metres further north there was a sheer two hundred-metre drop to the sea. The sun was very strong and I felt hungry, thirsty and a little at a loss. I could solve the first two problems, but I was having difficulty in collecting my thoughts. I opened one pack of dried fish and one of my bottles of drink, as I tried to sort out in my head everything that had happened.

If – and only if – the aeroplane crash hadn't been an accident, but rather a successful murder attempt, then that meant that five people had now been murdered. And there had been the break-in at my home and the warning shot in my office. It was unimaginable that the gunman had been trying to kill me, because no one misses like that. But why? Why had the two youngsters been killed, and why Mark Robbins and the crew of the aeroplane? And why did someone want to frighten me away? There was no doubt that this was all connected somehow, but I hadn't got a clue how. That Faroese people had done this I found hard to believe, however angry they were with the environmental organisations. But who could it be that was out to get these people?

I had only questions and no answers, and even though a wise man had once said that it's about asking the right questions rather than finding the right answers, that didn't help me out a great deal.

I ate the dried fish and drank my Hawaii Dream as I let the view over the outstanding beauty of the western side of Suðuroy settle into my soul.

Eighteen

I felt that I had been blinded by a burning light and that I was rolling over the edge of the cliff and falling and falling... Just before I hit the rocks I woke up.

My hands groped around on either side and I felt the cool grass beneath my palms. The sun was shining directly into my eyes, so I turned my head to one side so that I could open them. As carefully as I could I raised myself into a sitting position, as the uneasiness from the dream was still in my body and for all the world I didn't want to slip over the edge and turn that dream into reality. It was, however, not particularly steep where I was currently lying, so I knew that the danger wasn't great. On the other hand it was a short distance to the edge of the cliff.

It was gone eight o'clock. I had been asleep for almost three hours. The evening at Karl's house combined with a large meal had made my head heavy and I had lain down on my back in the warm weather. Even though the grass was cool, the heat from the sun and the warm jacket had meant that I hadn't become stiff from the cold. But now the sun was low and I shivered as I got up. Once I had shaken myself a couple of times and lit a cigarette, I was ready once again to meet reality.

The layers of basalt appeared razor-sharp in the evening sun, the rocks and skerries were sparkling like gold and the tuffstone was redder than ever. Nature was effervescent with springtime and hope. On the other hand there was not a soul to be seen.

I walked slowly up to the plane wreck, which lay black and gaunt on an area of flat land within the cordon. It felt a little strange to be alone with the remains, because just a short time before they had been surrounded by a crowd of people. But dinner and *Faroes Today* were much more attractive as the evening drew in. People could sit at home and enjoy the horror they had just been so close to. If they were lucky they'd also get to see themselves on some of the images on the television.

As I stood by the cordon and looked at the burned remains, a feeling of unease came over me. The crash and the ensuing fire had created total destruction. I was glad that the remains of the three on board had been taken away before I arrived. I couldn't even bring myself to think of the smell that the taxi driver had been talking about.

It would only be light for another hour or maybe an hour and a half, and I had to try to get down into the village to find shelter before darkness fell. Fortunately I had my mobile phone with me and could call the talkative taxi driver. Although I knew that mobiles were useful for many reasons, I wasn't really the best of friends with mine. I'd had a mobile for several years now, but I hardly ever had it on me and it was hardly ever on. But this time I had remembered it.

I walked over to the hillside to see the part of the plane that had escaped the crash almost intact. Other than the tail itself, that had G-HMMV on the side, there were also about two metres of the fuselage. I crossed the cordon to look at the smashed section itself and as soon as I looked into the opening of the wreck my blood ran cold. Half a metre in, in the area that I guessed had been the cargo hold, the floor was black and burned. So the tail hadn't been flung over here when the plane hit the ground at breakneck speed. It had been blown off from the inside.

I looked around, but couldn't see anyone. I was completely alone with the wreck.

There could be no doubt that the police had come to the same conclusion as I. Now we knew with certainty that five people had been killed. It was completely by chance that the plane hadn't come down in the middle of the ocean and never been found again. Presumably they had decided to make the most of the beautiful weather and undertake a sightseeing tour along Suðuroy's bird cliffs when the back part of the plane had been blown off.

Suddenly something hit the tail of the plane. And then I heard the shot.

Nineteen

I dropped to the ground and crawled as quickly as I could to the cover of the tail.

Whoever had fired the shot was somewhere up in the mountains above and only needed to wait for me to try to make a run for it. There was essentially nothing to hide behind. A mound here and a rock there – that was all. He could also have just come down here and finished me off if that was what he wanted. I had no way of defending myself.

Was it the same guy as in Tórshavn? Was it just another warning shot?

Still behind the plane's tail I got up and cautiously looked up towards the mountainside. Before I'd had a chance to see anyone at all, a bullet hit the edge of the metal so that it splintered. I immediately drew in my head.

Something warm ran down my cheek and when I reached up to see what it was, my fingers were coloured by blood. The splinters from that damn shot had cut me. I could forget about the idea that these were warning shots. This was serious.

There wasn't a soul to be seen. I looked in all the directions I dared to look in fear of what he might do next. But the result was the same. There was no one.

Maybe they'd heard the shots down in the village and would come to see what it was? It certainly wasn't hunting season, but from realising that to actually getting up from the sofa to investigate where the shots came from - that was a long way. No, I couldn't count on any help.

Who the hell would be trying to kill me? If that was what he was trying to do.

I took my coat off, rolled it up and held it above the edge of the tail, and immediately a bullet went through it.

This wasn't a game, and I'd have to make sure I could get out of this myself. I put the jacket back on; it now had four air holes in it.

What about my mobile phone? I could phone the police station in Tórshavn - I knew the number - and ask for help. The problem was that my mobile was in my bag and I had left that where I was when the first bullet was fired. About five to seven metres away. Much too far for me to attempt to go and get it.

It seemed a little strange that the gunman hadn't hit me with his first shot. He had clearly had shooting practice. On the other hand, I knew that it was difficult to shoot downwards and he had had to aim towards the sun. These incidental details dictated the difference between life and death.

I couldn't stay here, although one possibility would be to wait until darkness fell and I could get away. The problem was that whoever was waiting up there presumably hadn't intended to wait so long.

So what then?

If I tried to get away I would be shot, and if I stayed where I was, before long I would be staring down the barrel of a gun. A true dilemma.

It occurred to me that it wasn't completely unfeasible that I might be able to slip between the horns. It meant, however, that I would need to be able to see where the gunman was, and how was I supposed to do that? If I stuck my head out, that would be it for me. But if I could make a viewing hole in one way or another so that I could observe him without his knowledge... well, then...

The tail-end of the Cessna was on the ground and as it formed an arch, there was a possibility here. I got down on my knees, tore the grass away and started digging with a flat stone under the tail-piece. After about ten minutes I had made a hole and shortly afterwards I could see up to the middle of the mountainside. I couldn't see the top, but I didn't think that it mattered. Anyway, under the present circumstances, there wasn't much I could do about it.

For a while nothing happened. The mountainside looked as normal and peaceful as any other in the Faroes. And it was shining like gold in the evening sun. The only movements came from the scattered sheep. I was beginning to wonder whether the gunman might have given up his endeavour when I caught sight of something green moving.

On a steep section of the mountain I could see the back of someone climbing down. He was dressed in camouflage clothes and had a black backpack on. But where was his gun?

For a moment I had no idea what was going on – he had to be the one who was after me, unless there were several of them. My plan had been to wait precisely until the gunman was on a steep section and didn't have his weapon ready, and then I would run as fast as I could to the edge of the cliff and then hide under something or other. I hadn't been able to see any other way out. But now I was in doubt.

Then it dawned on me. His gun was in his backpack, and it would take more than a split-second to put it together. As this thought was going through my head, I jumped up and raced down towards the bird cliffs. I didn't turn around to see what the gunman was up to. I didn't dare. I ran faster than I had ever run before. I was running for my life.

When I got to the hillside above the bird cliffs, the plan was to stop, but I slipped on the dewy grass and went straight over the edge.

Twenty

It was dark when I woke up. And cold. I sat up and tried to look around. I could see a gleaming stripe of moonlight on the sea. On the other side I could feel a rock face. I reached up and touched a rock ceiling above me.

Where was I? What had happened?

Slowly my memory returned. I had fallen over the edge, but was nevertheless still alive. My body felt bruised and numb, but I hadn't broken anything. Presumably I was lying on a flat bit of the cliff face rather high up. Instead of ending up in the sea, I must have hit a projection and rolled under an overhang. The fall hadn't been far, but far enough for me to lose consciousness.

My fingers were stiff with the cold, and I tried to breathe on them to warm them up, but it didn't make much of a difference.

How was I going to get away from here? I stuck my head out and looked down. In the light of the moon I could see that there were about fifty steep metres between me and the sea. Upwards it was six at most, but it was vertical.

And then there was the gunman.

Was he lying in wait for me, or had he left, convinced I was dead? At the bottom of most of the bird cliffs there was a rocky beach where my lifeless body should be lying right now. When he didn't see a body, it wasn't unimaginable that he'd assumed I was hiding somewhere; that I hadn't fallen the whole way down, but had ended up part-way down. And that was exactly what had happened.

I looked at my watch. Twenty minutes to midnight. I had been unconscious for several hours. The question was whether he had had the patience to sit in the darkness for so long and wait for me to make myself known. That was what clever people called a 'good question'. Of course I couldn't know whether the person who shot at me across the harbour in Tórshavn and the person who was shooting at me here on Suðuroy's cliff tops were one and the same. The intention hadn't been the same: the first time to frighten and the second to kill. At the same time I had no idea who had been waiting to shoot me out here. Nevertheless, I suspected they were the same person and that when he saw I wasn't about to withdraw from the game, he had come to the conclusion that the best thing to do would be to finish me off.

But there was one thing I was sure of and that was that this person wasn't Faroese. He was acting much too professionally to be one of the usual hotheads in this country. Furthermore, at the police station they had said that the bullet that had been shot into my office wall was unusual. I had also seen the back of the man when he had climbed down the steep section and taken note of his backpack. A marksman with a rifle that could be taken apart so that it could be carried on his back was not a common sight here.

That the person who was trying to kill me was a professional could indicate that he wouldn't give up just like that. Before I decided how I was going to get out of here, I was going to have to find out whether or not he was still here.

A few metres away there were some guillemots on a shelf on the cliff. I found a little stone and threw it towards them. With whistling wings and characteristic cries the guillemots took flight, while I turned onto my back so that I could see the cliff edge. Shortly afterwards, firstly a gun barrel and then the outline of a head appeared on top of the cliff.

Twenty-One

I drew my head in immediately. That bastard had been sitting up there waiting for me to draw attention to myself, so that he could send me a greeting in lead. Undoubtedly with a steel core.

My heart was thumping so much that I was worried he'd be able to hear it. At the same time I knew that that was impossible, but when fear takes over, reason takes flight.

I couldn't stay here, but trying to climb up the cliff was unthinkable with very good reason. And just below the flat bit of cliff that I was lying on beneath the overhanging section there was a vertical drop. How it looked to the north I couldn't really determine in the darkness, but to the south I thought I could discern an inlet with pebbles. If I could get there, it wasn't inconceivable that I might be able to get away.

I looked cautiously up the side of the cliff but couldn't see anyone. But I was in no doubt that he was nearby. I gently eased myself out and could see that the first part of the journey was a combination of grass-covered rock ledges and ledges of eroded tuff. The former you could rely on if you were careful, but the latter less so - you only had to look at it and it crumbled.

Carefully I moved step by step along a grass-covered ledge, and for a while it went well. But then I came to a section where there was a rock sticking out of the grass and it became more difficult. There wasn't much to hold on to and even less to put your feet on. But this was the only way. I'd have to go around the cliff face.

For a moment I listened to see whether I could hear anything, but other than the gentle crashing of the waves it was completely silent. I felt around the rock with my fingers and grabbed a little knoll and then moved my right foot bit by bit until it seemed to be in a crack. I pulled myself round, trying to divide my weight between my hands and my feet. It worked. Hand by hand and foot by foot I moved around the rock with a verse from the old 'Kall og svein ungi' ballad going round and round in my head:

> *If you had hung from the mountain!*
> *On a good climbing rope.*
> *Simple stocking yarn!*
> *With yourself on the end.*

Although I didn't have much stocking yarn with me, I made it to a grass ledge and from there it was much easier to move and I could pick up some speed as I went down the slope, down to the bay which in the moonlight clearly showed itself to be large. I reckoned I had got through the worst and no longer paid so much attention to where I placed my feet. At that point the ground suddenly became tuffstone and I set off a minor stone slide. I was close to going down with it, but I managed to grab hold of the grass.

The sound of the small stones plummeting down the cliffs and puffin nesting areas sounded to my ears like a landslide, although only a few birds reacted. But someone else did hear it and a bullet hit a rock just by my left foot, whistling as it ricocheted out into the sea.

Now I started climbing down with some real speed, and I slid and rolled down towards the bay, while several shots were fired in my direction. One of them came so close that I felt it go through my hair. Fortunately the terrain turned inwards again almost immediately and I was under cover. Temporarily at least.

Not long afterwards I was standing on the pebbles and could see that the bay was wide and easy to climb out of. If it hadn't been for the gunman, of course. Trying to climb up directly from the bay would mean certain death. I'd have to head further south and into a steeper area again, where there would be possible cover for me.

As quickly as the uneven ground allowed, I hurried across the bay, fully aware of the fact that it resembled a lit stage now that the moon was in the west. But something must have hindered the gunman, because I made it over to the rocks at the coast intact, where the landscape once again rose up. After a few hundred metres I came to bird cliffs once again, and I wondered whether I should perhaps try to climb up to the grass-covered southern arm of the fjord.

I paused for a moment and leaned back against the cliff face. I wasn't only filthy, but was also close to becoming exhausted. I needed to have a rethink. But there wasn't much time for any thoughts, because at that moment I thought I could see something move over on the shore.

Then everything was as it was before. I held my breath and waited. If I squinted and strained my eyes, I could see something darker than the pebbles. During the First World War, the soldiers who were waiting in the trenches learned not to look directly in the direction from which they thought an attack might come, but just to one side. I decided to try that trick.

For a time nothing happened, but I could still make out that shadow. A little while later I was convinced that there was nothing out of the ordinary and I'd be able to climb up the steep, grassy section. Just then the dark silhouette moved a few paces and then stood still again. He was there!

The gunman clearly didn't know where I was, but presumably supposed I was nearby. So he was scouting the whole bay for signs of movement. My overcoat was a similar shade of grey to the cliffs, so it was hard to see me if I stayed still. And there wasn't much else to do at that point.

It felt as if hours passed. My body became stiffer and stiffer. I hardly dared blink. The stars were shining in the sky as though competing with the moon to light up the night. I wanted to tell both parties where to go.

And so, finally, after perhaps a quarter of an hour, the bent shadow began to move upwards. A short time later and he was gone. I was suddenly aware of how I was panting for breath and realised that I had hardly breathed at all while I had been keeping an eye on that dark figure. Now there was only one way to go and that was south to the bird cliffs.

The first stretch didn't present any particular problems, but then the way became steeper and steeper, eventually becoming almost vertical. But there was no other way.

What saved me and allowed me to get higher were the grass-covered rock shelves. I didn't dare put my foot on the areas where there was tuff, but there was so much grass everywhere that I could grab hold of it and heave myself up rock shelf by rock shelf. I had got about a hundred metres up when I heard the shot. Where the bullet had ended up, I didn't know, but it didn't hit me. This game couldn't carry on, as sooner or later the gunman would hit his target.

When the gunman hadn't been able to see me further inside the bay, he had presumably gone out to the shore again and a figure on the bird cliffs had caught his attention.

That was it for me. The only thing I could do to avoid being shot was to jump into the deep. And I wouldn't come out of that alive. I groped like mad around the cliff face, feeling that the weapon was probably being targeted right on my back. Then I noticed that there was an opening a little to the right and I moved in that direction.

The bullet hit the cliff exactly where I had been less than a second before.

The opening was roughly the same size as the peephole on a church tower, and I stuck my arm in to feel around. The cliff wall was about thirty centimetres thick here, but after that I couldn't feel anything. I reached in as far as I could, but my hand was simply waving about in the air. What if it went down a long way inside? It didn't matter. The situation could hardly get worse.

I grabbed hold of both sides of the opening and pulled myself in through the hole, falling into deep nothingness.

Twenty-Two

That's what it felt like, even though I fell a metre and a half at most and didn't get as much as a scratch. I sat up. The ground beneath me was uneven and from where I was sitting, I couldn't reach any wall.

Where on earth had I ended up? This wasn't a puffin hole, but maybe a grotto that had been created with the Faroes millions of years ago. If that was the case, there would hardly be any other way out than the way I had come in.

Suddenly I remembered my lighter, my magnificent plastic lighter that I hadn't left in my bag up by the wreck. In the light of the flame I could see that it wasn't far to the walls or the roof. I was just somewhere where I couldn't reach them. But I could see that the hole went further into the mountain and it became clear to me that it had been created by human hands.

There were remains of wooden posts and supports under parts of the roof. I was in a coal mine. I remembered hearing many years ago that while mining for coal they had broken through into the bird cliffs in the west. I had found one of these openings.

I turned the lighter off. It was no more than half full and I might need it for a long while yet. For the time being I was safe, but I had no idea how I would find my way to the exit on the other side of the mountain. But there was nothing else to do other than go for it. Before I set off on my exodus, I lit a Prince to calm my nerves and to relieve the tiredness and the hunger.

A short time later I was bent over on my way into the mountain, hoping that I hadn't become too confused as I moved along the tunnels and that I would soon find something to indicate that I was on the right track. Hoping I wouldn't wander around inside a mountain on Suðuroy for all eternity.

I lit my lighter, looked as far ahead as I could, turned it off and walked for ten metres, and then lit it again. I still couldn't walk upright and there were no tracks for coal wagons on the ground. They had either taken them away once they had stopped using this tunnel or they had never been there. After about two hundred metres, after walking several times through puddles, I came into a larger tunnel with tracks and now I could straighten out my back. Lovely.

Then another question came to me: which way should I go? Left or right? I turned off the lighter and tried to see whether I could detect any light from either direction, but then I remembered that it was the middle of the night. I also tried to listen out in case there was something to hear, but apart from the odd drop of water, it was perfectly still. Only the sound of a water drop now and again. Other than that, just stillness.

I didn't know anything about coal mining on Suðuroy and therefore didn't have any idea either which way I should go. If I chose the wrong direction I ran the risk of wading around in here for hours. Maybe for days? I went to the left.

At first everything went fine. I felt my way along one cart track and only used my light now and again. So far the ground had been fairly even, but now I was walking downhill. The ground became worse and worse. It had been a good number of years since coal had been mined here and in some places the roof had caved in. I was forced to use my lighter just to move forwards, and in some places I had to climb over piles of rocks.

I passed one side tunnel after another and was almost certain that I was going the right way, when suddenly the path ahead was blocked. The roof had collapsed and formed a blockade without an opening. I didn't dare think of how many tonnes would need to be moved for me to be able to get through. If I threw myself into this act of madness, probably just more would fall down and I'd still not make it out.

The only option was to go back to the nearest side tunnel

and hope that it connected to another on the other side of the fallen rock.

The side tunnel had no tracks and was so low that I couldn't walk upright, but after only fifty metres I found a tunnel that ran parallel with the main tunnel. I entered it and, after a relatively short stretch, there was a tunnel that led back to the main tunnel. Rather happy with myself, I followed it. But alas: where the side tunnel joined the main one more of the roof had fallen in, and there was nothing I could do about it. Back to the parallel tunnel.

History repeated itself with the next two side tunnels. It looked like a large part of the main tunnel had collapsed. What if the whole thing had come down? Was there any way out of here at all if the main tunnel was blocked?

My tiredness really caught up with me at this point and I began to doubt that I would ever get out of this mountain. At one place water trickled down the wall in a constant stream and I filled my hands. It was good water and I drank until I was no longer thirsty.

I sat on a rock which had undoubtedly fallen from the roof and smoked a cigarette while I had a think. Trying every single side tunnel to the main tunnel would take a very long time. Even though the parallel tunnel was low and narrow, it was probably best to follow it all the way along to see where I ended up.

I started to think about Frodo and his friends who walked through the dwarves' deserted mountain in *The Lord of the Rings*. Although they had Gandalf to light the way for them and give them directions, they still had orcs and a Balrog to fight against. I didn't think I was likely to meet anyone like that in this mine, but maybe a nice hulder? We'd have to see.

I threw down the cigarette butt and got up, lit my lighter and stumbled as I made my way along the passage, still unable to stand upright. It was low and tight in many places, but it was still possible to move forwards. One side tunnel after the other opened up on either side, but I determinedly held my course to the bitter end.

And it was bitter. At one point the tunnel abruptly came to

an end and it was clear that it had never been any longer. So I went back a few metres and into a side tunnel that would lead me to the main one. After fifty metres it was the same old story. The main tunnel was shut off.

It was a real disappointment and for a moment I was close to giving up. But my resolve returned. There was no way on earth that I'd let some arsehole gunman force me to end up as a skeleton in a deserted coal mine.

I turned on my heels and went straight back to the parallel passage and crossed it into another side tunnel. After a short time it became seriously difficult to move forwards, but I wriggled and crawled between the roof and the fallen rock. I scraped my hands and knees and ruined what was left of my clothes. At regular intervals I lit the lighter, but there were no side tunnels to be seen.

Suddenly I thought I saw a glimpse of light out of the corner of my right eye in the pitch-black darkness. I took a step backwards and saw it again. I went up to the wall and through a little hole I saw darkness, with a bluish light in the centre. Stars. This time I didn't curse them.

Now I could also feel a breeze through the hole and took in how fresh the air was. I lit the lighter and had to shield the flame so that it wouldn't go out. In the light I could see that it wasn't part of the ceiling that had collapsed, but just a stone slide from the wall. Most of it was gravel and small stones.

With my hands and feet I scooped and dug my way through the pile so that I could get through. The outermost part of the corridor had come down and was so low that I had to crawl to get out into the fresh air.

Opposite the entrance lay what was left of a post and I was just about to push that to one side when I caught sight of the silhouette of a person about twenty metres away. With full clarity under the starry and moonlit night I saw the gunman in camouflage clothes crouched down behind a rock with the side of his body towards me. On the rock his gun was ready.

Twenty-Three

When was this going to end?

I crawled a short stretch backwards into the mine. The gunman had clearly done his homework before coming to Suðuroy. Someone who didn't know the area would never have known that I had gone into a mine tunnel that would open out onto the west side of the mountain. He knew the mine and its tunnels and knew they crossed straight through the mountain. But one thing he didn't know was that part of the main tunnel had collapsed and that I had emerged from an older part of the mine.

He was lying upon a rise while the entrance to the mine was in a smaller gorge, where a load of rock had come down. It wouldn't be possible to get down towards the village, but if I carefully crawled up the hill to the left it wasn't unthinkable that I'd be able to sneak away.

Inch by inch I crept out of the mine and then lay there for a while with my nose pressed to the earth. There were no sounds coming from the gunman. I chose not to look that way. I crawled and slid further. And then waited again, listening.

How long it took me to get up the gorge, over the peak and down into a hollow on the other side, I didn't know. But I did know that this was a case of life and death and therefore for that time my existence consisted of crawling and listening. Nothing else.

Once out of sight, I wondered what I could now do to get away. If I walked in a large arch around where the gunman was and then down towards Trongisvágur, I should make it. But it would take hours for someone like me who didn't know these parts. If I chose instead to make for the plane wreck, my bag and my mobile phone, I could make contact with the outside world within half an hour. Of course, that would only be possible if the gunman hadn't taken my bag. I guessed that he had his hands full trying to come after me, when I had just flown over the edge of the cliff at full pelt and therefore hadn't noticed the shoulder bag in the grass.

I was desperate to light a cigarette, but I didn't dare. Instead I gritted my teeth and rushed as fast as I could towards the plane wreck.

The moon was going down, but the stars were shining with full strength and out here in the middle of nature where there was no light pollution to get in the way, I could see too many to count. And suddenly, despite my tiredness and pain here and there, I was filled with joy – partly because I had escaped with my life and partly because the landscape was so overwhelming and never-ending. For the last quarter of an hour, until I caught sight of the tail of the plane, I sang aloud to myself:

Fair is creation,
Fairer God's heaven,
Blest is the marching pilgrim throng.
Onward through lovely
Regions of beauty
Go we to Paradise with song! (J.C. Aaberg)

All verses straight through. Several times. If you were being ironic, you might say maybe I only knew the hymn because it was so short. And that would not be entirely wrong. But nevertheless the song expressed the pure joy of being alive. Of existing.

My bag was exactly where I had left it, and a moment later my mobile phone made a connection and I called the police station in Tórshavn.

The phone rang several times before a sleepy voice answered it: 'Police.'

'I'm up on the bird cliffs west of Tvøroyri,' I said. 'A gunman has been after me since last night.'

104

'I see,' growled the voice on the other end. 'April Fools' Day was a while ago now. You have to find something else to do than make prank calls to us.'

'Wait, wait!' I yelled quickly, because I could tell that the officer was about to put the receiver down. 'I'm not joking. You can call Karl Olsen and tell him that Hannis Martinsson has been attacked on Suðuroy. We know each other.'

'Karl's asleep, and I'm not just going to phone him at five o'clock in the morning.'

Only now did I realise what the time was. It hadn't occurred to me since I woke up under the shelter of the rock. I had had too much going on.

There was silence on the other end of the line. Then came the hesitant question, 'Did you say that your name was Hannis Martinsson?'

'Yes.'

Then there was another pause.

'Piddi í Útistovu was going around here last night cursing a man with that name. If that's you, I wouldn't be in a hurry to meet him.'

'I know Piddi,' I said. 'And I doubt he's ever said anything nice about me. Or to me for that matter.'

The man on the other end laughed. That had to be progress.

'So do you believe me?'

The laughter stopped.

'Where did you say you were, and what has happened?' came a professional voice.

'I'm west of Tvøroyri, close to the place they call "The Telescope". A man has tried to shoot me several times. He's still nearby and if you can get some from here to hurry over, you should get him. If you speak to Karl, you can tell him that I think it's the same guy who fired into my office on Sunday.'

'I heard about that,' said the officer, and you could hear in his voice that he was now awake and interested. 'I'll phone Karl, he can sleep some other time, and if he says that's ok, we'll contact the police on Suðuroy.'

Now we were getting somewhere.

'Give me your number and don't turn off your phone,' he added finally.

I gave him my number and leaned back against the tail of the plane to wait. One cigarette later I heard the sirens from a police car in the distance drawing closer.

As the sky reddened with the sun in the eastern sky, I thought to myself how great it was that the police could be so discreet when they needed to be.

Twenty-Four

There was a furious gale outside and the wind whistled as it passed through shrouds and fenders on the boats out in the bay. The jetties moved as though alive and at Vágsbotnur a good few men were wading around in thigh-boots where the harbour area stood under water, so that you couldn't tell the difference between the quayside and the harbour. Others stood in the shelter of houses and evaluated the chances of their boat making it. That kind of weather wasn't common around Walpurgis Tide, but a storm had come from Greenland and turned east by the Faroe Islands and had now hit with full power from the south-east. The worst wind direction in Tórshavn.

But in here it was calm. The radiators were red-hot and I had put masking tape over all the gaps around the windows so that the whole office didn't fly around. For now only an empty paint tin was needed to catch the drops from above.

While I watched the battle on the harbour and over by the shipyard, where they were fighting to moor the rusty longliner, I hummed:

How glorious in the Faroes at Walpurgis Tide,
The earth awakens, that maiden so fair.

Well, the earth had certainly woken up, but it was no fair young maiden. Rather a fury of the worst calibre.

I cut my song. If I wasn't careful I'd end up like everyone else in the country – in a choir. And as far as that was concerned, I'd always been told that I didn't have a tuneful note in me.

I tasted my whisky and observed the smoke from my

cigarette. It twisted and turned as it rose. It was well insulated here, if I said so myself. And I did just that. Now I was becoming aware that my Scottish drink was starting to have an influence on me, even though it was the middle of the afternoon. Although I thought I'd earned a little one, I had to be careful. No one knew what was waiting for me out there.

I had bought the bottle of whisky at Drelnes before travelling north again with *Smyril*. That I hadn't seen the state alcohol shop, *Rúsdrekkasølan*, when I arrived, I couldn't understand, but fortunately I managed to get provisions for the trip north. It said Highland Park on the black label on the bottle. Below that was a picture of islands in a sunset. It could almost have been the Faroe Islands.

My years in Denmark had given me a taste for single malt, and that was possible because prices had become so low in Denmark. Here it was also possible, because although the price for regular spirits was more or less double what it was in Denmark, the more expensive types cost more or less the same. The selection wasn't large, but Highland Park was going to be just fine.

Naturally the gunman had been scared off when the two police officers showed up. But I showed them the shot that had hit the tail of the plane and together we drove over to the coal mine where I pointed to the place where he had been lying in wait. But there were no foot prints to be seen – or anything else.

Whether or not they believed me was a different story altogether, but they had managed to get the bullet out of the tail of the plane. At the station I had had a shower, borrowed some clothes so that I no longer resembled a scarecrow and been given something to eat. While they were speaking to Tórshavn, I had the chance to lie down on a sofa. I was completely gone until I was awoken at about midday.

The officers that had come to get me from the bird cliffs were tall and young and more or less what you would expect – you wouldn't be able to distinguish between them and fifty other police officers in the Faroes – but, going on appearances, the one that woke me certainly wasn't from our time. He was so big that when I opened my eyes and saw him leaning over me I had an acute attack of claustrophobia. And I hadn't even had that in the mine. As he straightened himself out, it looked as if his head was touching the ceiling.

He reminded me of a Viking chief. Or at least he looked like how we imagine them to look. Fortunately there was neither an axe nor a sword in his hand.

His blue eyes gleamed and he smiled through his large, red beard which went down to his chest.

'Six foot six and eighteen and a half stone. That's it.'

I sat up and asked eloquently, 'Huh?'

'Those are the questions everyone wants answers to when they meet me for the first time.'

He was in a uniform that could have been used as a circus tent when he was on leave and offered me a hand that was the same size as a large saucepan lid.

'Kim Christensen,' he introduced himself in a voice that matched his appearance. It was like a stone slide that began down in his stomach, rose up through his throat and culminated when he opened his mouth. Right now he was speaking quietly, but it was obvious that you wouldn't want to be standing in front of him when he was shouting.

'Hannis Martinsson,' I said, wondering where my right hand had gone. Next to Kim Christensen I felt like a very little younger brother.

'The on-duty officer has told me your story.' He smiled. 'Up north they're saying that what you're saying is not completely implausible, but they also tell me that you have an incredible ability to poke your nose into all kinds of situations that don't really concern you.'

He looked directly into my eyes.

'Everything I have said is *true*,' I said, with emphasis on that final word. 'Not particularly funny, fairly improbable, but true.'

'Well then, there we have it.' He rubbed his hands. 'Let's go back to mine to get a bite to eat and then we'll go to Drelnes.'

'A bite to eat' was eight eggs, a double packet of bacon, half a dozen sausages and half a loaf of rye bread. With his food he drank a pot of coffee. His wife, who had prepared the sumptuous meal, wasn't much taller than his navel, but she was lively and warm. Nevertheless, it didn't go down too well when I said I wasn't hungry, but that a glass of milk would be lovely. I thought I heard her mumble something along the lines of 'Typical northerner', as she went to the fridge.

In the car on the way to Drelnes, Kim Christensen told me that I wasn't the only reason he was driving to the ferry port. The plan was that we were to look at the fellow passengers as they boarded so that I could let him know whether I recognised the gunman. After all, this was my pursuer's first opportunity to get off the island.

For the whole journey to Drelnes I sat with my hands clasped tightly around the handle on the door so that I wouldn't fall onto the massive police officer. His car wasn't new and with this driver the suspension had become so weak that there was a noticeable tilt towards the driver's seat. Whenever he turned to the left, it felt like I was sitting on a steep mountainside.

It was no later than half-past one when we got out of the car at Drelnes. *Smyril* wasn't due to sail for another two hours, but Kim wanted to make sure that no one got on board without us seeing them.

It was while we were waiting that I realised that *Rúsdrekkasølan* was close by and that it would soon be open. Kim Christensen said I could pay a little visit to the shop, as long as I promised to hurry.

A few minutes later I was back with two carrier bags. In one I had two bottles of Highland Park and six Tuborg Golds in the other. The large police officer had got changed into a dark brown knitted jumper, grey trousers and clogs while we had been at his house. He reckoned that if he were to have a can of Tuborg in his hand he would be completely anonymous. That people would think he was one of the many layabouts that drink their days away. I tilted my head back and looked at him. I had my doubts, but I didn't say anything.

We leaned against the wall of a house and drank the beers as empty lorries and vans drove onto the ferry. By the time they started to untie the mooring ropes, hardly any foot passengers had got on board, and certainly no one I recognised from the bird cliffs.

Kim said goodbye and told me he would let his wife know that I drank other things besides milk.

As I boarded – the last to do so – I thought to myself that it wasn't often necessary to try to convince someone of that fact.

Twenty-Five

Now I could hear shouting from outside. I went over to the window and looked out. The rusty longliner, which had once been yellow, had broken free of its rear moorings. The wind had taken hold of the stern and turned the ship around. Now it was in danger of coming free completely. If that happened, it would end up on the slipway having crushed everything in its path.

As I stood there in my shirt sleeves watching as they struggled by the shipyard, a rare feeling of peace came over me. What remained of the whirlwind had moved over the bay, the showers were constant, the jetties sought to break free and on the longliner they fought like crazy to cast the ropes to land. But none of this affected me any more than if it had been a film I was watching on TV from my armchair. Here it was calm – and I had my whisky and cigarettes.

Maybe the whisky was beginning to make its effects felt?

As soon as I had come into land at Eystara Bryggja I headed up to the police station. Fortunately it was Karl I had to deal with, rather than Piddi. I gave him the bullet from the plane's tail-end, as the Viking on Suðuroy had asked me to, and told him the whole story.

During the telling Karl only interrupted me a few times when he needed something explained further. Otherwise he listened in silence.

'I don't really know what to think,' he said once I had finished. 'It all sounds rather unlikely. You go to Suðuroy off your own bat to look at the plane wreck and then, as evening approaches and you are alone, someone starts shooting at you. The only possibility I can see is that the gunman followed you down south and waited for his opportunity. But that doesn't really make sense – here in Tórshavn he only fires warning shots, while on Suðuroy he does his utmost to finish you off.'

'Maybe it's precisely because I went to Suðuroy that he decided that warning shots were no longer enough.'

'Maybe, maybe,' mumbled Karl.

We sat there for a while without either of us saying anything, as Karl twisted the bullet between the thumb and index finger on his right hand.

'We've heard back from Denmark,' he broke the silence, took a piece of paper and put it on the desk. 'The bullet that was fired into the office is a 223 calibre. According to the analysis, the cartridge was a GP90 with a steel core of 63 grain, which is the same as 4.08 grams. It's Swiss ammunition, so they reckon it was probably fired from an SIG 550 sniper rifle, a weapon for specialists. SIG stands for *Schweizerische Industrie Gesellschaft*. The rifle has a telescopic sight, is easy to dismantle and reassemble again and is usually transported in a small steel case that resembles a laptop case. So you can walk around happily with one of these and no one is any the wiser.'

'And this,' he continued, placing the bullet from Suðuroy in the palm of his left hand and stretching it out towards me, 'looks like it's of the same type.'

'Who on earth sent a specialist to the Faroes to kill me?' A chill ran down my spine.

'Don't flatter yourself,' Karl grinned, although there was no laughter in his eyes. 'This individual presumably had something to do with Mark Robbins and the dead bodies found among the whales. You just got caught up in it. We have no idea how it all fits together. Not yet anyway,' he added.

'What about the plane? From what I could see, the tail-end had been blown off before the plane came down.'

Karl looked at me. 'You are observant, aren't you? Naturally the investigations have not yet been completed, but it seems fairly clear that there was an explosion on board the plane. Unfortunately for the people who put the bomb on there, the plane was above land when it exploded. If it had come down over the sea, we would probably never have heard anything more about it.'

For a short time we both sat there in our thoughts. Mine weren't particularly cheerful.

After a while Karl asked with a chuckle, 'What the hell have you got on? You look like someone in an amateur play in one of the villages.'

I looked down at myself and had to admit that he was right. My trousers were too short, but were tightly tied with a belt around my waist because they were too large. My red and black checked shirt was much too big, while the arms of my coat didn't reach down to my wrists. I looked like I belonged in a farce.

I was exhausted and everything that needed to be said had been said. I asked Karl to say hello to Katrin from me and to thank her once again for the wonderful meal I had when I was last there, said goodbye and walked out the door.

As I made my way down the corridor I heard a female voice calling after me.

'Hannis, wait!'

I recognised the voice and a shudder went through me.

Twenty-Six

The glass was empty, but this time it was my will that won the victory. I put the bottle in the bottom drawer of my desk. Coffee. I needed coffee to get some clarity in my head. I couldn't get that here, so I'd need to go somewhere else. Why not Eyskarið?

While I put my black padded jacket on – I had of course ruined my coat on Suðuroy – I heard a powerful rain shower hammer down on the roof. Drops began to fall at great frequency into the paint tin, but that wasn't a problem. I simply emptied it before setting off.

The woman who had called after me at the police station was a beautiful, black-haired woman in uniform. Her face was just as pale as before, but a little thinner, and with no wrinkles other than laughter lines by her eyes. Her red lips were enticing and there was no trace of grey in her hair. It was Duruta, who had once been my girlfriend and whom I hadn't seen since I moved to Denmark.

I stopped outside the Seaman's Home – or Hotel Tórshavn, as it called itself these days – and looked at the harbour. It looked as if they had managed to get the longliner under control, although a number of smaller boats had broken free. A wild dance was taking place on several of the jetties, where men had their hands full trying to stay on their feet while simultaneously trying to catch hold of the lost boats.

A powerful smell of pizza came from the restaurant in the basement of the former seaman's home, and it felt somewhat unreal in light of the battle taking place outside. I pulled the zip of my jacket right up to my neck and with the south-east wind on my back I walked up Tórsgøta.

Duruta and I had looked at each other, and I was strongly reminded of what I was wearing. But Duruta just touched the wound on my cheek with the tips of her fingers.

'You've hurt yourself,' she said, with warm sympathy in her voice.

'Yes, someone tried to kill me on Suðuroy. That's also why I'm wearing these clothes,' I hastened to add.

'I've heard about that,' she said. 'News travels quickly around this station.' She examined me with her sparkling, dark brown eyes. 'Why haven't you visited me?'

She clearly knew that a few days had passed since I came home. Karl or Katrin must have told her that.

'I've only just got back and I've had so much to do, sorting out the office and the house...' I faltered. 'But I was planning to pop in.' That last part was a half-truth, because even though I had thought about her several times, I never would have dared visit. 'I didn't know whether you'd got married and had a family and I didn't want to come along and disturb you,' I tried to make my excuses.

'Even if I'd got married, you could still visit,' she said teasingly. 'We know each other well enough.'

I could feel that I was blushing and had no idea what to say.

'Nah, take it easy,' Duruta laughed. 'I'm not married and I still have the one daughter. Her name is Turið and she's in the first year at Eysturskúlin. We live on Sodnhústún, you know, by the SMS shopping centre.'

She looked at her watch and exclaimed, 'Oh no, I have to go, I'm so late.'

She gave the cheek with the wound a quick kiss and hurried along the corridor. Just before she reached the end she turned around and called, 'Come and visit one day!'

The meeting with Duruta had stoked the fire that had never completely gone out. On the one hand I wanted to get close to her, on the other I had got so burned last time I was here. I didn't particularly want to go through those feelings again.

The rain had stopped for a moment and I stood overlooking the Gamli Kirkjugarður cemetery, looking out to the fjord. The wind had calmed down somewhat, but the whole fjord was foaming and down by the jetties the men would need to fight a little longer yet.

In Eyskarið, however, it was quiet. The radio was on, of course, but so low that you could hardly hear it. Three men were sitting in a corner playing cards, but there were no sounds coming from the billiard tables upstairs. There was no one behind the bar either. The coffee pot, on the other hand, was half-full and I went in, took a cup and sat a little distance away from the card players, whom I didn't really know as I had only spoken to them once or twice.

Both the next day's *Dimmalætting* and *Blaðið* were on the table and I sat down and looked at them – not that there was much of interest in them, even though they were much better than they used to be. A big traffic accident was on the front page of both papers, where it said that the Faroes were top of the league when it came to traffic deaths. One traffic advisor said that something needed to be done, while the journalist in one of the papers seemed to want to boast that the Faroes occupied this prime position. Then there was something about fishing, the obituaries, birthdays and a few lines of foreign news.

Dimmalætting contained a wealth of readers' letters, particularly on religious matters, but there was nothing new in that. Otherwise there were just the pages of advertisements which still filled most of the paper.

But a change had taken place in the last few years. Now all of the people who wanted independence from Denmark had started writing in *Dimmalætting*. Previously they would never even have looked at the paper, particularly if there was someone watching, but now it looked as if they had become so independence-minded that they were unionist.

'So, old boy, you're reading *Amtstidende for Færøerne*?' Haraldur came up the stairs from the basement, referring to the paper by its old Danish name.

'Why not? You've got to get your wisdom from somewhere – university doesn't cover everything.'

'Well, I don't think much of the wisdom you're aspiring to!' Haraldur laughed.

Jógvan Isaksen

'And what about you? Working tonight?' I asked.

'Yeah, they wanted me to help sort out the membership lists, but that's going to take quite some time. I just came up to get a beer and then I'll go back down again.' He looked questioningly at my cup. 'Are you sick or something?'

'No, I've sat drinking whisky for most of the afternoon. At some stage enough has to be enough.'

'If you say so, if you say so,' he mumbled with something resembling sorrow in his voice. He walked over to the bar and called out as he slammed his palm on the counter: 'Service!'

Quick steps could be heard coming down the stairs and the young fair-haired girl that had tended the bar on Saturday evening came half-running.

'I thought it was you. Now you can't even watch MTV in peace,' she said, with a playful smile.

'The working masses need their drinks, or they'll perish,' Haraldur objected.

'How in the world are you part of the working masses? As far as I'm aware you've always done whatever you felt like doing.' The girl placed a Veðrur beer and a double Gammel Dansk on the counter. She knew Haraldur.

'The rudeness of young people knows no boundaries these days,' Haraldur smiled to himself as he sat down beside me. 'Well, it doesn't look like you're in top form.' Haraldur looked at my cheek, which by now had scabbed over. 'What sort of scuffle have you been involved in?'

I told him quickly about the two intruders and the gunman and what it has been like getting through the mine.

He sat in thought for a while, fiddling with the label on the beer bottle. Then the girl behind the bar turned the radio up and a choir singing 'How Glorious are the Faroes at Walpurgis Tide' blared from the speakers.

'I know just as little as you about how this all fits together,' Haraldur said at last. 'But I want to help you as much as I can, when and if I can. These bloody environmental organisations mustn't think that they can just come to the Faroes and do whatever suits them.'

I mumbled something about it being unlikely that the

118

environmental organisations would kill one of their own, but my quiet protest disappeared in the noise of the choir.

'We're going to meet with the leaders of the pilot whale hunt tomorrow at four o'clock,' Haraldur was almost shouting now. 'At my house!' He stood up and went over to the bar, 'And that's enough of that!' he said, as he turned the radio down. The girl had disappeared again. She was probably upstairs watching MTV, while those of us downstairs were beaten by a flood of voices.

'Choir singing is like one of the plagues of Egypt. You can't take a step without hearing choir singing. Every single event starts and ends with choir singing.' Haraldur drank the rest of the bitter schnapps. 'Have the nerve to turn a radio on, and you'll have four-part harmony thrown in your face. Be so bold as to venture into town on Ólav's Wake, and you'll hit a choir no matter which way you turn. And worst of all at midnight on Vaglið Square.'

Haraldur took a mouthful of beer, then folded his hands and twiddled his thumbs. For a while, only the singing of 'Spring's Mild Breeze' could be heard. Then he laughed to himself:

'But otherwise you wouldn't actually think our choirs were ever in this country. I mean, they get so much money for trips abroad that they don't need to spend much time up here in the cold. As soon as someone gets the idea to go abroad and have a good time, one, two, three, piles of money are put forward from private and public funds so that forty to fifty people can have a laugh overseas for several weeks. The only thing they have to do in return is sing a song or two between drinks.'

I agreed with Haraldur completely and was presumably one of very few Faroese people never to have sung in a choir. All that talk about alcohol made me want something other than coffee. But I was resolute.

Haraldur laughed again. 'You should have sung in a choir, Hannis. Free trips and free drinks.'

I told him that I was as enthusiastic about choir singing as he was, but that maybe if you were standing in the middle of a load of singers, you didn't hear as much of the bawling. Maybe that was why there were so many choir singers in the Faroes?

We both laughed.

Twenty-Seven

A TV debate about whether the Faroes were on their way to becoming a developing country in terms of their fishing industry had finished and I had turned off the set. The programme was quite shocking in that it showed how exposed we were economically. Previously we had been a modern society, filleting and packing fish, but one fish factory after the other had closed down because the fish was sold untreated to other countries. They paid a better price than the Faroese and now people who were paid much less were filleting Faroese fish. Globalisation had hit the Faroes and no one was really sure what to do about it.

It wasn't unthinkable that the late Mark Robbins had been right when he said that his people could cripple the Faroes if it suited them. As things stood, it was uphill all the way.

I was at home, trying to stop thinking about what had happened to me, because I knew nowhere near enough for it to lead anywhere. My conclusion was that I had to find out more about the two dead activists. Maybe someone at the Heljareyga Guest House could help me? And perhaps the people at Sound Salmon?

I turned on the CD player and Leonard Cohen started singing 'The Stranger Song'. Out in the kitchen I made myself a gin and tonic and was met by 'who is reaching for the sky just to surrender' when I came back into the living room again. I had brought an armchair up from the basement and I sat down in it.

Maybe I should just get away from the whole thing? Travel somewhere for a while and hope that it had passed over by the time I got back? 'Never!' I said to myself. In addition to the break-ins here and at the office and the warning shots, an idiot had repeatedly tried to kill me on Suðuroy's bird cliffs. I would not and could not just accept that. This was my life and there were limits to what I would put up with.

Of course I could have chosen a different life, with a wife, kids and a house. I could have gone to the teacher-training college after I had finished sixth-form college, you could do that then, and behaved myself at some school or other and gone to the beer clubs at the weekend. Or I could have got a place at a bank, aged sixteen, seventeen – I knew several people that had done that – and worn a jacket and tie ever since. No, that would have been a fate worse than death. And I would probably have been fired ages ago. Certainly, in any case, during the most recent crisis.

I sipped the gin.

I couldn't have sat here like this if I was married. Or at least my wife would have had to be away on a course or something. On the other hand, that happened so frequently these days, that maybe I could have after all.

Maybe some would say that would be better than sitting in a beer club every night of the week. But if I had got married when I was young, you could guarantee that I would have been divorced by now, so I'd be sitting in the beer clubs anyway.

In *The Maltese Falcon* Sam Spade tells the story of a man on a trip who wants to get something to eat at about midday, but suddenly disappears without a trace. His wife and children are able to get by, because he owned his own house and business. Some years later Spade happens upon the man, who now has a new wife, children and a new business. He tells Spade that on his way to the restaurant he passed a site where they were building a new high-rise tower. A metal girding fell several storeys and landed right next to him. It didn't hit him, but a splinter from the pavement hit his cheek, giving him a scar.

The shock of the event got the man thinking about how it was sheer chance that dictated whether you lived or died and that he would have to arrange things accordingly. For about two years he travelled around, but then he moved back to the same state he had lived in previously and got married again. His new wife wasn't exactly like his first, but almost. His new life wasn't exactly like his first, but almost.

You can't escape your fate, I thought, and touched the scab on my cheek.

I was exhausted and tomorrow was going to be a long day, so I went upstairs to get into bed. On my bedside table was *Finnegan's Wake*, which I had hauled up to bed, in case I had any trouble sleeping. For several years I had tried to read that book, but had never got any further than the first few pages. Thanks to *Finnegan's Wake* I had never lacked sleep.

My mobile phone was also on the bedside table. I turned it on and wondered whether I should call Duruta. As far as the Faroese were concerned, it wasn't particularly late, so why not?

An envelope icon flashed in a corner at the bottom of the screen. It had been doing that for a while and I hadn't a clue what it meant. How could I get rid of it? I went into the *Menu* where I eventually discovered that an envelope meant I had a message on my voicemail. Presumably from the telephone company.

The screen asked whether I wanted to listen to the message, save it or delete it. Most of all I just wanted to get rid of it, but now that I'd got this service, I might as well try it.

As soon as I heard the voice, which spoke in English, I recognised it.

'My name is Joost Boidin. I'm the Dutchman you spoke with earlier today at the Heljareyga Guest House. We need to talk. Can you meet me at midnight by the empty, yellow concrete building above Boðanes? It's of the greatest importance that you come. Both of us are in danger.'

Now I was wide awake. I listened to the message from Joost Boidin twice more. Then I tried to find out when he left it. After a lot of fumbling I discovered that the message had been left on Saturday evening at ten minutes to ten. By then I'd gone to Eyskarið to play cards with Haraldur.

Why did I have to be so bloody useless with technology? I was so used to various things flashing on the screen that I hadn't paid it any attention.

Now it was Wednesday evening. Why hadn't the Dutchman got in contact with me? I had been in Tórshavn for the whole of Sunday and got back from Suðuroy yesterday around dinnertime.

I went into *Menu* again to see whether there were any other messages, but as far as I could see, it was just the one.

I was going to have to go down to Heljareyga to see whether Joost Boidin was there.

Twenty-Eight

The blue front door was unlocked although it was almost eleven. I went up the stairs, which creaked as much as they did last Saturday, but other than that, no sound could be heard. There was a light on in the kitchen and I opened the fridge. The things I had seen the Dutchman put in there almost five days ago were still there.

Then I suddenly remembered the postcard I had put in my pocket last time I was here, the one that had been sent from Hawaii to Stewart Peters, wishing him all the best for his 'hush-hush project'. Where was that? I vaguely remembered putting it on the kitchen table at home, but it wasn't there any longer. Had the guy who broke in to my house taken it? Was it the postcard he was after? It didn't sound very likely, but I was almost certain that he'd taken it.

Then I heard a rustle of paper.

I went into the corridor to listen. Dead silent.

I knocked on the closest door. No answer. The next one. Nothing there either. The third door led into the attic, which looked out over Dr Jakobsensgøta.

I stood stock-still and listened.

Nothing.

Then I heard someone looking through a newspaper. The sound came from the room at the end of the corridor, to the left as you came up the stairs.

I knocked on the door.

'Qui est-ce?' asked a dark female voice.

'Je suis Hannis Martinsson', I answered. 'Est qu'il y a possible de vous parlez?'

My French wasn't particularly good, but I heard steps inside

125

before the door opened.

A fair-haired woman in her mid-thirties looked at me with dark blue eyes. She wasn't much less than six foot, slim and wearing a grey tracksuit with a pink stripe down the arms and legs. Her jacket had a zip and was tight. The trousers just as tight-fitting. She was barefoot.

Her straight hair was clipped just below her ears, framing her large eyes and straight nose. Her broad lips were half-open, showing straight, white teeth.

She was beautiful and I almost forgot myself.

'Oui?' she asked, smiling.

She was charming. Finally I got out: 'Could we speak English? My French isn't very good.'

'Certainly,' she replied. 'I'm just as happy speaking English as French.' Her language was fluent American English, with no trace of French.

'Forgive me for bothering you, but I'm looking for Joost Boidin?'

'For whom?' She looked at me questioningly, and I noticed that she wasn't wearing any make-up. At least not as far as I could see.

'That tall, red-headed Dutchman.'

'Oh, him. I've seen him in the corridor, but I haven't spoken to him.' She smiled at me and I felt like I'd been given a prize. 'I didn't know he was Dutch.'

I looked over her shoulder into the room. Directly opposite was a window with mustard-coloured curtains and under it was a coffee table, which was almost covered in very large black and white photographs.

'You take photographs?' I asked.

She turned around and looked at the coffee table. Then she looked at me seriously. 'Yes, I'm a professional photographer. Freelance. I travel to various countries and now I'm here in the beautiful Sheep Islands.'

As she said the last part, her face lit up with a smile.

'Do you know Alan, who also lives here?' I asked hurriedly, before I got lost in her face.

'No, I don't know anyone that lives here. I only sleep here

and eat out at restaurants in town. Both Hotel Hafnia and Hotel Tórshavn were fully booked when I arrived – some oil conference or something – and I didn't want to be outside the town, so I ended up here.'

She motioned with her hand in a way that said 'That's life!' I saw that her nails were short with no nail polish. She wasn't being derogatory, neither with her words nor her hand movements. She was just stating things as they were.

'And now,' she added, 'I need to get back to work. I've promised some pictures to a French magazine.'

She took a step back and was about to close the door.

'Hang on,' I said quickly. I didn't want her to disappear from sight. 'What about the two people that were found dead by the whales? Did you know them?'

'No, only by sight.' Now her eyes were thoughtful. 'I was living here then, but as I said, I've not had anything to do with the other people up here.'

She smiled apologetically and closed the door. It was as though someone had turned out the light.

For a moment I stood there staring into the brown-stained door. Then I pulled myself together and knocked on the two remaining doors. No reaction.

With a feeling that I had missed something, I walked down the stairs.

Twenty-Nine

Down at Vaglið Square I managed to get a taxi. The wind hadn't died down and there were frequent heavy showers, so I didn't really feel like walking over to the Lágargarður care home, which was close to the yellow concrete building.

The driver was a plump man, aged around fifty with a cloth cap. He was listening to Jim Reeves' 'Distant Drums' when I disturbed him. It was just like in the days of my youth. He turned the sound down.

'Where are you going?'

'Over to Lágargarður.'

His engine was already going. He put the car in gear and we drove off along Áarvegur.

'Who are you visiting?'

'I'm not visiting anyone.'

'But what are you going to do at Lágargarður at this time of night?'

He wasn't going to give up.

'I'm not going to Lágargarður, but to the yellow building by the side of it.'

'Ah, where the cobbler lived. Yep, built during the war to keep an eye out for those Germans, but now the whole thing's in disrepair. My dad told me…'

While the driver carried on talking about who had lived in which house and when, I began to wonder whether I was quite the full shilling. Instead of staying at home in my warm bed, I was on my way to a derelict house. Just because Joost Boidin had wanted to meet me there on Saturday night, that didn't mean he would be there late on Wednesday. Everything indicated that he hadn't been at Heljareyga since I spoke to him on Saturday, but there was no one to ask about his whereabouts. So I was going over to the house to investigate and once I'd done that and found nothing, I was going to go home and stay there well into tomorrow morning.

The driver was now talking about building works on the site where the yellow house was currently standing.

'They're going to build a load of terraced houses. They'll be expensive, I can tell you that much. Not for your average Joe. But why would a building owner think about ordinary people? No one else does unless an election's on the way. Then anything is possible, but as soon as it's over, it's all forgotten.'

He stopped the car near the old people's home.

'That's as far as I can go. You can't drive the last bit.'

Suddenly the heavens opened and I asked the driver whether he might be able to wait for me. He could just leave the meter running. Better pay a little more than have to walk in this weather.

That wasn't a problem, as long as I didn't take long. I assured him it would take ten, fifteen minutes tops.

The path to the house was a muddy puddle and before long my shoes weren't fit to be seen. Together the wind and rain made sure I was also cold and drenched, so I wasn't in the best of moods. I cursed and swore, but managed to get to the shelter of the house.

It was a special building, to put it mildly. It was clear that it was one of the few buildings from the Second World War that was still standing. All of the British barracks had gone and only the foundations remained of where they had kept their cannon and ammunition. But this three-story building, which had a row of windows at the top facing the sea, had survived. Although, according to the driver, its days were numbered.

There were no windows into the basement – without a doubt it had also functioned as a bomb shelter – and on the middle floor the windows had been boarded up. As I walked around the building and into the wind, I thought I could see that there were window panes at the top.

On the side of the building that faced inland, there were

some concrete steps that led up to a ramshackle door. When I pushed it, it yielded with a squeak. It was so dark that I could hardly see. A torch would have been very useful at this point, but I didn't have one, and I didn't feel like going back to the taxi to ask whether the driver had one.

I went in and felt as though I was standing in junk up to my ankles. But on the other hand, it was completely still in here, so I took out my lighter and lit it.

It was clear that someone had been staying here. The middle floor consisted of one large room. Some old, dirty mattresses lay along one wall and in the corner there was a stove. Old newspapers, broken bottles and cigarette butts were everywhere and in one place I thought I could make out faeces. The walls were covered in graffiti. Presumably this had functioned as a place for young people to hide to smoke weed and worse. But no Dutchman.

Along the wall that contained the door I had entered through, there was a flight of stairs leading up. They were concrete, narrow and had no handrail.

With my lighter still alight, I walked up the stairs. When I reached the top I realised that things were different. There was no graffiti up here. The walls hadn't been painted recently, but they were untouched. A door stood ajar, just next to where I had come up, and I looked inside. The room was about fourteen square metres and was well ordered. On the floor there was a mattress, which looked new, and a little table under a window which looked inland. Behind the door there was a sink and a mirror and inside something that resembled a cupboard, there was a little toilet bowl. There was an oil stove on the floor, but it wasn't lit. Otherwise there was nothing in the room. Here it was so tidy that it was almost unnerving when compared to all the filth downstairs.

I turned the sink tap on and water ran out. Rather odd in a house that apparently no one had lived in for a long time.

From the landing there was one other door. It was locked. The lock was old school with a keyhole, but even though I tried to look through it, I couldn't see anything.

I turned the lighter off, which had become rather hot, and

stood in the darkness, wondering what to do. The wind was beating at the building, which was particularly exposed, but no air was coming in. Someone must have seen to that.

In darkness I walked down the stairs and didn't light the lighter again until I was at the bottom. In the light I looked around to see whether there was something that could be used to prise the upstairs door open.

On one of the boards that had been nailed to the windows there was a large, bent nail sticking out. I wriggled it back and forth until it came out. Then upstairs again to see what I was capable of.

To start with, things didn't go according to plan, and I realised that the fifteen minutes I had promised the driver had probably passed now. If this didn't work, I could come back in daylight. Suddenly it seemed as though the bent end of the nail had reached something that would move. I turned it with all my might and the lock clicked. I pushed the handle down and the door opened.

A violent heat hit me together with a chokingly powerful, cloying stench. A little light was coming in from the windows, but not enough to be able to see anything. The lighter would need to prove its worth once again and with that in my left hand I stepped carefully into the heat, holding my nose with my right hand.

In the middle of the floor was an oil stove, which was red hot and had clearly been on for some time. Over by the wall to the left was a sofa with bedding on it and next to that a dining table and four chairs. Along the opposite wall was a kitchen counter with a sink and a gas oven. The room was just as tidy as the one next door.

Under the window there was a pile of clothes on the floor. I took a few steps closer. It was a man, and I recognised the clothes. A patterned Faroese jumper, jeans and hiking boots. I had found Joost Boidin.

He was on his back and his face seemed strangely dark. Was it blackened? Or was it dried blood?

I walked over to the body and a black cloud rose up. Hundreds of shiny, black bluebottles. A white skull with small chunks of flesh on it was smiling up at me. Where the eyes had been were now two dark holes.

Thirty

The taxi driver and I stood in the shelter of the yellow building waiting for the police. The driver had been somewhat annoyed when I came over to the car, moaning that I had been away for at least half an hour and that he had other things to do than sit there waiting for me. But when I asked him to call the police and told him that there was a dead man in the house, he shut up.

Soon his curiosity got the better of him and he said that it would be better if we waited for the police over by the house and not in the warm car. Without a doubt he was worried that he was going to miss out on something if he didn't get as close to the body as possible. He had a large torch in the car and was now shining it up and down the yellow wall.

You could see from his face that he was desperate to get inside, but when he mumbled something about going in to investigate, I had cut him short and told him we would wait outside.

I had lit a cigarette and tried to control my gagging reflex. How the Dutchman had been killed I didn't know, because I had been in too much of a hurry to get away. I knew even less about why he had been killed. Or what he had to do with the whole thing. Or even what the 'whole thing' actually was. I had only questions and no answers. When it came to it, I was probably one of the great philosophers.

After a few minutes we could hear the sound of sirens and soon afterwards a car drove past the old people's home at great speed and further up the muddy road. The flashing lights illuminated the whole neighbourhood and it was certainly only the most senile that wouldn't have been woken by the sound.

The two that got out of the car were young and in uniform. They were both above average height and, judging by their appearance, were physically fit. One was dark-haired, the other fair. The fair one asked who had found the deceased and I told him. He asked the taxi driver if he had anything to do with any of this and as he was so short-sighted as to say that he hadn't, the officer asked him to go down to the police station and make a statement.

The driver, who by now realised that he shouldn't have said that, began to wave his light around as he protested that he had brought the man who found the body over and that he therefore had a right to be there. He was a citizen with rights and responsibilities and they couldn't just send him away.

The dark-haired officer interrupted him, told him to turn off the bloody light and to get himself down to the police station. Otherwise he'd be arrested.

The driver complained, but walked bow-legged and rocking down the muddy path.

The officers were standing by the concrete steps and it didn't look as if they were planning to do anything else.

'Aren't you going in?' I asked.

'No,' said the fair one with a northern accent. 'Karl'll be here soon and a doctor and some technicians are on their way over. We'll wait here.'

Then there was silence.

It hadn't rained for a while and the wind had dropped a lot. Now it was more of a fresh breeze. In the sky the clouds were still moving at a brisk speed, but there were openings between them and you could see stars. The weather would be good tomorrow.

Car headlights were drawing near and before long Karl Olsen was standing in front of me. His hair was all over the place and he was unshaven. Dragged straight from his bed.

'Now, old friend, we're not going to be losing our jobs while you're in the country,' he said sarcastically. 'Who have you found dead in there?'

I told him what I knew about Joost Boidin from the

Netherlands, who I had met at Heljareyga and who had left a message on my phone. I told him that my mobile and I didn't co-operate particularly well and that I therefore hadn't heard the message until that evening. And that I had been to Heljareyga and had met a female photographer who spoke French and English and said she didn't know anything about the Dutchman.

'The reason you first went to Heljareyga was because the two that were found among the whales had lived there?' Karl looked pensively at me.

'Yes, but I didn't find out anything about them. The Dutchman who's upstairs here,' I pointed at the top floor of the building, 'said he'd only been here for a week and didn't know them. And tonight the photographer said that she didn't know anything about anyone because she only slept at Heljareyga.'

'I've spoken to the photographer,' Karl smiled. 'Pretty, isn't she?'

I nodded in agreement.

'But I haven't met this Dutch guy,' he continued, deep in thought. 'What about the Scot, Alan McLeod? You didn't speak to him?'

'No, he wasn't home… Neither on Saturday nor tonight.'

'No, I can believe it. He doesn't waste his time at home when beer clubs and pubs are open. He's a good guitar player and knows a load of Scottish folk songs. You know, like "I've been a wild rover for many a year…"' Karl half-sang.

'I thought that was an Irish song.'

'Whatever.' Now Karl was serious. 'I think that this Alan is important. He works at the Prime Minister's Office by day and drinks and sings folk songs at night. I definitely want to talk to him. I'm going to go up and see what you've found, before too many people come along and destroy everything.' He put on thin rubber gloves. 'You can come too if you don't touch anything.'

Just the thought of Joost Boidin's skull started my stomach turning.

'I'd rather wait here,' I said, and took out my packet of

cigarettes.

'OK,' said Karl, with a little sarcastic smile. 'You can also go down to the station and wait and we'll talk later. If nothing else, you'll get a cup of coffee there.' He disappeared through the entrance with the ramshackle door.

I lit a cigarette and walked towards Jónas Broncksgøta and the police station, while thoughts of environmental organisations and murder went round and round in my head.

Thirty-One

It was midday on Thursday and I was sitting in the National Library reading about the whale hunt. I thought I should prepare myself a little for the meeting with the hunt's leaders. I had asked a librarian to help me find the material I was after. She was in her forties, short and dark-haired, with a friendly smile. She made it clear that there was no lack of information. The problem was rather the reverse, selecting what was wanted so as not to drown in it all. On the table before me were books and booklets about the whale hunt nowadays and from a historical perspective. I had also been given a folder of newspaper cuttings about the whales and various protests against the Faroes. According to the librarian, they had collated the cuttings in order to help schoolchildren writing essays about the subject. Before she left me, she said that if I needed it I could have access to a computer and the internet.

The radio was playing and I heard that they were predicting good weather for the next few days, with perhaps the odd shower. The midday music began with Franz Schubert's so-called 'Trout Quintet' – wonderful music for working.

I picked up the folder with the cuttings and opened it. Most of it was from *Dimmalætting* and *Blaðið*, but there was also some foreign material. It quickly became clear to me how Mark Robbins could have been so certain in his conclusion that the Faroes could be pushed into an impossible situation.

It was probably because I'd spent so many years abroad that I hadn't really noticed the strength of the forces the Faroes were fighting against. Of course I had also come across articles about the Faroese and whale hunts in foreign newspapers, but it wasn't often that I could be bothered to read them. And if a television programme about it came on, I would change the channel immediately. My attitude was that foreigners didn't have a clue what they were talking about when it came to the whale hunt. On the other hand, these people who knew nothing far outnumbered the Faroese. In relation to the forces we were up against, we were just a tiny speck.

The man who spoke out most strongly against the Faroes was the leader of an organisation that had sunk whaling boats in several places around the world. The Faroese had tried to talk to the man and explain that the pilot whale wasn't threatened in any way, but his conclusion was that whales should never be killed under any circumstances. The Faroese authorities tried to point out that that was a ridiculous idea and that the islanders couldn't all become vegetarians, but the man wouldn't budge. The last we'd heard of him was that he had bought a small submarine to use, amongst other things, against the Faroese.

It sounded so violent, so warlike. Maybe it was a joke after all, I thought to myself. But then directly afterwards I read a short piece in which it said that a member of the British Labour government had said that it would be better if the Faroese ate each other rather than whales.

But it wasn't just members of the Labour party that had declared war on the Faroe Islands. Famous actors and musicians offered their support all over the place, and when a Faroese football team went to play against a team from the British military a few years back, orders came from the Ministry of Defence to cancel the game, saying, 'We can't play against you, because you kill whales!'

So it was worse to kill whales than people? Did animals now have more rights than people? For the Faroese this was a very alien thought.

Another clip reported that a German firm which had been looking for oil near the Faroes had given the most extreme environmental organisations an assurance that they would try to convince the Faroese to stop killing whales. One

American company that wouldn't bow to these organisations was accused on a website of helping the Faroese to murder whales.

I fancied a cigarette, but you weren't allowed to smoke at the National Library. Maybe you'd never been allowed to smoke there? When I was a child you had to be ten years old to get a library card and from that day on I had been a regular guest there several times a week. But I couldn't remember whether people had smoked there.

The environmental organisations that were after us came from across the world, but the most aggressive came from the United Kingdom and Germany. The French and Swiss didn't hold back either and one Alpine organisation maintained that the whale hunt was a bloody relic of the Viking Age.

Clearly there was no limit to what people were prepared to accuse the Faroese of in the fight to ban the whale hunt. At one medical conference in the United States, one paper stated that the Faroese were so aggressive and killed pilot whales because they had so much mercury in their blood. The statement was repeated in an article in *Doctors' Weekly*, a Danish medical magazine, where a Danish doctor said that the Faroese could use this to hide the fact that they were actually more primitive than other peoples.

In one piece from the BBC, it said that one of the United Kingdom's most well-known natural scientists maintained that it was impossible to kill whales in a humane way, so all whale hunting should stop.

As I was thinking about the killing of whales in a humane way, the radio was turned up and the news came on. The main story was that several fish factories had closed, because they were unable to sell their products. The boycott of the Faroes was creating problems in every sphere of life. The ISA disease was causing havoc at the fishing farms and a murder had taken place.

They had an interview with a fish exporter who said that we would be forced to acknowledge what the whale hunt cost us. Faroese fish products were being excluded from the big markets because several shop chains had implemented policies not to buy Faroese goods. The European market had evidently had enough of the Faroes. The exporter finished by asking whether the whale hunt was so important to us that we were prepared to sacrifice jobs, welfare and our health. His last point was presumably related to the fact that the whale meat and blubber were so full of heavy metals that they almost shouldn't be eaten. After this came an interview with the director of *Vinnuhúsið*, the House of Industry, who confirmed that the whale hunt was a drag on Faroese exports. The problem wasn't new, but it was growing the whole time, and Faroese products were being boycotted in more and more markets. The director called on the authorities to carry out an investigation to determine just what it cost Faroese society to kill whales.

While they spoke about problems in the fishing industry, pictures of Joost Boidin's grinning skull appeared in my mind and a shudder ran up my spine. What about the gunman? Where was he? Luckily I wasn't sitting by the window and apart from the librarian I was the only one in the library.

They hadn't been unfriendly at the police station last night, but neither had they been particularly enthusiastic. They gave me coffee and asked me to wait until Karl came. I had read most of *Illustrated Science*, which had been lying on a table, when Karl came by. My thoughts were shifted from pyramids and Pompeii to Faroese daily life at Walpurgis Tide.

Karl had heard my explanation once again and I had asked him how the Dutchman had been killed and when.

'The doctor says he'd been lying in that room for about five days and that it was the high temperature that made the bluebottles eat his face. His forehead was split, so he had presumably received a powerful blow to the middle of his face. And something pointed and sharp was stuck through his throat under his ear. Presumably he was knocked down first and then killed. The blow to his face also broke his nose, so blood ran out. Then the flies came.'

On the radio they were now saying that a foreigner had been found dead in a house next to Lágargarður. A shudder ran through me again at the thought of Joost Boidin's fate, but nevertheless I caught the newsreader saying that the deceased had worked at Sound Salmon.

Thirty-Two

It hadn't occurred to me to ask the Dutchman where he worked. Or why he was working here at all. Why in the world hadn't he said something when I asked about the two Brits? He had only said that he had just arrived and that they had died before that. Why didn't he say that he worked at the same place as the two of them?

It was becoming clearer and clearer that I needed to go to speak to someone at Sound Salmon. But for now I was planning to read through the material in front of me and go to my meeting with the leaders of the pilot whale hunt.

In one book there was a long article on whaling statistics from 1584 until a few years ago. The article opened by quoting a few lines from *Seyðabrævið*, the Sheep Letter, of 1298, where it stated how much of a whale that had been driven in to land belonged to the landowner. Various sources were quoted to show that pilot whales had been killed since the earliest times. One source, however, claimed that pilot whale hunting hardly existed in the Faroes before 1400. Around that time two Venetian noblemen, Nicolo and Antonio Zeno, were on the islands, one from 1391 to 1395 and the other from 1391 to 1405. They had both retold their journeys in detail, written about Faroese fishing and about how the Faroese exported fish to other countries in Europe. They didn't mention pilot whales at all, but they probably would have if they were common. By and large most sources from the 1600s onwards discuss the pilot whales.

I knew that sources on Faroese history from the settlement until the end of the sixteenth century were few and far between. Truth be told, I had no idea that Marco Polo's fellow townsmen had visited the Faroes only a hundred years after he had visited Kublai Khan in China. So even then there was a connection between China and the Faroe Islands! I pictured Marco Polo, his father and uncle travelling through Armenia, Persia, Afghanistan and along the Silk Road to Beijing. War and sickness weren't the only obstacles – there was the heat in the deserts, the cold and snow in the mountains and the rivers and gorges. And the fellow countrymen of this unique person had visited the Faroes! Just the thought of it almost made my head spin and I suspected that the Faroes had a rich medieval history that we knew very little about.

Right, I needed to get back on the right path. Out of the Middle Ages, which until a short moment ago had seemed dark and monotonous, but which now shone promisingly with a wealth of facets. It didn't take much for my imagination to run wild.

Back to reality.

The Faroese whaling statistics were unique. From 1584 until the present day, every single whale hunted was counted and registered. There was, however, a short gap between 1641 and 1708 where we only had a few figures. In comparison with other fishing records, these were really something else. If we made a graph of eleven year average figures we would have a regularly undulating curve with four peaks: 1614-21, 1724-30, 1840-45 and 1936-69. The main reason for there being a high approximately every hundred years was presumably due to the movement patterns of the squid that the whales lived on, and that was connected to the sea's temperature and currents. The overall conclusion was that the Faroese had killed approximately 850 whales a year over 400 years, but that the whale population was not threatened by that.

The problem was that the environmental organisations didn't care about the Faroese whale hunt statistics. Whichever way you looked at it, whales were not to be killed. In some ways it seemed to me to be a very modern mindset, part of humanity's general alienation from nature. On the other hand, foreigners had never been particularly happy about the Faroese whale hunt, so maybe this attitude wasn't so new

after all? In one book there was a quote from the German Carl
Julian Graba's diary from 1828:

> *Down by the beach it was teeming with people who had come
> to see the entertaining whale hunt. We chose a good position
> from where we could see everything up close. The closer the
> whales got to the bay and the land, the more agitated they
> became. They packed together into a group and no longer
> paid any attention to the throwing of stones or the splashing
> of the oars. The distances between the boats surrounding
> these poor slaughter victims became shorter. The whales were
> slowly moving towards the bay and could sense danger. Once
> the whales had come in to the Vestaravágur bay, which is
> only approx. 250 foot wide and twice as long, they no longer
> allowed themselves to be driven like a flock of sheep, but
> prepared to turn. Now the deciding moment was near. Worry,
> fear, hope and the desire to kill shone from the face of every
> Faroeman. With wild yelling they started to cut the whales;
> every boat rowed at speed into the group. The men stuck their
> broad whaling spears into those whales that were not so close
> to the boat that they could smash it with a single tail-strike. The
> wounded animals shot forward at breakneck speed, the whole
> pod followed and beached themselves at Vestaravágur. Now
> a terrible scene commenced. All boats hurried to the whales,
> sailing between them without any thought, the men stabbing
> at the whales boldly. The men who were standing on the shore
> then waded out until over waist-level towards the wounded
> animals, hacking at them with a steel hook, which had a rope
> tied to it, and now three to four men hauled the whale onto
> land and cut its throat. In its deathly battle, the dying beast
> whipped up the sea with its tail, sending foam everywhere; the
> crystal-clear water in the bay was coloured red with blood and
> bursts of blood from their breathing holes shot high into the
> air. Like soldiers in battle lose all humane feelings and become
> predatory animals, so this activity brought the Faroese to rage
> and senselessness. About 30 boats, 300 men and 80 dead
> and still living whales found themselves in an area only a few
> square rods large. Shouting and noise everywhere; in clothes*

and with faces and hands coloured by blood, these otherwise so pleasant Faroemen resembled cannibals from the Pacific islands; there was not the slightest trace of compassion in them during this terrible bloodbath. But when one man was knocked down by the tail of one of the lethally wounded whales and a boat was crushed, the last part of this tragedy was played out with greater caution.

If people writing almost two hundred years ago wrote about the whale hunt in these terms, it was understandable that people expressed themselves more strongly in our milder days. Perhaps the Faroese were the only ones that couldn't see it? Was this part of our tradition so ingrained in us that we thought it had to be like that?

Other sources referred to investigations that stated that the pilot whale population in the North Atlantic was more than 800,000 whales, and that NAMMCO (the North Atlantic Marine Mammal Commission) and ICES (International Council for the Exploration of the Sea) estimated that the Faroese hunt, which affected approximately 0.1 per cent of the population, didn't make any difference. Blubber and whale meat still had great importance for Faroese households and covered about 10-20 per cent of meat consumption. Out in some of the villages the percentage was much higher.

It didn't make much of a difference, however, to maintain that we weren't hurting the whale population if that wasn't really what it was about. On one occasion a collection of signatures in the United States was discussed in order to encourage the Faroese not to kill whales, but to be like other civilised people and buy their meat at the supermarket! But whatever happened, chances were that we would have to stop killing and eating whales in the end – not because we were pushed into doing so, but because the pollution of the seas had become so great that whale meat could almost no longer be eaten. Several doctors advised against eating blubber because it contained so much mercury. And whale meat shouldn't be eaten more often than once a month. Unwitting transgressors in those countries which were trying to stop us from killing whales would maybe make us stop eating them?

In recent years a lot had been done to try to make the whale hunt more humane. The whaling spear was banned and the steel hook had been replaced by a ball hook, which was only to be used to cut into the whale's breathing hole. The environmentalists, however, said that this was where the whale was particularly sensitive, so it was actually just as bad. If you could see that a pod of whales didn't want to swim towards land, you were to let them go, but of course this didn't always happen. In *Blaðið* there was one article about a pod of whales in Miðvágur in the middle of the nineties. The killing should have been over within 15-20 minutes, but instead it took three hours. They didn't manage to persuade the whales to swim to land – everything became confused and the hunt was torturous for the animals and the hunters. In the end the whales were so agitated that some of them sank without having had their throats cut. Some tried to get the pod to swim out again, but that also failed, so all that was left was to cut and drag the whales and then cut their throats, even though it was far too deep. *Blaðið's* conclusion was that this was animal torture of the type that should never take place in a civilised country.

When I was growing up there were essentially no Faroese people that called the whale hunt into question, even though the hunts at Eystaravágur were so gruesome and brutal that people fainted. For us in those days that was just how things were. Now doctors, people in industry and newspapers were questioning the practice. A shift had taken place.

For a while I sat looking over to the window and across to the house roofs and down to Bryggjubakki. The sun was shining beautifully and there was only a gentle breeze causing the leaves on the trees in the garden on the opposite side to move. On the radio they were playing music from the sixties and that suited me just fine.

There were several books that I hadn't gone through, but I doubted that I could get any more from them. The Faroese predicament was absolutely clear and I didn't think the leaders of the pilot whale hunt would be able to give me anything new. I quickly looked through a couple of books and fixed upon one that said that changes in Faroese society could be seen in the various descriptions of the whale hunt.

In one account from the second half of the 1800s, people were most worried that the whales could escape. No one was concerned with whether it might be wrong to kill the whales. But the hunt was described as being so violent that women and priests shouldn't be present for it. The text carried a hint of a solidarity which is absent from later reports of the hunt. Our existence no longer relies on hunting to the extent that it used to, and in some instances the hunt is described as mindless murder. In the most recent accounts the writer was no longer a participant but an observer and the reports were now full of hate for the practice.

Just as Faroese society had changed over the previous hundreds of years, so had the perception of the pilot whale hunt. It was no longer a necessity to survive and all that remained was unpleasant theatre. If these were the attitudes of the Faroese, what on earth were foreigners to think?

I leaned back in my chair and noticed that there were now several of us at the country's leading library. A young dark-haired man was sitting reading newspapers on a screen and a middle-aged Swedish-speaking woman was asking over by the counter for material on 'the hero Sigurd' and 'the snake Fafner'. And behind one of the librarians I saw a man of around sixty with thin grey hair, who was hurrying through the reading room to the staffroom. He was obviously trying to avoid being caught by any visitors' questions. The danger wasn't particularly great as there were only three of us there.

Now I became aware that the radio had been turned off and that the only sound was the buzzing of the neon lights. It was time to go. It was only just past two o'clock, but I had all the information I wanted about the Faroese and pilot whales. I put on my padded jacket and thanked the librarian for her help. She was busy explaining to the Swedish woman in the peculiarly Faroese form of Danish that Sigurd was called Sjúrður in Faroese and Fafner was Frænir.

147

Jógvan Isaksen

Outside I lit a cigarette and, rather pleased with myself, walked down to the creek by Rættará and further to Kafé Karlsborg at Vágsbotnur, where I was planning to get a bite to eat. Maybe I could even sit at one of the tables outside and enjoy the sun? If I closed my eyes I could imagine I was back in Rome, having a rather more peaceful time of it.

Thirty-Three

At Úti á Reyni, where Haraldur lived, things had changed somewhat. The little hallway in the old house was tidy – the first time I had experienced that. Boots, clogs and shoes stood along the wall and on a coat rack there were two jackets and a parka. I took my shoes off and went into the living room, where I was met by Haraldur.

'You're so early that we'll have time for a beer before the other two get here.' He went out into the little kitchen while I looked around.

I almost didn't recognise the place. The living room, which constituted most of the house, was spick and span. Previously, wooden longliner bins used to fill up the hallway, while the living room was a mass of clothes, dismantled shotguns and genealogical tables. Now it was so tidy that the house could easily have been used in an advertisement for cleaning products. On the desk, which was usually covered in forms for genealogical tables, there was now a black computer. Opposite the sofa, where I had sat down, was a large, grey television that I didn't recall seeing before.

'It looks a little different to how it used to look here,' I said, motioning with my hand. If I didn't know better, I would have sworn that Haraldur was blushing.

'You know, Sanna,' he mumbled and placed two Veðrur beers on the coffee table. 'Faroese women like it when everything's shiny and it makes no difference to me.' He groaned as he sat back in an armchair opposite me.

Once he had tasted his beer, he continued. 'Sanna hasn't moved in properly. She has a place in Hoyvík, but she comes here quite often. And it's not far from here to where she works at the government offices. She sleeps here from time to time, and....'

Haraldur seemed quite uneasy. Talking about himself and women clearly wasn't one of his favourite topics. I showed him mercy and changed the subject.

'What about tracing back your family? Have you given up on that now?' I took a large mouthful from the bottle. Sanna hadn't yet taught Haraldur to put glasses out on the table.

'No, no, but Sanna's taught me how to use the computer for that, and it's much easier to get hold of information and contact people via e-mail.' He was becoming more lively now.

'How far back have you got?' I asked, with irony in my voice.

But Haraldur was far too interested in the subject to notice my tone.

'I can tell you that I've got back to a Norwegian Viking at the beginning of the 900s, who seems to be my mother's ancestor. Brynjolf the Far-travelled was his name.'

'Are you a descendent of Tróndur or Sigmundur?'

'What do you mean?' Haraldur looked at me in confusion.

'If you've traced your family back to 900, you must also know whether you're a descendent of Tróndur or Sigmundur. They were alive around the year 1000.'

Haraldur stared briefly into space, but then became animated once again. 'Ah, you bloody scoundrel, sitting there, embarrassing decent people,' he laughed in good humour. 'No, I can tell you that for those of us that live in this country, our family heritage is of importance. But a vagabond like you wouldn't know anything about that.'

I was about to tell him that my family tree was at least as long as his when there was a heavy knock at the door and the door into the hallway was opened. The leaders of the pilot whale hunt had arrived.

I heard them kick the shoes off their feet and then they came into the living room. They leaned forward so that they wouldn't hit their heads on the doorframe. The house wasn't just old and crooked, but also low. Both men were in their fifties, of average height, plump and with full beards. One had curly, fair hair and a bright smile and one was dark-haired with a more serious appearance.

'This is great,' said the one with curly hair. 'Sun outside and beer inside.' He looked around. 'I thought there was something different when I was out in the hallway and now I can see that everything's changed. Where's all your junk gone? Have you got a cleaner or have you got married?' His accent wasn't a Tórshavn accent, but it wasn't far off. Presumably he was from one of the villages just north of Tórshavn.

Haraldur didn't answer, but muttered something about fetching some beer.

'If you also had a schnapps, that wouldn't be the end of the world,' the comedian added. He dropped down onto the sofa beside me.

'Hermann Hansen,' he said, offering me his hand.

'Hannis Martinsson,' I said, stretching out mine. Straight away he tried to squeeze as hard as he could, but I squeezed back and for a moment we sat there squeezing away.

'Enough of that crap, Hermann!' growled the dark-haired one in an Eysturoy accent.

'I just wanted to see whether there was any power in this city boy,' said Hermann before letting go. I took my hand back, and although it hurt a little bit, I didn't let on.

'You guys wrestling there on the sofa?' Haraldur came in with a tray and four beers, a bottle of *brennivín* and a large schnapps glass.

'As usual, Hermann's acting the fool,' said the man from Eysturoy, who had sat down on the chair on the other side of the table. 'The name's Óli Justinussen.' He looked over to me. 'I'm one of the leaders of the pilot whale hunt here and I'm also a vet. The other leader is the one who tried to crush your hand. What else he does, I have no idea. He changes jobs more frequently than the rest of us change our underwear.'

'Then you go a bloody long time without taking your underwear off,' said Hermann. 'I've been a driving instructor for the past three years.'

He took an generous schnapps from Haraldur, said cheers and emptied his glass. He then sipped his beer, rubbed his hands and said, with joy in his voice, 'That was just what I needed.'

Óli Justinussen said a short and sweet 'Cheers', emptied his glass and leaned back in anticipation in his chair. Once Haraldur and I had also had an quick one, there was silence for a short time, even though the driving instructor looked like he wanted to say something several times. The expression on the vet's face made sure he kept quiet.

Now it was up to me.

I began to tell them about Mark Robbins' visit to my office and that he wanted me to work for GOS.

'Guardians of the Sea are bloody liars!' said curly-headed Hermann fiercely. An angry look from the vet stopped him.

I told them that this was because the two youngsters that had been found among the whales at the quayside had been members of GOS. I told them that Mark Robbins' plane had crashed and that I had been shot at several times. I left out the bit about Joost Boidin. I didn't think there was any need to drag him into it.

'What's the connection between the two kids found among the whales and the shots at you?' Óli Justinussen asked.

'Actually I don't have a clue about that. And neither do the police. This meeting with you is an attempt to investigate all possibilities, because I can't work out any connection.'

'Maybe those youngsters shouldn't have been killed, but when they only come here to cause problems, what can you expect?' Hermann was speaking quickly and heatedly.

'You think that a whale hunter cut their throats?' I retaliated.

'You better watch it, you – an errand boy for people that want to cause problems for the Faroes and accuse the rest of us of being murderers.' Hermann had turned around on the sofa and his face was now no more than 20 centimetres from mine. There was absolutely no smile to see.

'Come on,' said Óli Justinussen sedately. 'He just asked you a question. You have to put up with that.'

'I don't know what I have to put up with. But I don't much like being accused of murder.'

'That's not what I was saying,' I said, seeking to placate the man. 'It's just that when you say that the murdered youngsters were kind of asking for it, you have to understand that I'm going to ask whether you guys did it. It's not because I think you did, but I have to ask, because I haven't got the foggiest what's going on here.'

'We didn't kill the Brits and I don't know anyone that would have. There may well be some that could imagine doing it, but that's not the same thing at all. We're not idiots.'

'You have no idea how the two of them ended up with the whales on the quayside?' I looked over to the vet.

'No, we've asked around, but no one's seen anything. We had finished the marking just after dinner time and from then until the notes were issued at about nine, there was no one there. We haven't found a single person that was there between eight and nine.' He sipped his beer. 'So whoever put the dead bodies among the whales' innards was able to do so in peace and quiet.'

Thirty-Four

I hadn't expected much from the meeting with the leaders of the pilot whale hunt, but I'd hoped for something at least.

'What about the environmental organisations? Do you have anything to do with them?' I asked cautiously.

'The environmental organisations!' Hermann exclaimed. 'We've had nothing but trouble from them for years. We try to inform them, inform them, inform them, but it makes no difference. The aim of most of the organisations is to get publicity from their attacks on the Faroes, so that they can finance their lives of luxury. They're not afraid to lie to get themselves cash. They don't want to base their arguments on scientific investigations and if they're not going to do that, it's not worth talking to them.' He banged his fist down firmly on the coffee table, making the bottles rattle.

'Let me have another schnapps,' he said to Haraldur.

Haraldur had been sitting there with a smile on his face – presumably he was used to Hermann and his opinions on the environmentalists.

Once the schnapps had made its way down, Hermann continued. 'We've been doing our own policing when it comes to the whale hunt. We have improved our killing methods considerably and we do what we can to inform the world about the hunt. It's a viable hunt. These people say that the whales feel pain, but the Faroese know how to kill a whale quickly and humanely. We have nothing to hide and now that the environmental organisations are trying to get people to stop buying our fish products, it's even more necessary for us to kill whales. Trying to get these foreigners to understand anything at all is hopeless.' He shrugged his shoulders despairingly.

'What can be done?' I asked. 'Do we bend to their will and do what they want?'

'Hell no! Never.' Hermann picked up his beer and downed it.

The vet chipped in cool-headedly. 'It's not beyond the realms of possibility that the rest of the world can force us to stop killing whales, but we certainly won't give up voluntarily. The debate about the extent to which we can harvest natural resources is completely new. It's a problem we haven't had before, presumably because there was no point before. For a modern city-dweller, nature is something you watch on TV. It's not something you touch. Having animal blood on your hands is now a mortal sin. And then this European and American missionary spirit builds up and this... warped worldview is forced onto anyone that thinks otherwise.'

Haraldur had gone back into the kitchen for more beers and asked whether we'd like to have some schnapps as well. Everyone approved his suggestion.

The vet continued: 'In a way, these environmental organisations have something in common with Hinduism, where the rights of the animal are to be defended. Physical pain is considered the worst thing of all. That has never been the Christian perspective. The leading voices in these groups accuse us of differentiating between species. "Speciesism" it's called. They reckon it's arrogant and morally reprehensible to act "as though we humans are something special". In reality we're just mammals, like so many other species. That gives us no right to kill other animals. That is clearly a Hindu worldview, while Christianity has always spoken about man's right to the world he lives in. The disunity on the right to harvest Earth's natural resources is just one little pawn in a cultural battle in which people who are completely removed from nature demand that we act like them.'

We sat in silence for a moment, thinking about the world's folly. Outside the sun was shining and two oystercatchers screeched as they flew by.

'If everyone thinks like the environmentalists, what can we

do?' I broke the silence. 'I mean, who cares about the Faroese and the Greenlanders? There's no more than 100,000 of us, compared to six billion.'

'There are more of us than that,' said Óli Justinussen. 'The Icelanders, Norwegians and Japanese hunt whales too. But the environmentalists don't go after the Norwegians or the Japanese. Norway has its oil wealth and the Japanese have the world's second largest economy. The Icelanders have almost given up their hunt, which leaves just the Faroes and Greenland. Both countries are part of the Kingdom of Denmark and both are therefore represented by Denmark on international whaling commissions. Denmark has never hunted whales, so you can imagine how eager they are to defend us.'

'We should have demanded independence years ago,' added Hermann. 'Then we'd be able to decide everything ourselves. Then there'd be no Danish diplomacy, just a fist to the face.' He punched the air with a clenched fist and it was obvious that he was getting drunk.

The vet carried on regardless. 'Only a tiny percentage of the thousands who are supporting the crusade against whaling have ever seen a whale. For them, the whale is a silhouette on the horizon, big, beautiful and mysterious, something that has earned the right to live. These people have no idea that some whale species are threatened and others have never been anywhere close to it. Anything that involves whales arouses feelings that don't appear – with the exception of a few confused souls – when we talk about fish, for example. We have feelings for warm-blooded animals that we don't have for cold-blooded animals.'

'What do you say, Haraldur?' asked Hermann suddenly. 'Are we sinning every time we catch a cod or haddock? That would be a crying shame.' He laughed to himself.

The vet still wasn't going to let himself get distracted. 'Whales are enchanting because they live in water, in the sea. Psychologists say that water represents our primeval instincts. Those experiences we feel belong to our deepest subconscious, recalling in one way or another the embryonic stage in the womb. In that way, the whale hunt is up against powerful forces, both economic and psychological. There is no good reason for giving up the hunt, but many bad ones.'

'Let's have another schnapps and talk about something else.' That was Hermann, of course.

After we had sipped our drinks, the others started to talk about the fishing industry in the fjords. I sat back in thought, trying to summarise all I knew about environmental organisations and whales.

One thing was clear – the environmentalists would go to great lengths to stop the Faroese whale hunt, but killing their own was a step too far. I did know that these people had come to the islands with the aim of creating problems, and that they had done. But something other than whaling had to be behind it.

The only concrete thing I had was that three people had been killed: Jenny, Stewart and Joost. All three had worked at Sound Salmon. According to what he'd said, Joost had only been here for a week or so, but the other two had been here for almost three months. If I could find out what they'd been up to, maybe it would become clear?

And then there was the Scot, Alan, who worked in the Prime Minister's Office during the day and played in pubs by night. Was he a Jekyll and Hyde? I needed to speak to him and I needed to go to Sound Salmon.

Part Two

We have one of the best environments in the world for salmon farming. We had perhaps Europe's lowest production price before ISA hit.

Representative of the House of Industry

Thirty-Five

If I got nothing else out of the meeting with the leaders of the pilot whale hunt, at least I had a hangover. Haraldur had been very generous with his pouring and for dinner he'd put lamb ribs on the pan. Both leaders had phoned home saying that unfortunately they wouldn't be able to be home for dinner, because they were in a whaling meeting that was taking ages. The vet, Óli Justinussen, still had a completely clear head, but the driving instructor, Hermann Hansen, had had slightly slurred speech when he phoned to tell his wife about the meeting he couldn't leave.

One headache tablet had made its way down and I sat at the steering wheel in my new hire car, thinking that I probably should have taken another. But now it was too late. When I was younger, I had no idea what a hangover was, but once in a while I did get one now. I turned from Vegurin Langi into Hvítanesvegur and set course for Sund.

Ever since I had arrived home I had thought about buying a car, but my economic situation wasn't particularly great, so I had hired a Toyota Camry instead. A fantastic automatic car – but that colour! It was mauve, so I feared it would be recognisable everywhere. But the guy that rented me the car reckoned that Tórshavn was full of cars just like that, so I'd just disappear into the mass. I had my doubts.

Friday morning. It wasn't yet eleven o'clock, so as far as I was concerned, that was early morning. It was overcast and mild, with next to no wind. Not much traffic about, just the odd car zooming by now and again. I cast a look down to Hvítanes as I drove by. In the days of my youth Hvítanes was far away from Tórshavn, but today the village was a suburb of the capital. It still looked the same though. Colourful houses surrounded by the greenest of green.

We had had such a good time at Haraldur's that it was almost one o'clock when we left. Sanna had come along about half-way through the evening, but when she saw what we were up to, she said she'd leave us in peace. She kissed Haraldur on the cheek and hurried off. We tried to tease Haraldur, telling him that his days of freedom were now over and that he was now under the thumb, like all married men. Soon he wouldn't be allowed to go out fishing, but would be forced to stay at home and have dinner on the table ready for when the lady of the house arrived home from work. But Haraldur was clearly so happy about his present situation that our comments didn't affect him and we soon gave up. Instead we told stories about people we knew and that was also fun.

I hadn't phoned Sound Salmon in advance, because I thought I'd just get the answerphone, and I couldn't be doing with that. You were much more likely to get to have a conversation with someone if you went in person. My hopes were not particularly high, however, in light of all that had happened the previous five, six days. Every time I thought I could see an opportunity to make some sense of what was going on, it disappeared like dew before the sun. Or died.

I was soon able to drive down to Sund and the Sound Salmon fish farm. There were fish rings out in much of the fjord, most by the opening. Out by a group of three rings there was a boat. It looked as if I would be able to see someone.

I drove onto the quay area and parked the car right by the wharf. I got out, lit a cigarette and examined my surroundings. On the other side of the fjord was the village of Kaldbak, which I hardly knew anything about. Even though I had grown up in Tórshavn, the village had never really meant anything to me. Back then there was no road to Kaldbak, but several times a year I had pulled in there on one of the Tórshavn Dairy and Margarine Factory's milk boats on the way to Eysturoy. But I had never been ashore there. Later, when a road had come, I drove there once just to see it, but the village still meant nothing to me. Nothing. The reason for this was probably because I didn't know anyone from Kaldbak, so there was no reason to have any opinion on the place. Without a doubt it was a fine village, but for me it was just some houses which were far away from everything.

The boat had started to head towards the land, and I turned my back to the fjord and looked at the Sound Salmon building. It was south-facing by a steep cliff face and was a grey two-storey building with a gently pitched roof. There were skylights on both sides of the central roof ridge. On the east-facing gable, above two red wide doors, was a huge green plywood salmon, splashing about. Above it said in large letters, 'Sound Salmon', and beneath, in English, 'From the purest waters in the world'.

The building was about twenty-five metres long, and just around the corner by the main entrance, there was a door and three windows side by side. Otherwise there was nothing on the long wall. I went over and grabbed the door handle. It was locked. Nearby there was an old, dark blue van with the firm's logo on the side. I walked south of the building and saw that on this side there was a continuous row of windows, both upstairs and downstairs, but no door.

Behind the building a large area of cliff had been blown away towards the main road. Where the rock had been was now a collection of containers. Some were painted white with the picture of the green salmon and Sound Salmon's slogan on the side, while the rest were a mixture of red, blue and a lot of rust. There were also some fish rings here, with their posts pointing into the air.

Now I could hear the boat and I walked to the edge of the quayside to meet it.

The water foamed as the blue fishing boat came at full speed, and just as I was wondering whether he was going to steer straight into the wharf, he went into reverse and the boat came in smoothly by the quayside. The boat was about 35 foot long and 15 foot wide. At the front there was a little wheelhouse and behind that a fairly large deck with a crane. A man in blue overalls and a cloth cap came out of the wheelhouse and threw the front mooring rope to me. I tied it around the bollard. The same thing happened with the rope at the back.

'Have you been out to feed the salmon?' I asked.

The man jumped onto land and I could see now that he was forty at most. The cloth cap had fooled me into believing he was older. His face was blotchy and his stomach bulged under the overalls. He investigated me with his brown eyes. Then he put his hand in his breast pocket and took out a packet of Samson tobacco.

'No,' he said, putting the correct amount of tobacco onto some rolling paper. 'We only feed them in the evening. It's best to do it half an hour before sunset.' With his left hand he put the packet of tobacco back in his pocket and held the paper to his lips with the right, moistened the sticky edge with his tongue and rolled the cigarette together on his thigh, shoved it into the corner of his mouth and lit it with a stormlighter. I had seen it done before, but I was equally impressed every time. Personally, I always had to use two hands when rolling a cigarette, and even though I had tried many times in my youth to learn the art of doing it with one hand, I never succeeded.

'Nope, I was repairing the hole in the fencing above one of the rings. The seals are good at getting in and eating whatever they can. They never come when we're nearby, so it's impossible to get them within weapon range. Some reckon that the seals know when we're carrying weapons, so they dive down. They can be under water for a good hour or longer.'

'Do you work for Sound Salmon?' I asked.

'Yes, I'm the feedmaster, responsible for feeding and keeping an eye on the rings. I don't have much to do with all that other stuff.'

'All that other stuff? What do you mean?'

'Catching the salmon, killing it and preparing it for export.'

We had drifted towards the building and the man took out a key and opened the door.

'Do you want a cup of coffee?' he asked as he stepped inside. 'I've got a coffee machine in here.'

A hospitable man, I thought to myself. I took him up on his offer.

Inside the entrance hall there were two regular doors to the right. On the first it said Office in metal lettering, on the second Toilet. In the end wall there was a closed steel door. We went into the office, which was fairly large with several computers. The feedmaster took two mugs and filled them with coffee.

'Do you take anything in it?' He leaned over a little fridge and took a carton of milk out.

'No, I've always heard that drinking black coffee makes you beautiful.'

'I see, I see,' he smiled, filling his own mug with milk. 'I'm not about to take part in any beauty competition. Don't think I've been invited.'

He sat down heavily in an armchair. 'I suppose you're here on some kind of errand, coming to Sund? Are you from the police?'

'No, I'm not, but why did you ask that?' I pulled an office chair over to me.

'A lot of strange things have happened here, and now that Dutch guy has died too.' He sipped his coffee.

'What do you mean about a lot of strange things happening?'

'What do I know, but until about three weeks ago, everything here was fine and dandy. Sonni said we were looking to expand. He said we were the only fishery that hadn't been hit by ISA and that we were going to be rich. I reckon he meant that he'd be rich.' The man in overalls with a cloth cap chuckled.

'Sonni is in charge here?'

'Yep, and owns most of it, if you can say that. I reckon that the bank or the Norwegians probably own the lion's share or more.'

'Where are all the other workers?'

'They've all been fired. I'm the only one left,' said the feedmaster, stubbing out his cigarette on an ashtray. 'Sonni said that now that the Dutch guy has been killed too… You've heard about the two Brits?' He looked at me inquisitively.

'Yes, I have, but what does Sound Salmon have to do with their deaths?'

'I don't know, but first two Brits die and then a Dutchman and they all worked here. That's not right.'

'But what were the foreigners doing?'

'I don't know. Something or other upstairs.' He pointed upwards.

'And what's that?' Now I was seriously curious.

'I don't know. Never been up there. It's always locked. I just come here.' He indicated the office. 'And of course into the gutting room downstairs, where we keep the dried food, but upstairs I've never seen.'

'The Brits and the Dutchman, they worked up there?'

'As far as I'm aware they did.' He got up. 'I'm off home for dinner. The wife's doing fermented fish with mutton tallow.' He looked at his watch. 'What did you want?'

'Nothing in particular. Just wanted to talk to the boss about the deaths.'

'You won't get hold of him today. He took the evening flight to Denmark last night and won't be back before Monday.'

'Why did he go yesterday?'

'Don't ask me. No one tells me anything. But when I got here yesterday afternoon, Sonni was here and he told me that he was going away for a few days and that I should just carry on as normal. As if I haven't always done that!'

The feedmaster went over to a desk and looked at a chart:

'You can see here that over a thousand salmon should have been caught last week.' He pointed at the chart with his index finger. I took the opportunity to turn the handle on one of the windows so that it pointed upwards.

'What happens if they're not caught?'

'It's too crowded for them and it's pure cannibalism. In the fish ring that I just repaired the fencing on, they were swimming low in the water. That's usually a sign that they're trying to get away, but can't because of the seine net.' He shook his head. 'It can't carry on like this.'

I had nothing to say to that, so instead I said goodbye to the worried, yet friendly man and went on my way.

Thirty-Six

I wanted to talk to the Scot, Alan McLeod, who worked in the Prime Minister's Office, but I didn't really know how to find him, now that it was lunchtime. In earlier days, everyone used to eat dinner in the middle of the day and Tórshavn was one large traffic jam. There were still many, like the feedmaster at Sund, who went home to eat, but it was rarely for a hot meal, and in most workplaces the pattern resembled those in other Nordic countries. You had a break of half an hour and then you could leave earlier. The reason for the change was that in only a few homes was one of the couple at home and able to have hot food waiting ready. It was simply not worth trying to have dinner in the middle of the day. Nevertheless, it was still the case that older people preferred to have their main meal together with the radio news at twenty past twelve, but most of them had retired a long time previously.

But there was one good thing about what remained of the midday break. There were always loads of parking spaces to choose from at this time. There were no problems down at Kongabrúgvin and the news had just started as I pulled up the car by the side of the old Sjóvinnubankin, which now housed the Trygd insurance company.

The weather hadn't changed, overcast and mild, so I sauntered along, looking at the boats by the jetties. Even though *Smyril* still hadn't sailed off to Suðuroy, the area on the other side of the harbour looked strangely empty, now that the new *Norrøna* passenger ship wasn't there. There was something wrong with the proportions. The passenger tower of the transport terminal was massive in relation to the Suðuroy ferry, which fitted in well with the general surroundings. When *Norrøna* was in, the ship and the tower matched, but the rest looked like a Lilliput land. *Norrøna* had ushered in a time of horror vacui, as the harbour area only looked right when there was an enormous ship visiting. If there was to be congruence between the ship and its surroundings, those responsible didn't decide to get a smaller ship, but to make everything else larger. Away with the small, old buildings and in with the new large foreign-looking ones! Then you could easily blow up part of the Tinganes peninsula to give the ships of the future space to turn.

As I passed the old Stokkastova log house and walked up to the little stone-covered square by the country's highest authority, I could hear the news coming through the window of Skansapakkhúsið. They had got as far as the troubles in the Middle East.

The main entrance into the Prime Minister's Office was in the rebuilt Sjó- and Vektarbúð. On a sign in the pane of the door, it said that it was open from 8 to 4, Monday to Thursday, and 8 to 3 on a Friday. A great change had taken place since the days when you were lucky to catch the short morning opening hours and the even shorter afternoon slot.

Just inside the door, a beautiful spiral staircase led upstairs. The banister was wooden and had been painted a shiny white. It was the kind of staircase that most women dreamed about but never got. Clearly no expense was spared here, and it was just as nice as at a modern care home.

Behind a teak counter to the left by the window, there was a young girl by a computer. The radio had now got to the music event listings and there were more than a few of those on a Friday. When the girl caught sight of me, she got up and came over to the counter. She was in her twenties, her hair shining in various shades of brown and her face was well-proportioned and classical. Her eyes were large and wide and you could detect some green in the brown. She had a black velvet choker with a silver medallion around her neck. She was wearing a thin black blouse with lace frills and three-quarter-length trousers that were just as thin. On her feet she had silver sandals with very narrow straps. She looked like she was on her way out to a party or something like that, and I felt a little sting at the thought that she was no longer a possibility for me.

'Yes?' she asked obligingly.

'I'd like to speak to Alan McLeod.'

'Oh, Alan.' Her whole face lit up, revealing her straight, chalk-white teeth.

'Alan usually eats at Café Natúr. He says that he can't be doing with a lunchbox. He says those are some of the stupidest things he's ever come across.' She laughed to herself.

It was clear that the sun shone out of Alan as far as this young, beautiful woman was concerned. That was an excellent reason for me not to like him.

'Blimey. You up already?' It was Haraldur's Sanna, as I had started to call her. 'You must be able to take it better than most people if you're not staying in bed all day, hiding under the covers.' She laughed good-naturedly.

'Oh, you know, practice,' I said, trying to dodge further questions.

'Yes, it must be. I've just been to Haraldur's. He was still in bed snoring away, so I left him there. He can clean up himself – his house looks like a pigsty.'

There was no anger in Sanna's voice, just bewilderment over how stupidly men could behave.

I didn't know what to say, so I said goodbye to the two indulgent women and went on my way.

Café Natúr was located in a beautiful old building with a grass roof which together with the old Hotel Djurhuus formed a bottleneck just before Kongabrúgvin. It was very narrow between the two buildings and there was just one pavement, which was hardly more than half a metre across, alongside Café Natúr. Sometimes you felt you were risking your life if you needed to cross the road and then move sideways along the building, so that a car's wing-mirror wouldn't hit you.

Inside Café Natúr there were a number of people and the music from the radio thundered between the walls. A hoarse English voice was singing to an accompaniment of guitars and strings. Alan McLeod was easy to identify. He was in a black jacket with silver buttons on the sleeves and on both sides of the jacket's opening. Underneath that he had a red tartan waistcoat and a green tie. Even though he wasn't in a kilt – he had dark trousers on – he shone bright with colour as he sat there. He was well-built with fair, curly hair and a beard. He was in his thirties. He was sitting together with four others at a table in the middle of the room and had just said something that had made the others burst out laughing.

I went over to the table and asked the fair-headed one whether he was Alan McLeod.

'Yes, I'm Alan McLeod,' he said in broken Faroese.

'Can I have a word?' I indicated towards a little table by the inner wall.

'That's OK,' he replied falteringly, as though he were looking for the words.

He got up and I could see that he was at least six foot two and broad-shouldered. His blue eyes shone as he smiled: 'I'm not so good at Faroese, I've only been here for three months.'

The four at the table, presumably colleagues judging by their clothes, with suits and ties, had started to talk about a principal who was completely hopeless and got involved in all kinds of things that didn't concern her. Alan and I were forgotten already.

We sat by the little table and I told him in English who I was and asked whether he had known Jenny McEwan and Stewart Peters.

'Yes, I did,' he answered in an obvious Scottish accent. 'They were almost Scots, of course, and we lived in the same place. But they were so confoundedly serious and only spoke about stopping the whale hunt. I came here to Café Natúr with them now and again for one of the music evenings, or to Eyskarið or Bakkus, but I couldn't get them to sing or drink.' He laughed to himself. 'Most of the time we just spoke over breakfast at Heljareyga. About studying in Scotland, or someone we all knew, or something like that.'

'You have no idea why they were killed?'

'No, it was a shock, and now that Dutch guy's dead as well. I hadn't really had the chance to speak to him.'

'What about Robin Nimier, who also lives at Heljareyga?'

Alan McLeod's face lit up. 'She's pretty, isn't she? Unfortunately I've hardly spoken to her. I'm only ever really at Heljareyga to sleep and she's probably not there much more than that. And she doesn't seem to go out to experience Tórshavn's nightlife.'

'Alan!' The four at the table in the middle had got up. 'Lunch is over.'

The Scot took out a little gold pocket watch and looked at it. 'I have to go.' He put the watch back in his pocket.

'How is it that you work at the Prime Minister's Office?' I asked as we got up.

'There's an exchange agreement between Scotland and the Faroes, whereby we exchange officials. I have an M.A. in Social Sciences and work for the Scottish government in Edinburgh. You know, we also want home rule.'

He said the last part with a smile and was on the heels of the other four as they walked through the door.

I ordered a baguette with cheese and ham and a large draught beer. While I waited for the food to come, I wondered whether Alan McLeod had actually told me anything at all.

Thirty-Seven

It was gone two in the morning when I parked the car by the SEV electric company's buildings at Sund. It was only about two hundred metres to Sound Salmon and I thought it was better if my car wasn't directly outside, should anyone happen to come along.

Between SEV and Sound Salmon stood Sund's only house. It was black with a green roof, white windows and shutters and looked like a farmhouse. There were no lights on in the house, but on the main road and down by the quayside there were lamp posts. Even though there were no people around and only a few cars up on the main road, I still tried to stay by the edge of the road, as far away from the streetlights as possible.

I hadn't wasted my time that afternoon. I had left Café Natúr and gone straight to the town library to use one of their computers. I'd first gone onto nummar.fo and asked the computer to search for Sonni. About fifteen names and addresses appeared, but only one of them was linked to Sound Salmon. Sonni Christiansen.

I did a Google search for Sonni Christiansen and received hundreds of hits. It turned out that he had been in fish farming from the beginning, and while others had gone bankrupt and lost their farming rights, he had been able to stay afloat. Several years ago he had sold part of his business and some newspapers speculated that he had sold much more than the permitted third. Foreigners were only allowed to own 33 per cent of a fishing business. Several sources said that this was the only way he would have managed to become a wealthy man, owning most of the land in several small villages. In

an interview Sonni said that these stories were born out of
jealousy and that he had worked hard and got good results. It
was his skill that had meant that Sound Salmon was the only
fishery in the Faroes not to have been hit by ISA.

Afterwards I had found the website of the University
of Stirling and the phone number for the Institute of
Aquaculture. I had then gone to my office at úti í Bakka and
called the Scottish university. Via several receptionists I got
through to a professor who had taught both Jenny McEwan
and Stewart Peters. When he found out that I was calling
from the Faroes, he yelled at me for coming from a nation
of 'barbaric heathens', that didn't care whether they cut the
throats of whales or people. After a while I was able to calm
him down and tell him that I was trying to find out who had
killed his former students. The professor's voice became
somewhat milder and I was able to ask him a few questions.
He told me that the students were 'specialists in infectious
salmon anaemia', or ISA.

The sky was heavily overcast, but from time to time a
crescent moon could be seen. I had my black padded jacket
on, with dark jeans and hiking boots. The lamp posts stopped
long before the Sound Salmon building, which therefore lay
in darkness. That suited me just fine.

When I had turned the handle of the pivot window so that
it wasn't closed, it was just on impulse. I hadn't had any firm
plan to break into the company's building, but just thought
it somewhat mysterious that the man who fed the fish had
never been up there. That he didn't know what went on up
there. Therefore, it would be very helpful if I could get in
when it suited me.

Even though the salmon farms were not really of any great
interest to me, I still knew the great importance they had
had for the Faroese economy. And in recent years the ISA
abbreviation had become more and more common in the
media. I knew that it was a terrible disease that had hit almost
all the fisheries in the country and left the Faroese salmon
export in tatters. Sound Salmon, however, hadn't been hit
and they had employed ISA specialists. At the same time,

these specialists had also been sent by Guardians of the Sea to fight the whale hunt. How all of this fitted together, I had no idea, but maybe there was an answer to be found on the secretive first floor of the Sound Salmon building?

I pushed the tips of my fingers into the space between the window and the frame and opened it. Soon afterwards I was standing on the floor on the other side of the now closed window. I took out a little torch and lit up the way over to the door and into the entrance hall. At the far side I took hold of the handle on the steel door and it opened. I had feared that it would be locked and now felt that I had won a half-victory.

The gutting room was large and along the wall opposite me there was a row of steel tables and washing bowls. There was a strong smell of fish. Part of the space on my side of the room was taken up by an office and a toilet, but about seven metres into the room the wall ended, forming an indentation in the rest of the hall. Where the hall started there were sacks of dry food piled up towards the ceiling. Further in there were three large grey vats with blue canvas edging. I went over to one of the vats and looked inside. It was empty. Not a fish and not a drop of seawater. Maybe the baths were intended to be used for young salmon? Either way, there was nothing here now.

I shone the light around the hall and caught sight of a steel staircase right in the corner. I went over to it, and walked up the four metres or so to another steel door. I tried to push the door, but it didn't open. I shook the padlock and got the same result. What now?

I stood there for a moment, wondering whether there was anything to do. I soon came to the conclusion that I hadn't come so far in the middle of the night, including breaking in to the place, just to be stumped by a bloody padlock.

Down in the hall I looked for a tool. Such a large operation was bound to have a load of different tools. On a magnetic metal board on the wall above the tables there were about thirty filleting knives and underneath this about the same number of grindstones on a wooden shelf. But none of this could be used for my purposes. I caught sight of a large wooden cupboard under the stairs and when I opened it, a load of spanners and screwdrivers appeared right before my eyes. Beneath these it was full of cutting nippers, but they weren't particularly large. There was also a hacksaw, but the padlock was so big that it would take a long time. At the bottom of the cupboard I saw two red rods about a metre long. I grabbed hold of them and stood there with an overgrown pair of cutting nippers in my hands.

In one motion I cut the padlock off and could now enter the Promised Land. At first glance, it didn't look particularly promising. A long, broad, empty corridor from one end to the other became apparent in the little bit of light that was coming in from the roof windows. To the right there was a door. I opened it and illuminated the room behind it with my torch. Toilet and bathroom. I went back a few steps into the corridor and went to the next door, which was also the last. It was locked.

This place was unbelievably secretive. A lock on almost every door. Now I was starting to go crazy. The door was a normal inner door and the lock was a normal Yale lock. I took a step back and kicked the door with all my might, roughly where the lock was. The frame broke into pieces with a crash and the door flew open. I could hide the fact that the padlock was missing, but not this. Right now I didn't care whether anyone could see that I'd been there.

Thirty-Eight

It was a large room and in the torchlight I could see that it was a research laboratory. The smell was the characteristic indeterminate combination of various chemicals. Beneath the windows on the long wall, there were several tables with sinks and between them fridges and freezers. On other tables there were computers. Printers, microscopes, glass flasks, gas burners and everywhere there was a mass of leads and cables. Where there was space on the wall there were shelves full of plastic bottles in various colours, brown and yellow cardboard boxes, pots, books, buckets and a lot of other things that, to my eyes, looked like junk. Most of the tables and much of the floor were covered in a mess of paper and A4 folders. There wasn't space to put a foot down without stepping on a document or a folder.

Someone had been trying to find something very quickly before leaving. I was fairly certain that this was Sonni Christiansen and I would have put money on him not coming back on Monday as the feedmaster had said. Sonni Christiansen had left the Faroes for ever. But why? And had he found what he was looking for?

I picked up some of the paper from the floor, 'Export quantities in terms of rounded weight: October 1999'. Another had the corresponding figures for March 2002. I tried to look in a few of the A4 folders, but the information about young salmon and the number of salmon in the fishing rings didn't mean anything to me. It was clear, however, that not all of the equipment and instruments on this floor were just used for counting salmon and encouraging their export. But what had they been used for?

For a while I went back and forth opening a cupboard door here and a drawer there, but I was none the wiser. In one corner there was a workplace with a microscope, computer, laptop and fridge on one side, a red office chair and a metal cupboard under the desk on the other. I sat down on the chair and started to look more closely at what was here. In the fridge there were about twelve test tubes in a stand at the top, while there were food remains below. According to the date on a milk carton, none of this had been touched for about three weeks. I hurriedly closed the door.

In the metal cupboard there was letter paper and envelopes, but nothing else. A map of the Faroes from the Faroese Food, Veterinary and Environmental Agency with an overview of young salmon stations and fishing areas was taped to the wall and on a little pin board by the side of it hung a sign saying, 'Summary of the ISA-Outbreak'. The laptop was open and I drew my finger across the screen. There was a thick layer of dust. That hadn't been touched for weeks either. I lit a cigarette. It didn't matter now that I had kicked the door in.

There could hardly be any doubt that Sonni had been in a hurry to leave and seeing that three of his employees had been murdered within a few weeks, maybe that wasn't so strange. On the other hand something very mysterious had been going on up here, but it was difficult for me to see what. Maybe the police would get a specialist in to investigate the case? But how could I tell them that they needed to look here? Well, there was no point worrying about tomorrow.

On the wall above the fridge there was a little set of shelves, of which the bottom one, with ringbinders, had fallen onto the fridge. Some files had ended up on the floor. The top shelf, however, looked untouched and I got up to read the text on the spine of the light grey binders. On about ten of them it said, 'Exp. Weight, DKK', followed by a year. In the middle of the shelf, two binders were sticking out a little, and despite all the chaos elsewhere, I felt the need to straighten them. I pushed my palm up against them, but they didn't move. They were getting caught on something.

I put out my cigarette on a metal lid which was on the desk, took out one folder and shone the torch into the space. There was something there. I took two more folders out and put my hand in to retrieve the object. It was an ordinary blue diary with a hard spine, but the text on the cover made it a little unusual for our part of the world. On the top it read 'The GOS Diary', and further down 'Stop Whaling!' There was no doubt that it had belonged to one of the British biologists.

Other than the humming of the fridges and other machines the only sounds were coming from infrequent and distant cars up on the main road. At one point I thought I heard one of them slow down and for a moment I listened out to see whether it was turning down this way. After a couple of minutes with no sound from outside, I calmed down and opened the diary.

Just inside the cover there was a short list of telephone numbers. The top number I recognised from the University of Stirling. Then there were three Faroese numbers, which had names alongside: Sound Salmon, the Prime Minister's Office and Heljareyga. At the end there was a mobile number next to the name Stewart. Without a doubt this was Jenny's diary.

Why the Prime Minister's Office? Alan McLeod? I could make guesses from here to eternity, but that would make no difference. Instead I carried on flicking through the pages.

In January there were only one or two notes. 'Meetings' with certain people, whose names were only marked with initials. I had no idea who most of them were, but from the middle of the month for about two weeks the initials MR appeared several times. Mark Robbins, I guessed.

At the end of January it said, 'Edinburgh-London 10.15; Gatwick-Copenhagen 14.35; Copenhagen-FI 19.15'. I took FI to mean the Faroe Islands and this day to be the one they had arrived on.

The next few pages were blank, but on 11 February there were the letters FH-FI-FJ, on the twelfth, AE-DE-DF, and on the thirteenth, Z-EE. On the fourteenth there was nothing, but on the fifteenth, sixteenth and seventeenth, the letters were back. Then there was break of a few days before the letters

179

appeared again. This pattern continued right up until the middle of April, but then there were no more. The rest of the diary was blank. With good reason.

The letters were written with different pens and pencils, but the handwriting was the same. Some kind of logbook, perhaps? Recording what?

It meant nothing to me, but if it was a code I would need to find the key to it. I took hold of the middle pages and shook the book, but the only thing that fell out was the folded overview of the year at the back. As I tried to put it back again with one hand as I was holding the torch with the other, I saw that there was some writing on the last blank page, just before the overview.

It was no easier to understand. The writing on this page consisted entirely of numbers. Nine lines with the same pen. I flicked through the last few pages of the diary, but there were only these figures. No indication whatsoever as to how they might be interpreted.

I shut the diary and put it in the inside pocket of my jacket. I was almost certain that the diary was what Sonni Christiansen had been looking for before he disappeared. Now it was a case of finding out what the letters and numbers meant. But not right now.

I looked at my watch. It was quarter past three, so it was high time to go home and get to bed. I lit the way before me down the stairs and through the gutting room before turning the torch off as I reached the outside door in the little entrance hall. Once I was outside I took a rock and smashed the pane in the window I had climbed through. Then I opened it a little. Maybe they'd believe that there had been a break-in.

As I walked over to the car, I thought about how I could get Karl to investigate where Sonni Christiansen had gone. I could try to imply that something very strange had happened at Sound Salmon and that the boss had disappeared into the big, wide world. Or something along those lines.

I opened the car door and got in. I had just put the key in the ignition and was about to turn it, when the windscreen shattered into hundreds of pieces and something white-hot grazed my cheek.

Thirty-Nine

Fortunately I hadn't fastened my seatbelt and when the next shot hit the headrest I was lying down across the front seats. Ever since I had come back from Suðuroy I had suspected that the gunman was going to try again. That it should happen right now, was, however, completely unexpected and this time he had me. That the bullet had only grazed me meant that its course must have been altered when it hit the windscreen. On the other hand, I had no way at all of getting out of the car without him seeing me. Or did I?

The car was parked a little crookedly in relation to the road and the shot had come from the large rocks down by the shore. Even if the gunman was in front of the car, he was also below it, and the car was on a slight hill. If I could ease myself out through the car door that faced inland, there was a possibility that I could get behind the SEV building and away. A very small possibility.

I heard scraping from down by the shore, so it was just a question of time before I had the weapon pressed against my temple. I had to get away quickly. But first I had to ensure that the light in the car wouldn't come on when I opened the door. The switch on the roof was in the central position, as usual, which meant that the light came on when the doors opened, but was otherwise off. So there were two options. If I flicked the switch one way, the light wouldn't come on whatever happened, but if I flicked it the other way, it would come on. The problem was that I didn't have a clue which way I should flick it. Left? Right? I had to make a decision.

I stretched my hand up and flicked the switch to the right. Nothing happened. And nothing outside the car either, where I could hear footsteps on the gravel. I opened the door carefully and the car stayed dark. Then I dragged myself out through the gap, arms first, before crawling on all fours the short stretch to the electricity building and then, bent over, I ran up to the main road. There were no cars to be seen. I crossed the road and hid behind a rock.

By now the gunman should have discovered that he hadn't hit me and that I had disappeared. He was probably also aware that I was somewhere close by. At regular intervals the moon became evident through the clouds, illuminating the whole bay. It was during one of these moments that I detected the silhouette of a person coming up the road.

After a short time it was dark again and I hurried up the hill towards the steep mountainside. I hoped that the gunman would think I had headed towards Tórshavn in the expectation that I might be picked up by a car.

It was hard work going uphill, and my many years in big cities had not exactly made me a mountain hiker. I was fine getting over small ledges, but before long I encountered a large rock face. About ten metres high. I was going to try to climb it anyway, but as I stretched my hand up to grab hold of a little overhang, a projectile hit the rock. I dropped to the ground, cursing the moon that, while only half-sized, had lit up the land and sea.

Now it dawned on me that I hadn't heard any shot. Not before in the car either. The weapon obviously had a silencer on it, and that had saved me. Although the silencer meant I couldn't hear anything, it also meant that the weapon was not quite as accurate.

The moon had gone behind the clouds and I ran south below the rock face. Or was it southwest? That kind of irrelevant thought always came to me when I was under pressure. So what? It wasn't far to the Sundsá River, I knew, and if I could get into the little gorge that it had cut into the land, I would be hidden for a short time at least.

Puffing and groaning I ran for my life while trying to forget that someone was aiming at me. When I reached the river I slid on the grass down into the gorge. At the same speed I continued upwards with the aim of reaching the larger valley that was higher up. I knew the valley well as I had camped there as a scout several times. You just needed to continue along the river and then you'd get to the Oyggjarvegur road.

Fortunately there wasn't much water in the river, so I was able to keep myself below the bankside almost the whole way up. The last part was particularly steep and now I was beginning to feel tired. I fell and crawled, trying to draw comfort from the fact that I had probably got away from the gunman. Just then, there were sparks from a rock right by the side of me. The adrenaline was pumping even harder and with a real effort of strength I fought my way up those last few metres and over the edge.

I lay down flat to catch my breath. At the same time I was aware that I couldn't stay there because the gunman would be here before long. For a fraction of a second I thought about grabbing a suitably large rock and smashing it into his head. The impulse was quickly dismissed, because the man was certainly far too experienced for me to be able to hit him.

On the other hand, I knew that the valley was so large and so open that if I started to run I'd be shot as soon as the moon came into view. I had to hide somewhere and it needed to be somewhere close by. I had no time for anything else.

I hadn't got up into the valley itself yet, but in the moonlight I could see that I was on a slope of about one hundred metres. A little bit to one side the base of the cliff jutted out and the ground below looked rocky, but then the clouds covered the moon again and I couldn't see anything. I got up and set off in the direction in which I thought I had seen some rocks. When I got there, I could make out a load of large rocks and I felt my way between them. Now I would need to find some kind of opening that I could crawl into or under. It was the latter. In front of me a rock of the size of an average outhouse had evidently fallen and landed on a part of it that jutted out. This rock together with the large ones all around it formed a little hole. I thought I could hear a faint noise from above the river so I threw myself into the hole.

At first I thought that I would only be able to stay where

I was, but then I realised that the hole led around a corner. I therefore slid on my stomach further and further under the rock and into the hillside. I was on rock, but after about three metres or so, there was no longer rock above my head, but soil. Shortly afterwards, the space became so narrow that my shoulders rubbed on either side. I moved back a little and managed to turn myself around. Then I pushed myself back into the hole as far as I could go. I was now about five metres from the entrance and the hole had a corner in it. I would have to be unusually unlucky for someone to find me here.

There was nothing else to do but wait for the dawn to come in a few hours. By that time, hopefully the gunman would have taken his gun apart and gone home.

I strained my ears to pick up noise from the would-be assassin to find out whether he was nearby, or whether he had continued up towards Oyggjarvegur. There were no sounds to be heard. I wanted to light a cigarette, but knew that it wasn't possible. Now I started to think about my mobile phone which, of course, was at home. I cursed myself silently and promised myself that I would never leave without my phone again. At the same time I knew that it was a promise I would never keep. I had had that mobile for ten years and almost never had it on me. That habit would be difficult to change.

Who knew what sort of a hole I had my legs in? Maybe it was for a hare? I felt how my legs tingled at the thought that there might be a hare inside. But didn't they always have several exits? And who said that a hare lived here anyway?

Now I did hear something and I held my breath. I could hear cautious footsteps in the gravel which stopped when the ground became grass. Now there was someone right by the entrance to the hole. I suspected that the individual had stopped. Everything was still for a moment. Complete silence. Then I heard his clothes rustling as he bent forward. He looked into the opening of the hole, but there shouldn't have been any trace of me as the ground was rock.

Then a blinding light filled the outer section of the hole.

Forty

The light didn't quite reach me, but I lay as quiet as a mouse and stared at the rock. The gunman must have been completely convinced that he had the upper hand, otherwise he would never have shone a light. I heard scraping at the entrance to the hole as though he were feeling around. I held my breath. The light disappeared and footsteps moved away.

I felt as though I hadn't taken a breath for several minutes, but in reality it was a matter of seconds. He didn't seem the type to give up, so I'd need to be prepared to stay here for a while yet. Maybe until mid-morning?

It was only four or five degrees outside, but in my hiding hole it was a little milder. Nevertheless, I could feel that my toes were becoming stiff from the cold and that my feet were wet. I had been in so much of a hurry to get up beside the river that I hadn't watched where I was walking. I had definitely gone through some puddles on my way. The padded jacket was warm, so there were no problems with the top half of my body, and I tried to wriggle my legs a little to keep the cold at bay. But it didn't make a massive difference. Firstly, it was too narrow and secondly I feared being heard outside my hiding place. Instead I took out my packet of cigarettes and took the filter and paper off a cigarette. I put the tobacco in my mouth as if it were chewing tobacco. I could remember from my childhood that I had seen older men do that. It didn't taste particularly great, but it felt as if the tobacco managed to be both numbing and stimulating at the same time. After a while I had no feeling on the inside of my bottom lip and it was as though a calming warmth went through my whole body. I didn't feel hungry. Not yet anyway.

It was the third time I had been shot at and I still had no idea why. Of course it had something to do with the two youngsters, the two that had been found with their throats cut among the whales. But how did it all fit together? I couldn't see it. I could connect Mark Robbins with the two biologists, but he was a different matter. If it had only been the first two then it could have been some kind of revenge from an insane whale hunter, but the fact that Mark Robbins' plane had been brought down might indicate something bigger.

Although Mark Robbins hadn't said anything about Sound Salmon – he hadn't actually said very much about anything – maybe I should be thinking in that direction if I wanted to find some meaning in the turn of events. Jenny McEwan, Stewart Peters and Joost Boidin had all worked at Sound Salmon and they were all dead. Maybe their deaths didn't have anything to do with the whale hunt, but with what had happened at the fish farm. Only Sonni Christiansen could answer that question and he'd fled abroad. I needed to get hold of Karl so that the police could start looking for him.

Almost immediately I realised that Sound Salmon could hardly be the answer to all the questions. Why did Mark Robbins need to be taken out? And why did I? We hadn't been anywhere near anything to do with the fishery when we were blown to pieces and hunted on the bird cliffs respectively on Suðuroy. I felt my pocket with Jenny McEwan's diary in it. Maybe there was something in that that would help untangle this mess? For now, Sound Salmon was the only thing I had to hold onto.

Now the tobacco really didn't taste very good any more and I spat it out. I felt shattered and rested my head on my arms. Maybe I could take a nap? I tried to twist and turn to find a position in which I was more comfortable, but I didn't really succeed. It was best when I was on my back, but even then the hardness of the floor was too evident. I tried to make the best of it and in my thoughts I was out in the world: sunny days on the Mediterranean with pasta and red wine. In my mind I saw Rome and the French Côte d'Azur with strolls by the water's edge. I half-slept occasionally but was never completely gone.

Now and again there came a sound from outside, but I didn't know whether it was the gunman or a sheep. A few times Duruta's face also came to mind and I wondered who her daughter's father was. Someone or other over at the police station? Duruta had been married to an officer who had been knocked down and killed by a youngster. Maybe she kept to her own?

I pictured Duruta as she put her fingers on the wound on my cheek and the I thought about the shot which had almost finished me off. I felt my face and noticed a scratch on my cheek. Now I had wounds on both sides of my face. In Germany they'd think I belonged to the upper class with duelling scars from my study days. Here they would probably think I had cut myself while shaving because my hands were shaking too much after a heavy night in town.

It was gone half five and it was starting to get brighter. The light cautiously eased itself in through the entrance of the hole and there was also a beam of light coming in from above. Presumably there was an opening between the rocks and the cliff. I didn't dare crawl out from my hiding place, but tried to do a little bit of aerobics with my arms and legs. It helped warm me up a little, but only a little.

Outside I could hear birdsong, particularly the characteristic calling of the oystercatchers, and now and again some sheep bleated close by. That the sun was rising in the sky could be seen from the strength of the light in the opening, and the beam from above was like a spotlight.

Once it approached seven, I decided that enough was enough and I started to drag myself towards the entrance. I had got to the place where the hole turned and was now on my knees, when I heard a voice not too far away call:

'Hello! What are you shooting at here?'

Forty-One

The sniper was still there.

Just how close I discovered once I heard mumbling in English close to the hole.

He had worked out that I must have been hiding somewhere nearby and had sat down to wait. There was no doubting that this was a professional. On the other hand, I'd known that for several days.

'You're not allowed to shoot on outlying fields,' called the loud voice. 'You're not actually allowed to shoot at all at this time of year. If you don't clear off with that rifle, you'll be reported to the police.'

I heard barking from a dog.

Thank the Lord for the shepherd who had caught sight of the gunman. If he had come just a little later, I'd have been dead. I shuffled back into the hole. There was nothing else to do than stay here for a while longer. I didn't dare believe that I'd get away just because the shepherd had come. If I appeared, chances were we'd both be shot.

I heard the gunman move away from the hole and he said something or other.

'What did you say? Speak so that others can understand you.'

I heard the gunman say something else, but it was mixed with the barking of another dog.

'Shut up, Floy! Down, Snar! I can't hear a thing over you.' The dogs didn't stop, but the shepherd was obviously used to this, so he continued:

'Ah, English? You should have said.' He was clearly from somewhere frequently battered by the sea, because every word could be heard clearly, so it was though he was standing just by the rock. He now spoke in slow English. 'It's forbidden to shoot in this… Oh, what's the bloody word? … in this place.'

There was another mumble.

'I don't know, but you have to leave. Right now,' he added. 'Goodbye!'

It sounded as if the shepherd had got the gunman to go.

Now I heard sniffing around the entrance and the nose of a sheepdog came into view. Black and white. It growled and showed its teeth.

'Floy, where the hell are you?' The shepherd didn't come any closer, but his voice could be heard clearly from where I was.

'Floy!' he called threateningly and the dog moved backwards out of the hole.

'There you are. I should throw you off a cliff. No point having a dog that only gives tongue and otherwise hides when you need it.'

For a while I heard him continue to complain about the dog as they moved away from the hole.

The valley was large and open and the shepherd would probably keep an eye on the gunman until he disappeared. As far as I was concerned it was best to stay lying here. Maybe for the rest of the day. That wasn't an exciting prospect, but once so much time had gone, the man who was after me would definitely draw the conclusion that I had got away.

During the morning it became quite pleasant in the hole and I was able to sleep for a few hours. When I woke up my body was stiff from the hard ground and I ventured towards the entrance, where I could sit upright. Slowly the feeling returned to my limbs again, but I couldn't do anything to alleviate the thirst I was now feeling. The hunger I could stave off by chewing tobacco.

By mid-afternoon I had become so brave that I looked out of the opening of the hole. About two metres outside there was a little puddle in a rock. The water wasn't beautiful to look at, more green than clear, but I looked around cautiously and hurried the two metres on all fours. I could hear birds and sheep, but nothing else. I collected some water in my hands and drank. It was all right, even though it was muddy and lukewarm from the sun. I drank until I was no longer thirsty and then moved backwards back into the hole.

For a moment I wondered whether I should leave, but came to the conclusion that the gunman could easily be sitting somewhere up high with a telescope with a view over the whole valley. I stayed there, however desperate I was to leave.

Time didn't seem to be moving. The hours felt like years. I took the diary that I had found at Sound Salmon out of my pocket and there by the entrance I sat looking at it. I might as well use the time for something.

First I looked at the letters which appeared regularly between 11 February and 12 April, but I knew too little to be able to get anything out of them. Maybe the letters could be translated into numbers, but then they would need to be turned into something else and I had no idea about that. Instead I flicked to the back of the diary and looked at the numbers:

```
19 14 19 6 13 8 3 17 14 2 2 0
4 1 19 13 4 12 4 4 17 6 0 4 7
18 3 13 0 18 14 6 13 4 4 22 19
0 7 0 18 8 13 14 12 11 0 18 3 13 20 14
20 1 8 17 19 18 8 3 13 4 4 1 18
5 8 2 4 15 18 4 7 19 14 19 3 4 19
4 9 23 1 18 12 17 0 5 7 18 8 5 3 4 8
4 19 18 3 13 0 13 0 22 4 2 12 24 13 13
18 17 4 19 4 15 19 17 0 22
```

There could hardly be any doubt that this was a code, but if it was even a little advanced, my chances of cracking it here and now weren't great. On the other hand, the two youngsters had no real reason for creating a complicated code. They would probably need a simple system that was also easy to use. Letters and numbers alone would cover the real meaning, if someone was to look in the diary by chance. At the same time, the contents were so important that the whole of the first floor at Sound Salmon had been turned over to find the diary. Moreover, the letters were written over the course of two months, while the numbers looked as if they were written all at once. The possibility of finding some kind of meaning was therefore greater if I looked at these first.

I remembered how we wrote codes when we were kids. How we wrote with lemon juice and when the paper was warmed up the writing appeared. And there were those books with puzzles, much like the ones in the diary, where numbers needed to be added together in a certain way or there was some pattern that had to be determined. I couldn't see anything like that in the nine lines of numbers in the diary. The way in which the numbers had been written didn't indicate that they were to be added together in any way.

I tried to find a pattern in the numbers themselves. First 19, then 14 and then 19 again and then 6 and 13. There was five between the first three numbers, but then thirteen and seven. Was there a connection between the thirteen that separated the 19 and 6 and the number 13? I didn't think so. If that was the pattern, the code would be far too complicated. First and foremost it had to be simple.

'Meeeeh.' There was a sudden bleating near my ear and I had such a shock that I almost had a heart attack. A sheep was standing by the entrance chewing on a tuft of grass. It looked at me in a friendly but incurious fashion.

I had been so preoccupied by the numbers in the diary that I had blocked everything else out. And that could be dangerous. The sheep went its way, while I tried to see whether I could hear anything unusual. The wind had picked up a little and the grass whistled; far away I could hear a curlew. The sun was still shining and even though it didn't make it into the hole, it was still warm here. I didn't want to think about the gunman.

Simplicity, simplicity, I tried to tell myself. Just before it had occurred to me that the letters on the earlier pages could represent numbers. Why couldn't these numbers represent letters?

It wasn't going to be the Faroese alphabet in any case – if anyone at all actually knew what that was, I mumbled to myself. Both Jenny and Stewart were from Britain and were therefore presumably writing in English. I wrote the English alphabet from A to Z on a blank page. There were 26 letters. That fitted in well with the numbers in the coded passage, where no number was higher than 24. But I was straight into problems. The first line ended in 0 and which letter could that stand for?

If I left the zero for a moment and put letters in place of the numbers. The nineteenth letter was S, the fourteenth N, the nineteenth again, and then F and M. I took a break: SNSFM. That meant nothing. That the code might consist of several different parts wasn't a thought that filled me with joy.

From my coding days I remembered that e was the most common letter in English, and if you could locate that you could often crack the code. I sat there counting the numbers.

Immediately it became clear that 4 was the most common. It appeared eighteen times and then came 13, 18 and 19, which all appeared eleven times.

If we said that 4 represented the letter e, which was the fifth letter of the alphabet… Then it hit me, of course! 0 was a, and then 4 would become e. It was like winning the lottery. I started to put letters into the code:

```
T O T G N I D R O C C A
E B T N E M E E R G A E H
S D N A S O G N E E W T
```

It meant nothing. To me in any case. My previous enthusiasm had evaporated. I hadn't got anywhere.

I looked through the opening to the hole and saw that the shadows were growing longer. Evening was approaching, and once twilight was well and truly here, I would make a break for it.

As I sat there, I ran my fingers over the diary page with the numbers on it and noticed that something felt rough in the middle. On closer inspection I saw that a page had been ripped out, but so far in that I hadn't noticed it. There could be several reasons for tearing out a page, but I suspected that it had something to do with the code. That the text had first been written there and had then been coded. There was nothing to do but continue to replace the numbers with letters.

When I got to the last line, I vaguely sensed something. For a moment I sat there looking at the letters and then it was as though someone had turned the light on for me.

```
T O T G N I D R O C C A
E B T N E M E E R G A E H
S D N A S O G N E E W T
A H A S I N O M L A S D N U O
U B I R T S I D N E E B S
F I C E P S E H T O T D E T
E J Y B S M R A F H S I F D E I
E T S D N A N A W E C M Y N N
S R E T E P T R A W
```

The first part of the last line was the name Peters in reverse. Jenny had written the text first and had then reversed it line by line and replaced the letters with numbers. Simple and workable. Whoever found the diary would be forced to use up a lot of time deciphering the code.

I reversed the text and wrote it out letter by letter on a new page. Then I read the whole English text.

And got a shock.

Forty-Two

I knew that foreign organisations would go a long way to stop the whale hunt on the Faroes. But what the text revealed went far beyond anything I had imagined. It said:

> According to the agreement between GOS and Sound Salmon ISA has been distributed to the specified fish farms by Jenny McEwan and Stewart Peters.

Fish farms were of immeasurable importance to the Faroese economy and by destroying them the country would be weakened to the extent that it might just give in to outside pressure. That was what I presumed the people behind this must have been thinking. Mark Robbins and his chums had sent the two young biologists to the Faroes as a Trojan horse. They were to pretend they were working at Sound Salmon and protest against the whale hunt, like so many other foreigners. In reality they were to spread ISA to fish farms all over the country and thereby cause problems for the Faroese economy. Sound Salmon, with Sonni Christiansen at the helm, were undoubtedly well paid for the part they played, in addition to the fact that he was the only one who could export safe salmon. I didn't understand the fanaticism of the two youngsters, but understood even less why someone from the Faroes would take part in that kind of plot. It was clear that the death of the two Brits had caught Sonni Christiansen unawares and once the Dutchman had been added to the mix, it became too much and he left the country.

Right, Karl and the police would have to deal with him. As far as I was concerned, I just needed to get away from here.

I was starving and now that night was beginning to fall, the cold gradually started to return. The birds were silent and only a couple of sheep were bleating. The evening sun shone on individual rocks and rises, but in a short while it would be dark. I eased myself out of the hole and headed straight downwards. I knew that there was a little cliff face at the top, but that was better than wading upstream. The plan was to get down to my car, which was hopefully exactly where I had left it the night before.

When I got to the edge, I still thought it was a long way down, but the remaining evening light helped me see where I was treading. Step by step I climbed down to the first ledge. It also felt quite steep and I sat down and slid down to the next steep section on my backside. Now the light was seriously beginning to disappear, but I was able to make my way down the next bit too. Now it was no longer so steep and I was able to more or less run down to the main road.

Almost there, I stopped and looked around. A car was heading southwards and I had to fight the urge to stop it and ask them to take me with them. Instead I crouched down and made myself as small as possible. It was best not to get more people involved in this than necessary. The lights passed me by, accompanied by the thumping of Faroese rap music. Presumably someone from one of the villages on the way to a Saturday night party in Tórshavn.

I stayed crouched for a while, observing the cluster of buildings at Sund. There was no light from the farmer's house tonight either and there were no cars to be seen outside. Both Sound Salmon and the electricity company's buildings were completely dark. It was absolutely idyllic – if it hadn't been for the gunman who was probably lying in wait. On the other hand, he could just as easily have gone back to Tórshavn, or he was up on the Lambafjelli mountain or Gellingarklettur or… There was no point guessing where the gunman had gone. I got up and hurried across the road.

As I approached the coast, I could see that the car was where I had left it. I felt a shudder down my spine as I went over to the car and looked in. Yep, the keys were still in the ignition. The front seats were almost completely covered in splinters of glass from the windscreen. I brushed them away from the driver's seat and got in. In the rear-view mirror I could see that the rear window had also been hit. That had presumably been caused by one of the shots that had been aimed at me. A shudder went through me, but perhaps that was the cold.

The car started straight away and I slowly drove up to the main road where there was now some traffic. The vast majority heading south. Having no windscreen made a huge difference and I never went above 60km. One car after the other overtook me and several of them beeped their horns furiously. It wasn't normal for anyone to drive less than 80km an hour, particularly not on a Saturday night.

As I approached the town, I began to think about where I could go. I didn't dare go back to my place. The gunman – and any friends he might have – was definitely keeping an eye on my house. Then there was Haraldur. He'd been good in emergency situations previously, but Sanna would definitely be there now, so that wouldn't work as well. Karl was an obvious choice, of course. I would need to talk to him anyway about the ISA plot and about Sonni Christiansen.

When Hvítanesvegur came to an end, I turned left onto Eystari Ringvegur and then up the hill along Hoyvíksvegur where there was a residential area on the left-hand side. When I got to Katrin and Karl's house I could see that it was completely dark. No one home. The disappointment hit me hard. For a moment as I was driving towards their house, I thought I had come through it all, but now it was starting all over again.

I was hungry and tired and didn't know where to go. Then one face came to mind – Duruta. 'Come and visit one day,' she'd said. Maybe this wasn't quite 'one day' – it was almost half past ten – but the Faroese were known for going to bed late, so it would hardly be a problem on a Saturday night.

I put the car into gear and drove back on to Hoyvíksvegur and then, after a short stretch, on to Gripsvegur, where there were two cul-de-sacs with townhouses. The lowest one was

Sodnhústún. It was narrow and there were cars parked along the road. Nevertheless I eased into the road to see if there was a parking space somewhere, as the car would be far too exposed out on the main road. At the end of the road was a little turning area which I largely blocked as I parked my mauve Toyota Camry there. With its broken windows it looked like a stolen car that the thieves had just dumped there.

In which house might Duruta live? The way I looked right now, I didn't want to risk knocking on the wrong door. With scratches and stubble on my face and dirt on my jacket and trousers, I'd hardly be welcome. At the same time, I didn't know whether Duruta had visitors. Had she even meant it when she invited me round? Either way, I didn't know where else I could go.

In almost half of the houses the windows were dark, while from others there was music and noise. People were having fun. I was about to go into the little garden in front of the first house to find out whether I could see anything through a window when a voice addressed me:

'Are you looking for someone?'

I gave a start, even though I hadn't done anything wrong. Well, nothing particularly wrong. An older woman with white newly-permed hair was staring at me through thick glasses. She was wearing a light coat and had a dark scarf around her neck. She smiled.

'Yes, I'm looking for Duruta Danielsen's house. She has a daughter called Turið.'

'Oh yes. Turið often plays with my grandson when he visits. My daughter lives in Denmark, you know, but her son often comes to the Faroes to visit his grandmother. It's not easy when you're alone, my husband died almost ten years ago, and when all your grandchildren live in Denmark so you don't see them very often. But Pætur comes to visit several times a year because his mother works for an airline and can get cheap tickets. She takes him to the airport and asks a stewardess to keep an eye on him and then I meet him when he gets to the traffic terminal here in Tórshavn.'

The old lady continued to talk about her grandson, who

was clearly an exceptional child. I, however, was beginning to get impatient. When the friendly grandmother took a pause for breath, I quickly interjected:

'Where did you say Duruta lived?'

The woman had just opened her mouth to continue the story of her wonderful grandson, but I managed nevertheless to get her thoughts back to me. She turned and pointed to a house in the middle of a row just down the hill.

'She lives just there. You can see her daughter's bicycle in the garden.' She turned back. 'I live here.' She pointed to the second house in in the row above us.

'Thank you very much,' I said quickly and left the woman. It wasn't particularly polite, but I was tired.

The garden in front of Duruta's house was completely Mediterranean, with large pots and most of it covered with tiles. The orange bicycle had been placed up against one of the pots. On the middle and top floors the light was on. I walked up the few steps to the front door and listened. There was no sound to be heard. I rang the doorbell.

Forty-Three

At first I didn't know where I was. Flowered wallpaper and a low bookcase beside a white door. I turned around and looked straight into a lithograph of Zacharias Heinesen which was hanging in the middle of the wall above the bed. Double curtains with large flowers covered the window, but it was evident that the sun was shining outside. Then it dawned on me. I was at Duruta's house in the bedroom down in the basement.

I looked at the clock. It was almost nine. I got out of bed, walked over to the window and opened the curtains. Beautiful weather. I looked around for my clothes and remembered that Duruta had taken them and said something about washing them. A white dressing gown was hanging over the back of a chair and I put it on. I went into the hallway and could hear the tumble drier going in the utility room. Someone was up.

When I had turned up late last night, Duruta had sat me on a chair in the kitchen. She had given me two large glasses of Red Aalborg, which warmed me to the ends of my toes. While she buttered a couple of slices of rye bread with dried lamb's meat and salted mutton, which I ate with a ravenous appetite, I briefly told her my story. When I had explained to her that I didn't dare go back to mine while it was dark, she had said that she had a guest room down in the basement that I could sleep in. Once my hunger had been stilled, I felt sleepy, but Duruta said that first I should get undressed and have a shower. I remembered taking my clothes off and the shower, but I didn't remember any more than that.

I went up the steps and into the kitchen, where Duruta was standing ironing with her back to me. Her daughter was

200

eating cornflakes.

'Mum! The man's awake!'

The little girl called out while keeping her dark blue eyes firmly fixed on me. Her hair was the same colour as Duruta's, but was curlier, and her face darker. And then her eyes – those she didn't get from her brown-eyed mother.

Duruta turned around. 'Good morning! How did you sleep?'

She smiled. 'The best sleep I've had since coming back to the Faroes, I think.' It certainly felt like it.

'Mum says your name is Hannis. Is that right?'

The little girl's legs, that didn't reach the floor, were swinging and she stirred the bowl of cornflakes with her spoon.

'Yep, my name's Hannis and I've known your mother for a very long time.'

'I know. You used to live together.' She looked at me interrogatively. 'Are you moving in now?'

'Turið!' Duruta put down the iron and went over to the girl. 'You're not to ask such personal questions of strangers. Look,' she took the bowl and went into the living room with it, 'you can sit in here and watch cartoons while you eat.'

Turið stood there with her spoon in her hand. 'You're the first man who's slept here since we moved in,' she said, before turning about and running into the living room. Soon afterwards loud music and Daffy Duck's lisping could be heard.

Duruta came back into the kitchen and went over to the ironing board without looking at me. 'I just need to iron this shirt and then I'm done. There's coffee in the vacuum jug and French bread on the kitchen table.'

Once the coffee and two pieces of French bread had made their way down, Duruta hung the shirt on a chair – it was my shirt – and put the ironing board away. She sat down at the table.

'Do you remember how you got into bed yesterday?' Duruta smiled at me.

'No.'

'Once the shower had been silent for over quarter of an

hour and I hadn't heard anything from you, I went downstairs. Fortunately you hadn't locked the door to the bathroom. You were sitting on the toilet seat, fast asleep with the towel on your knees. I helped you into bed.'

'I was completely exhausted,' I excused myself.

'When I saw you on the steps last night it was like seeing a ghost.' She poured coffee into a mug. 'Filthy with dried blood on your face and almost transparent from tiredness. I had a real shock.' She gave me a serious look.

'I know,' I said. 'But as Karl wasn't at home I didn't know where else to turn.'

'Old grazing grounds?' Duruta asked. I thought I could hear a sting of something or other in her voice.

'That wasn't the idea,' I said. 'But I'll go straight away.'

'No, don't take it like that. I didn't mean anything by it.' She placed her hand on mine. 'You're always welcome, even if you look like you've been out fighting or been pulled through a muddy puddle.'

'I told you yesterday what had happened and that we need to get hold of Sonni Christiansen.'

'Yes,' said Duruta thoughtfully. 'I'm not in the criminal department but it looks as if Karl will be taking over there, so it's him you should speak to. By the way, I've heard rather a lot about you over at the station. And it hasn't all been good – particularly when it's come from Piddi.' She laughed and I felt an unusual feeling of warmth.

'What's been said in the media? Have they made anything of it on the radio?'

'Yes, they've spoken about the Dutch guy that was found dead in the house over at Lágargarður, but there hasn't been anything about why he was killed. I doubt that the people who are working on the case know anything about that.'

'What about the campaign against the Faroes?'

'That's another story.' Duruta sipped her coffee. 'Pressure on the Faroes is growing all the time and now several politicians have begun to maintain that we should stop the whale hunt. People in industry have had that opinion for several years, but that this should come from politicians is new. If we don't want to end up with an economy like it was a hundred years ago, it looks as if we'll need to bow to the environmental organisations.'

The noise from the living room hadn't become any quieter and now I thought I could hear Tom and Jerry fighting each other.

'You have a sweet daughter,' I said.

'Turið is fantastic,' Duruta smiled. 'She might be quite vocal, but she also knows how to be quiet.'

'What do you mean?'

'We don't live with her father and he doesn't visit. I have told her that's just how it is for us. It might be different for others in her school, but here it's just us. And she's never asked after him.'

I was going to say that she might well still think about her father, but thought it was best to keep my mouth shut on that. Instead I asked whether she had an internet connection.

The computer was in a study upstairs. We searched for the Faroese Food, Veterinary and Environmental Agency. I was still in the dressing gown, but had got hold of the diary I had found at Sound Salmon. The internet connection wasn't wonderful, but after a short time the homepage came up. Then I chose Fish Farms and a pdf of fisheries. I printed the two pages. The overview showed which fishery owned what, where the fisheries were and finally a number.

In the diary for 11 February it said: FH-FI-FJ. According to the key I had used for the numbers at the back of the book, where A was 0 and so on, these letters would be: 57-58-59. The fish farms with these numbers were all in Kollafjørður. I looked at 12 February: AE-DE-DF, which gave: 04-34-35. The first was in Lambavík and the second two were in Skálafjørður, so they were close together. 13 February: Z-EE, which gave 24 and 44. Both of these fish farms were near Kirkjubøur.

There couldn't be any doubt. The letters in Jenny McEwan's pocket diary stood for numbers that stood for fish farms in the list from the Food, Veterinary and Environmental Agency.

I went through the whole diary and found that one farm after the other had been infected with ISA. Only one centre hadn't been affected and that was Sound Salmon.

Duruta had gone downstairs while I sat with the computer and the diary and I heard her and Turið bickering about something or other. It was about ten o'clock now, so I thought it was probably about the time to ring Karl.

The phone rang for a while before anyone answered.

'Is that Karl? It's Hannis.'

'Mmph, huh?'

'It's Hannis. Wake up, Karl.'

'What's going on?' came a muffled voice from the receiver.

'I know why the two biologists and the Dutchman were killed.'

'What are you telling me?'

Now it was as though the cogs in his brain were beginning to turn, even if it was slow going.

'Hang on, hang on.' It sounded as though Karl was rethinking things. 'We didn't get to bed until almost six and now it's ten. Can't you phone back this afternoon?'

'No,' I said with determination. 'I need to speak to you now. It can't be soon enough.'

'Okay, okay,' Karl gave up. 'Phone in half an hour.'

I went downstairs to Duruta, who was now alone. Through the kitchen window I could see Turið cycling outside.

'Your clothes are ready.' Duruta pointed at the chairs around the dining table where in addition to the shirt there was now a pair of jeans and a duffle coat. On one chair were my socks and boxer shorts.

'That's why the tumble drier was going?' I smiled and Duruta nodded in affirmation.

'You're an angel,' I said, and I turned my back to my former girlfriend as I put my boxer shorts on. I was still wearing the dressing gown.

'It's amazing how shy you've become in your old age,' Duruta laughed behind me. 'Particularly when I think about what I saw last night.'

I didn't know what to say. The situation was a little embarrassing and my voice was thick when I finally said something.

'Karl asked me to phone back in half an hour. He'd clearly been out partying all night.'

'Oh, flip,' said Duruta, with one hand over her mouth. 'It was Piddi's leaving do last night. The whole police station was there. It had completely slipped my mind. I'm sorry about that.'

'It doesn't matter. He's woken me up so many times when I've got into bed late. But why weren't you there?'

'I'm not one for going out to these big parties and I need to stay at home with Turið once in a while. I can't always leave other people to look after her. As you know, I don't have any family in Tórshavn.'

Duruta looked serious, but then she added with a smile, 'But maybe you could babysit for me now and again when I have to work or go to a party?'

'Yeah, well, why not?' The question had caught me a little off-guard, so I didn't really know what to say. 'I'll go up and call Karl,' I said and slipped past Duruta, who gave a knowing smile.

Karl was in a better mood now, even if he sounded a little hoarse.

'Now I've had a headache tablet and a coffee, so I'm doing a little better. What were you saying?'

I told him the story of the diary I'd found at Sound Salmon. How I'd got into the building I skipped over – I could tell him that later – but I told him how I'd been shot at in the car and how I'd stayed hidden in the outfields the whole day yesterday. I also told him that Sonni Christiansen had made an agreement with GOS to spread ISA over the whole country.

'What shits,' exclaimed Karl. 'But you say that the feedmaster at Sound Salmon said that Sonni Christiansen flew to Denmark on Thursday evening?'

I told him that was right.

'I'll phone back in a moment. I just need to check something.'

Ten minutes later Karl phoned back.

'I've spoken to the airport. No Sonni Christiansen left the country on Thursday or any other day.'

Forty-Four

I parked the car above the village. The sea was dead calm and Kalsoy with its uneven mountain peaks was reflected in the water. In the sky there were just a few tufts of clouds which were slowly moving with their shadows forming new landscapes on the ground. Below me was the village of Elduvík, which was a perfect example of an idyll; about forty houses, if the outhouses were included, in two parts on either side of the river which wound through the deep-green valley. Where the river ran into the sea was a large beach with pebbles and a little landing spot on the eastern side. On the pebbles and on the grass above them, people were sitting on mats, while children ran about playing. Five or six cars stood parked on the road nearby. People from Tórshavn enjoying a Sunday out in the villages.

Duruta had lent me her black Golf on the condition that it wouldn't end up looking like the Toyota. She and Turið had wanted to come with me, but Duruta needed to work now that almost the entire station was out for the count after Piddi's party. She also had an arrangement with a friend who was going to take care of Turið. They used to take it in turns and ensure that they weren't working at the same time. The friend was a nurse. Duruta said the deal worked well because Turið and her friend's daughter were in the same class at school.

I had promised Karl that Duruta would take Jenny McEwan's pocket diary over to the police station and that I would head over there myself a little later once they were ready to interrogate me. In the meantime they would look for Sonni Christiansen, who had evidently become so frightened that he had gone into hiding. I told that to Duruta and said I'd quite like to speak to Sonni before the authorities got hold of him. Duruta looked hesitantly at me for a moment and then said that she shouldn't do what she was about to do, but she couldn't see that it would hinder the police in solving the case. She used the phone in the living room and came back after a short time to tell me that in addition to owning a load of land, Sonni Christiansen also owned a house, if not two, in Elduvík. And he used to go there at the weekends. I wanted to know how she knew that. She said she knew someone who had worked for Sonni.

It was almost two o'clock and it was time for the Sunday news. I turned on the radio and it belted out choral singing. I thought it was a song by Hans Andreas Djurhuus, but was so busy turning down the volume that I didn't catch which one it was. I wasn't expecting to get much from the news, because on a Sunday it was generally only random pieces that had been translated from foreign news companies.

First there was an overview of the afternoon's programming and then of the evening's and then the weather forecast. There would be a westerly wind for the rest of the day, but during the night it would become southerly with local fog. So Tórshavn would disappear – it really was a magnet for fog. The news started with a ferry in Pakistan that had capsized. Several hundred people had drowned. In South America a plane had crashed and several people had died there too. Somewhere in Norway people wanted permission to shoot wolves because they were attacking sheep. That was the closest it came to domestic news, even though we'd never had wolves on the islands. But we did have sheep. And history told us that we'd all come from Norway a thousand years ago, so naturally sheep matters in that part of Scandinavia would be of interest to us.

Before listeners' requests, there were some advertisements for prayer meetings, and then came a police announcement:

'The head of the Sound Salmon fish firm, Sonni Christiansen, is requested to make contact with the police. If anyone knows the whereabouts of Sonni Christiansen, we would like to hear from you. Please contact us on 351448.'

They hadn't found Sonni in Tórshavn. I hadn't expected them to, but it would take a while for them to get up here. I turned off the radio, put the car in gear and rolled down into the village.

Now the only problem was that I didn't know which house belonged to Sonni Christiansen, and there was no point asking any of the people who were sunbathing. I had to find someone from the village itself. I parked the car behind the other 'outsider' cars to the east of the river. This half of the village was smaller than the western side and the houses were newer. A person from Tórshavn who wants a house in a village isn't out for a new-build, but an old house with 'charm'. So I crossed the river to the western side, past the white wooden church and into the village.

Most of the houses were in good nick and there were new cars, where people had been able to squeeze them in. But there were no people, even though I could hear the listeners' requests show coming from several of the houses. Of course I could knock and ask, but that seemed a little awkward. I'd prefer to hail someone on the street and see how that went. Further into the village there were some ramshackle outhouses with rusty iron roofs, but as in most villages, these just added to the charm. I was from Tórshavn after all.

Once I'd come through the village I was on a road with a slope down to the beach on one side. The sun was baking and the noise from the children, mixed with the Swedish Vikingarna band singing about dancing on a Saturday night, made me think that it maybe wasn't so bad to live in a village like this one. Previously living anywhere in the Faroes other than in Tórshavn would have been considered a fate worse than death, but the peace, sun and the sea view here did seem tempting.

A powerful cough made me turn around. On the steps outside an ochre yellow house stood an older man in a Faroese cap. He spat and a lot came out. He came down towards the road and I went over to him. He was wearing a navy pin-striped suit from around the middle of the previous century, with a white shirt and a black tie. His shoes were black and polished.

'Excuse me!' I called. 'May I ask you something?'

We stopped and looked at each other. He was barely as tall as me, but broad across the shoulders. It was difficult to estimate his age, but he was near his eighties, I reckoned. He had tried to shave himself, but in several places the razor hadn't quite found the hairs. His eyes were bright and blue and he had small, dark lines from chewing tobacco in the corners of his mouth.

'What would the outsider like to know?'

'Do you know where Sonni Christiansen lives?'

'A friend of yours?' the old man asked. He looked at me inquisitively.

'I wouldn't say that. I've never met him, but I did hear that he might be here in the village.'

'Oh yes?' He coughed again and spat. 'I've just heard the news on the radio and the police said they wanted to talk to him.'

'Yes, and I'm working with the police,' I said. It wasn't a big lie. Duruta had told me about Sonni and Elduvík, and she was in the police.

'And what do you want with him?'

He wasn't going to give up without a fight. His eyes were fixed on me the whole time.

'There's something we want to talk to him about. Some irregularities that have taken place.'

The man smiled with his whole face and his tobacco-stained teeth came into view.

'I always suspected that. They come from Tórshavn with a load of money and buy one chunk of land after the other. He was after mine too, but I told him no. I always knew that something wasn't quite right there.'

'He has a house here in the village, doesn't he?'

'Yes, two, but he usually hangs about in Ólavshús, the red one with the grass roof.' He pointed to a large, older house nearby. Then he laughed to himself.

'And now that scoundrel's off to the nick. No surprises

there.'

I tried to protest a little, but the old boy wasn't listening to me and, in any case, there was no need to rain on his parade.

'I'll come down to Ólavshús with you, but I fear he's left the village now. I know he's been here for a few days, but I reckon I caught a glimpse of his car yesterday when he left.'

Once we had started to go down to the red house, he laughed again to himself. 'This is almost better than the sermon today.'

'The sermon?' I repeated.

'Yes, I was at church this morning. That's why I'm in my confirmation suit. I don't wear this every Sunday. But when a female priest comes to preach, and a good-looking one at that, you have to go to church. Also just to annoy those people who are against women priests.' He smiled at me. 'Those bloody Danish priests that rush up here trying to ban women from preaching in God's house. What on earth are they doing? Do they want us to become independent just to be free from them?'

He harked and spat as if to show what he thought about these men.

'It was a brilliant sermon she gave, that priest lady. I can tell you that,' he added.

'What did she speak about?' I tried to be polite.

'Now you're asking more than I can say. Something from the Gospel of St. John, I think. Something about women being sad before giving birth, but then all worry disappearing once the child's come. But I can tell you that ever since I was a little boy I've fallen asleep as soon as I've sat down on a church pew. It's good they don't have those people who go around prodding and poking anyone who's fallen asleep any more.' He laughed again.

We had now come to the red house, which was beautiful. It was long, with a whitewashed foundation and hatches that could be pulled over the barred windows. The door was locked and there was no car outside.

'But it was good and no one can say anything else about it.'

'What was good?' I asked, slightly confused.

'The priest's sermon, of course. What did you think I was talking about?'

I didn't know, but if people spoke like this in the smaller villages, then maybe I wasn't sure I wanted to move from Tórshavn after all.

'No, I was just thinking about Sonni. Where might he be?'

'I don't know, but he's up to no good wherever he is,' said the old man with the same smile. Now the tobacco trails reached down to his chin.

I said goodbye, walked down to my car and slowly drove out of the beautiful valley.

Forty-Five

Just after the cattle grid south of Funningsfjørður I met a police car, which in my rear-view mirror I saw driving to Elduvík. They would be at least as disappointed as me.

Who knew where Sonni Christiansen was hiding? It wasn't unthinkable that he had houses in other villages, but I'd have to find that out in Tórshavn. Or leave it to the police to find out. It wasn't my job to find out which dirty tricks the company director had played with GOS. On the other hand, they were presumably the reason why someone had tried to kill me several times. If I wanted to know why they were after my life, I needed to talk to Sonni. And then there was the thousand pounds from Mark Robbins. That was about twelve thousand kroner. I thought I had well and truly earned that now following my experiences on Suðuroy. The rest was unpaid overtime. Furthermore, Mark Robbins had been involved in the conspiracy against the Faroes. But why had he been killed?

For the whole journey south, as I drove under a clear blue sky, keeping an eye on the sheep along the side of the road, I tried to put everything that had happened to me over the past week in context. But by the time I came out on the Kaldbak side of the tunnel towards Tórshavn, I hadn't managed to make any kind of sense out of it all. Someone – GOS maybe? – wanted to put the Faroes in their place, and therefore ISA had been spread throughout the whole fishing industry. Various problems had sprung up on the way and Jenny and Stewart had been killed. Could it have been Sonni Christiansen? I found it had to believe that of someone from the Faroes, but maybe he'd been forced to because he had taken part

212

in the whole ISA plot. I didn't know. And I didn't know why Joost Boidin had been murdered. Or Mark Robbins. Or why someone had tried to wipe me off the face of the earth.

When I got to Sund I saw that the blue van was parked outside Sound Salmon and I turned the Golf on to the road down to the shore. I was going much too fast for that kind of whim, but fortunately the road was wide and the car had good grip, so it worked. I parked the Golf by the van and noticed that the fisheries boat had gone.

I went to the edge of the shore and saw that the boat was on its way back from the fish rings. Only now did it occur to me that I hadn't had a cigarette all day. I patted my pockets, but of course there was no cigarette. I had chewed the last ones under the rock and ingested so much nicotine that it had lasted until now. Or perhaps it was because Duruta had told me she'd stopped smoking once her daughter came along, by which she'd meant that I wasn't to smoke in the house. Whatever. I'd manage for a little while yet without tobacco.

It was the same feedmaster, but today the overalls were red and he had no cloth cap on his head. I caught the ropes and tied the boat.

'I heard on the radio that they're looking for Sonni,' was the first thing he said. 'Don't suppose you know why?' He looked at me questioningly. I stretched out my hand and helped him ashore.

'No, not really. But it has something to do with the fisheries,' I answered, which was more or less to do with the truth.

We walked over to the building.

'God knows what's happened up there. A big chaos of tools and papers.'

'You've been up there?'

'Yeah, we had a break-in on Friday night, so I had to go up to have a look. Someone or other had rooted through everything, but I've no idea whether anything was taken.'

He took out a key and opened the door. A plywood board had been placed over the broken window pane.

'They came in through there?' I asked.

'Yeah, they smashed the pane with a rock and opened

the window. Upstairs they broke the padlock with our own cutting nippers. Not particularly clever to have those lying around freely unless you want to help people break in.'

We went into the office.

'Coffee?' The feedmaster showed me a half-full coffee jug.

'Yes, please.'

He gave me a mug and then filled it. Then he took out the packet of Samson tobacco and rolled a cigarette with one hand. I was about to ask whether I could roll one myself, but thought I'd make a fool of myself once he saw how bad I was at rolling cigarettes. Instead I said:

'You've got your Sunday best on.'

'What do you mean?' He looked at me in bewilderment.

'Your overalls are red and not blue, like on Friday.'

'Yeah, you could say that,' he laughed. 'Actually I hadn't been planning to come here before tonight, but there was the break-in and it's hard enough to get the police to take a look. They were here yesterday afternoon. For fifteen minutes, perhaps, no more than that. They were busy, they said. And do you know where they were going?'

'To Piddi í Útistovu's party,' I said with a smile.

'How did you know that?' He gave me a surprised look.

'I have my sources,' I answered secretively.

'Ah, ok,' he looked doubtful. 'Never mind, but I wouldn't have come here this afternoon if there hadn't been such a commotion in one of the rings.'

'What sort of commotion?' A shudder ran through me.

'It's the ring I told you about last Friday, where the salmon was swimming so low. Now they're all trying to get to the surface, so it's like a battle.'

'Is it possible to get the salmon out?' I asked eagerly.

'Yeah, I'll empty the rings tomorrow, because it can't be left like this.'

'Could you empty that one ring today?'

'Yes, I could do that, but once we've got the salmon on board, what are we to do with it? There's no one to slaughter it before tomorrow.'

'We'll cross that bridge when we come to it,' I said and

hauled the feedmaster to his feet. 'Come on, hurry.'

Twenty minutes later we had a large hose in the ring and were sucking up salmon into a tank on the boat. When we thought we had them all, I asked whether he had a fishing telescope. He gave me a light yellow one made of plastic. I got down onto my knees to look into the seine net.

Down at the bottom there was a pile of white bones. Facing me on top was a skull.

Part Three

A high mortality rate among humans would be an advantage. It is our duty to bring one about. It is our species' responsibility towards the environment to eliminate 90 per cent of our effective strength.

William Aiken

Forty-Six

'"Ill weeds grow apace", my mother used to say when I was little.'

The man who was talking puffed violently on a large cigar and disappeared from time to time in billowing clouds of smoke.

'But…'

The man was so worked up that he didn't hear me.

'And I can tell you that she was right.' He turned about and stood in front of me. I was sitting on a chair. 'Now the same man has shot at you three times and you're still alive. If I wasn't a policeman, I'd give him a helping hand.'

He took the cigar out of his mouth and waved it about, as he previously had done with a pipe. It was dinner time on Sunday evening and the angry man was Piddi í Útistovu, who had the pleasure of having me in his care. We were alone in his office at the police station.

'We've found out from Denmark that both the bullet that was shot into your so-called office and the one that was dug out of the tail of the plane on Suðuroy are from the same weapon. Presumably an SIG 550 sniper gun.'

He paused and took a large puff on his cigar without taking his eyes off me. 'Why the hell anyone would bother to send a gunman after someone like you is beyond me. You're not worth hacking up into animal feed.'

'I don't know either,' I tried, but Piddi was listening just as much now as before.

'We've also found a bullet in the back seat of the car you wrecked. It's like the others.'

I couldn't be bothered to explain to him that it wasn't me

who ruined the car. And anyway, the car wasn't ruined, it was just battered.

He walked a few steps back and forth, pulled on the cigar and continued:

'You're a moron, a bloody idiot who doesn't know how to behave, but instead drags all sorts of budding criminals behind him. A good-for-nothing son of a bitch, who…'

'Come on!' I interposed loudly. 'I don't care for having all kinds of insults and swear words thrown at me.'

Piddi looked at me astonished. 'Swearing and insults? You think this is swearing? I'll tell you something for nothing. Only people from the north swear. For us from Suðuroy it's an art form. It's nothing like you guys mumbling your way through dirty words.'

He turned the cigar in his mouth with his fingers, took it out and examined it approvingly. 'It's a Churchill,' he said with a suddenly much softer voice.

I was completely baffled. I wasn't used to that tone from Piddi. 'Churchill? What do you mean?'

'I reckon you've heard of Churchill, even though you're a northerner?' he said with sarcasm in his voice. 'You know, the one who was the British Prime Minister during the war.'

'I know who Churchill is,' I answered.

'And what did Churchill always have in the corner of his mouth?'

'A cigar,' I answered, still confused. I wasn't exactly sure what was going on here.

'Exactly!' Now Piddi's whole face lit up. 'And this is a Churchill cigar from Davidoff.' He held the large cigar up to me. 'I got a box of them at the police station last night. The world's best Cuban cigars.' He looked pleased with himself.

'Wasn't it a leaving party?' I asked.

'Yes, and now you're wondering what Piddi's still doing here?' He inhaled from the cigar. 'I'll happily tell you. It's to confirm my decision to leave. I could have stayed for another two years, but just meeting you has made all doubt disappear like dew before the sun. I'm free from the police and free from you. So thank you for that.'

He stretched out his hand and I stood up and shook it. Then he disappeared through the door, smiling and smoking.

Nothing at this police station had ever surprised me more. It was as though Piddi were a different man. You often hear that strange things happen to people once they retire, but still…

'You've spoken to Piddi?' Karl was standing in the doorway laughing.

'Yeah, but he was a bit weird. I preferred the old Piddi.'

'He requested – or rather demanded – to be allowed to speak to you in private as a last favour from us colleagues. We had a man in the corridor, just in case he was going to attack you, but as far as I'm aware, he didn't do that.'

'First he screamed at me, as he usually does, and then he thanked me, and I haven't experienced that before.'

'Don't worry about it,' said Karl. 'Now you're free of each other. That's why he's so happy. And because he's allowed to smoke again. Don't forget that.'

'Maybe,' I answered doubtfully. It could be that Piddi had started to smoke again and therefore saw more joy in his existence, like Karl said, but that he would be so happy to be free of me felt like a dubious honour.

'And you've found another body?' Karl slid down onto a chair on the other side of the cluttered desk, leaned back and folded his hands behind his head.

'Have you found out whether it's Sonni Christiansen?' I hurried to ask, so that Karl wouldn't also criticise me on my habit of finding dead people.

'That was easy.' Karl smiled, pleased with himself. 'We just phoned the dentist and found out who had been responsible for looking after Sonni Christiansen's teeth. We asked for that person to go down to the clinic and sent a car with the skull from the fishing ring down there. In less than an hour we had had it confirmed that the skeleton belonged to the director of the fishery.'

'Do you know how he was killed?'

'No, we haven't got that far.' He fixed his gaze on me. 'It's no more than three, four hours since you found this gem for

221

us. And only three, four days since you found the Dutchman.'

In my mind I saw a black cloud that rose up and beneath it a smiling, white skull. A shudder ran through me.

'You don't know more about why he was found dead among the salmon?'

'No, we keep finding dead ends,' Karl sighed. 'When you phoned about the diary we thought we had a lead, but before we got to Sund, you'd found Sonni's body.'

'He must have been working with someone,' I tried.

'Yes,' said Karl discouraged. 'With Jenny McEwan, Stewart Peters, Mark Robbins and Joost Boidin. All dead. The role that Joost played we don't yet know, but the others all seem fairly clear. In any case it seems as though Jenny was afraid of something when she wrote the agreement in code in the diary. Some kind of insurance, but not particularly useable.'

'Whoever killed these people must still be in the country,' I chipped in. 'It must be a foreigner, so can't we just try that?'

'Have you any idea how many foreigners go backwards and forwards to the Faroes? And even if we say it's someone who's been here for three weeks or more, that's still a huge number. But we can limit it more if we assume that all three were the same murderer. If, on the other hand, we're dealing with three different murderers, everything becomes much more complicated, as they *all* could have gone back and forth.'

'And then there's whoever shot at me.'

'And then there's him,' said Karl with emphasis. 'We know that we're only looking at one person there because it's all the same gun. But we don't know whether he's got anything to do with the murderer or murderers. We do know that more than one person was involved when Jenny and Stewart were killed, because the bodies were carried to be left among the whales. Other than that we know nothing.'

'But you must know something?' I protested. 'You know that GOS is involved.'

'GOS, ha!' Karl snorted. 'They are so slippery that we can't count on anything where they're concerned. The Chief Constable himself phoned the headquarters in London, but they didn't know anything. Hardly even knew Mark Robbins, although they admitted that he had once worked for them. As far as they were aware he was now working by himself.'

'You let them get away that easy?'

'No, but even if the Chief Constable turns to Scotland Yard and they undertake an investigation, we still can't prove anything. And we still don't know how the various deaths are connected. As far as the Brits are concerned, the whale hunters killed the two youngsters, so why wouldn't they be responsible for the rest as well?'

Karl sighed and looked upwards for a moment. Then he loosened his hands from behind his head, looked directly at me and pointed with his right hand across the desk.

'The only thing we do have is you.' Then he smiled effusively. 'But you're also the murderers' only stumbling block.'

Forty-Seven

Being the murderers' only stumbling block was not a role I had coveted. Yes, it had been my lot for a number of days, but Karl actually expressing it in words didn't make things easier.

I was standing at the window in my office, smoking a cigarette and looking out over Vágsbotnur. I made sure I was partially hidden, just in case someone tried to hit me again. The danger wasn't great as there was thick fog. The people who passed by down at the quayside appeared fuzzily from the haze and disappeared again at the next moment. The sound of the foghorn on the jetty added an air of both cosiness and eeriness to the surroundings. It was gone eleven on Monday morning and Creedence Clearwater Revival's 'Bad Moon Rising' was coming from the transistor radio. It always made me happy that the Faroese radio broadcaster, Útvarp Føroya, had such suitably conservative tastes when it came to music. The music programmes were overwhelmingly characterised by good old tunes that you'd heard countless times before. But that you wanted to hear again.

When I was done at the police station last night, I had gone to Duruta's. I had told myself that the reason was to get my car, but in reality I was at a loss. When things ended between us about seven or eight years before, I had got the impression that she didn't care about me. That she didn't like my lifestyle. But now it looked as if she had nothing against me. And that she maybe even almost wanted a visit from me. I didn't really understand, but perhaps I wasn't supposed to.

Duruta had just come home from work and had picked up Turið, who was sitting in front of the television eating something chocolatey with a spoon. She was watching a

Danish film with Dirch Passer and Ghita Nørby. It looked like 'The Baroness from the Petrol Tank', which I'd seen as a little boy at the Sjónleikarhús theatre. Clearly not much had changed since then.

Under strong protestations Turið was sent to bed.

'You have to go to school early tomorrow morning.'

We sat in the kitchen, where I'd been given a bite to eat. I hadn't had anything since breakfast. After a short while I was overcome by tiredness. Being able to relax for a moment had made me tired. Duruta had offered me the room in the basement and I had accepted. I didn't feel much like going home alone.

I lay there thinking of Elduvík and the skeleton in the seine net and my thoughts had begun to float towards the direction of Dreamland, when I noticed that the door to my room had opened. Within a second, the quilt was moved to one side and a naked female body pressed against me. It was Duruta.

'I wanted to do this ever since I saw you over at the police station,' she whispered in my ear. 'If you don't want more than this, we can just lie here like this,' she added in such a low voice that I almost couldn't hear it.

I answered her by putting my arms around her and gently drawing her in towards me. I was also naked and soon afterwards it wasn't possible to see where one of us ended and the other began.

The heat from the night was still in my body, now as I was standing at the window trying to discern people in the fog. I thought to myself that maybe it hadn't been so stupid coming back to the Faroes. In any case, one person seemed to be happy about it. And that was a good start.

The fog eased a little and I saw a fair-haired woman in a long, light blue coat taking photographs down at the quayside. Her camera was on a tripod, so presumably she was a professional. As far as I could see, the lens was pointed straight into the fog, but fog was characteristic of the Faroe Islands after all. Then I suddenly realised that it was the woman who spoke French and American English. I grabbed my duffle coat and ran down the stairs onto the road and down to the quayside.

Robin Nimier was even more beautiful when she was lost in her work. The shining blue coat that went down to her ankles brought out the gold in her hair. She shone as she was standing there. I looked out into the harbour and saw that the outlines of the boats formed supernatural shadowy shapes in the fog. It wasn't just the fog she was taking photographs of.

'Capturing the Faroese sights?' I asked in English once I was close to her.

She looked up from the camera and smiled when she recognised me.

'The one looking for the Dutch guy.' Her smile disappeared. 'I heard that you found him.'

'Yes, I did. Too late, unfortunately.'

'I didn't know him, but it's always terrible when something like that happens.' She looked at me with a serious expression.

There wasn't much to add to that, so I took the conversation in a new direction.

'Interested in fog?'

'That too,' she answered. 'I'm trying to catch all the nuances in the Faroese weather. There's no point taking bright and colourful tourist pictures. You can get those anywhere, but this!' She waved her hand into the fog. 'This is particularly Faroese.'

At that moment the fog returned and we almost couldn't see the water.

'But when it's as thick as it is now, I can't do anything with it.' Her face lit up with a smile. 'Well, no one would be able to see if the picture was taken here or on the other side of the world.'

She removed the camera from the tripod and started to pack everything down. I didn't know what I was planning to get from her, but I didn't want just to let her go.

'What about a cup of coffee and a little something?' I asked and pointed to Café Karlsborg, which had just opened.

'Yeah, why not?' Robin Nimier smiled and handed me the tripod.

There were already some tourists sitting outside the café,

but we thought the weather required a table indoors. Once we had sat down, Robin Nimier shuddered a little.

'Your weather is changeable and fascinating, but couldn't it be a couple of degrees warmer? I grew up in Africa and there it's certainly a little warmer than here.'

'You speak fluent English and French. How did that come about?'

'My dad was French and my mum American. They met near the equator and I was the result. The reason why I'm running around so far north is because my mum was from Alaska and particularly when the temperature passed fifty degrees she would talk about snow and glaciers. But so far I've not been any further north than the Faroes. It's too cold.'

She smiled and it was as though the sun were shining.

We both asked for a cappuccino, even though the Italians maintain that it should never be drunk after eleven, and open sandwiches with sausage meat and dried lamb.

'How can it be that a foreigner like you eats dried lamb?' Foreigners often ate dried lamb when it was served to them, but choosing it voluntarily was unusual.

'You should hear what I ate in Africa when I was growing up. Dried lamb is great.' She swallowed half a slice of bread. Then she looked at me inquisitively.

'We've met twice and only talked about me. What I do, where I'm from. You haven't even told me what your name is.'

'I'm sorry about that. My name is Hannis Martinsson and I've lived abroad for many years, but now have an office here in Tórshavn and work as a consultant.'

'Consultant?'

'Yes, I advise, write articles about the Faroes and Faroese issues.'

'Like a journalist?'

'Yes, I used to work as a journalist for various papers, but now I'm freelance.'

'Like me,' Robin smiled.

'Something like that,' I tried to avoid any further questions.

We finished off the food in peace and I half-listened to the music. It was country and western music and I thought it was probably Johnny Cash.

'Have you spoken to your housemate at Heljareyga, Alan McLeod?' I had remembered that the number of the Prime Minister's Office had been in Jenny's diary. It might have had something to do with a work permit, but maybe there was a connection of another kind.

'I spoke to him last night, but he was heading out to sing or play at a pub somewhere, so we didn't say much. But he's very charming.'

'You don't know what he's doing here?'

'He said he was working at the Prime Minister's Office and that there was an exchange agreement with Scotland. And that he'd be going home again after the summer break.'

'You don't know any more about what he's up to?' I continued.

Now the woman on the other side of the table wasn't so friendly any more and her eyes became cold. 'Why are you sitting there asking me about people I hardly know? I thought we were going to get some food and have a nice time, but instead you're practically interrogating me.'

I was caught somewhat off-guard, but tried to protest. 'I wasn't trying to pry…'

Robin Nimier wasn't listening. 'If you want to know something about Alan McLean, you'll have to ask him yourself,' she said firmly. She got up. 'Thank you for the coffee and the sandwiches. I have to get back to work.'

She disappeared into the fog with her tripod and camera bag.

I was a little embarrassed, but I was also wondering why Robin Nimier had called Alan McLeod Alan McLean.

Forty-Eight

Back at the office I phoned Karl at the police station and asked whether he'd spoken to Alan McLeod, as he had said the other day. He had, but he couldn't see that there was anything amiss there. The man worked on international relations at the Prime Minister's Office and entertained people in the evenings with Scottish and Irish folk songs. A real wag.

'Where did he study?' I continued.

'Hang on. Let me look at the papers. It says here the University of Glasgow. What do you need that for?'

'I don't know. I'm just wondering what he's doing here.'

'Don't do anything stupid. We'll talk later,' said Karl, before cutting off the conversation.

I dialled directory enquiries and asked for the phone number of the University of Glasgow. Then I phoned them and asked to be put through to the Faculty of Social Sciences. After a fair bit of to-ing and fro-ing around different departments, I finally got through to Professor Firth. Judging by her voice, she was in her forties.

'You're asking about Alan McLeod?' she asked cautiously.

'Yes, I'm ringing from the Faroe Islands, from the Prime Minister's Office and there are one or two questions we'd like to have answered in connection with pay grades.'

'Can't you just ask Alan?' The voice was guarded. Maybe she'd been involved with the charmer at some point. That would make sense.

'Yes, but he's on a business trip to Greenland, so we thought it would be quicker to phone you.'

'Ah, OK, well then, that's OK. What would you like to know?'

'I understand that Alan McLeod has an MA in Social

Science?'

'He has a BA in Sociology. He wasn't here for long enough to get an MA.'

'Why does he say Social Science?'

'We don't usually call it that, but it's not completely wrong. Social Science is the name of the faculty and it contains a number of different disciplines. Sociology is one of them.'

'You say he wasn't with you for long. Do you know where he was before coming to you?'

The other end of the line went quiet.

'Professor Firth?' I asked after a pause.

'Yes… I don't know if I'm allowed to say it,' she said finally.

'What do you mean?'

'I don't know who you are and I promised Alan…'

There had definitely been something going on between Professor Firth and Alan McLeod.

'Well, I can just ask the female principal who went to Greenland with Alan McLeod.' I tried to stoke the fire. 'It was just the two of them, so I'm sure they're close to each other.'

Professor Firth wasn't unlike other women – or men for that matter – when it came to the touchy subject of a love-life. She took the bait.

'Has he found himself a new greenie girlfriend?' The voice on the phone from Glasgow was cutting.

'I don't know how much she has to do with the environment, but she's twenty-five and looks good.' Maybe that would get the Scottish professor so ruffled that she'd spill.

'That sounds right. I know what he's like, with his guitar and his women. He usually hangs out with hippy-types.'

Professor Firth now sounded like she was almost crying.

'But he promised me, that he wouldn't…' The voice stopped.

'Professor?' I was worried she might disappear.

'He was in the SAS,' she said laconically.

'The airline?' I asked in confusion.

'No, the Special Air Service.'

'The Special Air Service?' I repeated, as a load of images ran through my mind. This was unexpected.

'He went on raids in Bosnia and Sierra Leone. I promised I wouldn't tell anyone, but if he's going to lie and go on business trips with his lovers, I don't feel particularly bound by my promises.'

I thought of the old adage that hell hath no fury like a woman scorned. I ignored the fact that I had contributed to this particular instance.

'You can tell Alan McLeod, once he's back from his lovers' jaunt, that he's not to show his face at this university again.' Then the rejected professor hung up.

I leaned back in my chair and let the surprise sink in. Alan McLeod, the smiling party animal, had been trained by the extra-tough Special Air Service, so environmental organisations weren't unknown to him. But he had lied to me about his qualifications. Why? Because he didn't care? Because he got more money as an MA than a BA? I didn't know, but the fact he had been part of the SAS was interesting. Some of the rougher elements of the environmental organisations, the ones that sank whaling boats with bombs and by ramming them, had also often had their training from the military.

But the SAS was a special force, one which only took on the most hard-core of men, so it wasn't commonplace to find a former member of theirs working for the Prime Minister. Alan McLeod hadn't told the police about his past and was therefore unlikely to have told his colleagues in the government.

I knew that there were loads of books about the SAS and that some of its members had retold their experiences from during the Gulf War, where they had fought behind enemy lines. That was just something I had read in the newspapers. I didn't otherwise know very much about the force, although I did remember a news programme on the television from years ago, in which camouflaged SAS members stormed an occupied embassy in London. The terrorists had pretty much all been killed, while no members of the SAS had been wounded.

These guys were tough.

I opened the bottom drawer and put the bottle of single malt on the table. In the same drawer I found a clean glass and poured about an inch into it. Once I had tasted the noble drink, I lit a cigarette. Over recent years my desire to smoke had been increasingly connected to alcohol. I could usually last most of the day without smoking, but once I'd had a beer or other drink, I needed a cigarette.

What should I do now?

Once the cigarette had been finished and the glass of whisky emptied, I had decided that I needed to know more about Alan McLeod. He was the only crack in this sorry and seemingly closed story.

Forty-Nine

I paused in the corridor upstairs at Heljareyga. The only thing I could hear was the humming of the fridge. I didn't know whether new residents had moved in, but as it was early afternoon, it was highly unlikely that anyone was at home. I cautiously walked over to the kitchen and looked in. No one. The dormer roof was half-open and now that the fog had shrouded the land and its people, it was no more than eight degrees. It was cold in the kitchen. I opened the fridge. There were just a couple of things on two of the shelves. Joost Boidin's shelf had been cleared.

Back in the corridor I listened out for a while, but when the silence remained unaltered, I went over to Alan McLeod's room. I took out my pocket knife, stuck the blade into the gap between the door and the doorframe and managed to move the latch. In the next moment I was standing in the attic.

At first sight, everything looked as I had expected. The floor was covered in clothes and the rickety desk beneath the attic window was covered with newspapers, empty beer bottles, broken guitar strings and, in the middle of the mess, a pair of black shoes. Along the wall to the right there was a made bed with a light brown bedcover. On the bed there was a tartan dressing gown and a creased white t-shirt. In the corner to the left there was a worn guitar. There was a poster on each end wall. One showed The Dubliners in their young days and the other one was an election poster promoting the Scottish National Party with Sean Connery.

Something wasn't right. I stood there a moment longer and studied my surroundings. Then the penny dropped. The bed!

It was the blanket on the bed that did it. It was completely smooth, not a crease. The dressing gown and T-shirt had been purposefully placed on the bed to make it look a little disorderly. The clothes on the floor had been there for a while. As had the mess on the desk.

I went over to the desk and picked up a beer bottle. Dust on the neck. Then I dragged a finger across one of the newspapers. The end of my finger was grey with dust.

Alan McLeod had arranged his room so that a visitor would think it a real bachelor pad. But now he had been in the Faroes for several months and he was no longer so careful. His years in the military had left their mark and the bed was the most obvious example.

On the left side of the desk there was a green cardboard folder. I picked it up and looked in it. Personal documents. First and foremost, a copy of the agreement between the Scottish Parliament and the Faroese government. Then information on pay and sources of funding for extraordinary payments from the European Union to countries outside the union. Everything looked very normal. In the bottom drawer there was just Alan McLeod's British passport. The picture of him was as bad as they always are, so that was normal too. Nevertheless it did strike me as a little odd that the passport was only a few months old and that there wasn't a single stamp in it. But presumably he changed his passport every now and again, just like the rest of us.

Between the bed and the door there was a large double wardrobe. I opened the doors. There were three Scottish jackets on hangers. Two of them were black and looked like the one Alan had been wearing when I met him. The third was Bordeaux-red. Almost a dress jacket. At the bottom of the wardrobe there were several pairs of shoes standing dead straight next to one another. On one side of the wardrobe there were shelves, and here there were shirts, underwear and socks. All ironed and folded as though they had come straight from a launderette. On the bottom shelf there was something that I had first thought to be a large blanket with the same tartan pattern as on its owner's waistcoat. But it soon became clear that this was much longer than a normal blanket. This was a kilt. I had heard that kilts required a lot of material, but this was about eight metres.

By the bedhead there was a low bookcase with two shelves. On the top one there were about ten books with a small rock as a bookend. The volumes were so perfectly in line that I didn't dare touch them, but I tried to read their spines: Aldo Leopold's *A Sand Country Almanac*, John Lovelock's *Gaia*, Arne Næss' *The Shallow and the Deep, Long-Range Ecological Movement*, Hans Jonas' *The Imperative of Responsibility*, Christopher D. Stone's *Should Trees Have Standing?* and Michel Serres' *Le contrat naturel*.

Of these authors I only knew Arne Næss, who I knew to be somewhat extreme in his views on the environment. At sixth-form college I had read a history of philosophy that he had written, but I didn't remember having any real interest in nature or animal rights back then. I didn't know who the other authors were, but everything indicated that they were extremists.

I found a pen in my pocket and ripped a page out of one of the newspapers on the desk. It was hardly going to be missed. I made a note of the authors' names so that I could check who they were and put the pen and paper in my pocket.

For a while I stood there looking around me, wondering about the difference between the surface mess and the perfect and systematic order beneath it. This schizophrenia was far too perfect and artificial to believe. There was no real connection between the entertaining and guitar-playing Alan McLeod and his time in the military. There was no apparent explanation as to these two roles from what I could see. The books perhaps revealed something, but not enough. Other than the agreement and the passport in the drawer, there was nothing personal in the room. Yes, there was the guitar, but still…

I pulled the drawers out and looked underneath them, just in case there was something hidden there. Nothing. Then I unfastened the posters at the bottom and looked behind them. Nothing there either. Under and behind the clothes in the wardrobe, in jacket pockets and on top of the wardrobe.

Nothing.

Alan McLeod was clearly as white as the snow. Whiter than anyone else. But at the same time there was something else that was worrying me. I tried to work out what it was that was trying to make itself known right at the back of my mind.

I dropped that thought, walked over to the door, listened out to see whether there was anyone outside and then sneaked out. In the corridor I saw Robin Nimier's door and half-wondered whether I should also pay her room a visit. But I had to make sure I wasn't taking on too much. I had no idea when she might be home. Particularly in this foggy weather, where it could become difficult to take photographs. Instead I went into the kitchen.

Before long I had been through the kitchen cupboards, the microwave and the fridge. Nothing unusual, nothing personal.

I sat down on one of the chairs and looked across the table med the hotplates and stainless steel sink. That was the whole kitchen investigated. I found a cigarette in my pocket and lit it. It didn't matter if the residents knew that someone had been there. As I turned on my chair to reach out for a bowl to use as an ashtray, I saw it.

The postcard!

That was what had created unrest in my mind. Sub-consciously I had registered it when I was in the kitchen before, but I hadn't really taken notice of it.

The postcard with the ship with the multi-coloured stripe was exactly where it had been when I took it on the Saturday. Moreover, the drawing pin was in the exact same hole. But the card hadn't been on the notice board when I'd been there on Thursday. Or had it? I was beginning to doubt myself. Never mind. I loosened the drawing pin and took the postcard. The text on the reverse hadn't changed either: sunshine and sea on Hawaii and best wishes for a hush-hush plan from Matthew.

Whoever had committed the break-in at my house on Saturday night had put the postcard up on the noticeboard, so I could see it. Only two people lived up here: Alan McLeod and Robin Nimier. But it still wasn't necessarily one of them. A third person could easily be involved. And I had no idea who that might be.

But it didn't matter. Whoever was playing cat and mouse with me wasn't going to get away with it. Two could play at that game.

I put the postcard in my pocket and went on my way.

Fifty

My house looked just like I had left it on Friday morning. I didn't think anyone had been there, but to be on the safe side I locked the front door and the door down to the basement. The whole way down Jóannes Paturssonargøta I had had the tickling feeling down my spine that someone had a weapon aimed at me. I had to force myself to walk along the pavement at a normal pace and not start to run or hide in a garden. I whole time I tried to reassure myself that the fog was so thick that the gunman would need to get very close just to be able to see me.

Once the door was locked I felt a sense of relief and went straight into the kitchen to get my bottle of gin. I put it to my mouth and took a proper gulp. And then another, before I screwed the cap back on. Before long I was starting to feel relaxed. When I put the bottle back in the cupboard under the table, I noticed the bottle of Highland Park which stood there unopened. It didn't matter. The harsh taste of gin suited the situation. The milder Scottish drink could wait until better times.

I took the postcard out of my jacket pocket and put it back on the kitchen table where I thought I'd left it last. I didn't really know why, but knowing it was back somehow put my mind at ease. That I had been the one who took it and that someone else had actually put it back in its rightful place on the noticeboard made no difference to me. But it did matter why it had happened and who had done it. That the postcard had been removed from the kitchen at Heljareyga again would maybe lead to something or other that would hopefully help me work out what on earth was going on.

And then there was the page from the newspaper with the list of books and authors. I didn't have a computer, but maybe I could call someone and ask them? Who did I know that worked with animals and conservation? No one, really. The leaders of the pilot whale hunt were hardly the right people to ask. Certainly not the driving instructor, but maybe the vet? Then I remembered an old friend.

We'd had a lot to do with each other at school and in our first years in Denmark. Then he finished studying biology and moved back to the Faroes to teach and we lost contact. Jóanes Winther was definitely the right person.

My mobile phone was on the dining table staring at me, where it had been since last Friday, but I left it in peace and instead went into the living room to the old landline and phoned directory enquiries. A moment later I had Jóanes Winther's number.

The phone rang for so long that I was about to hang up when someone picked it up.

'Jóanes,' came the breathless voice on the other end.

'It's Hannis Martinsson, Jóanes. Remember me? It's been a while!'

'Hannis! It must be at least ten years since I last saw you. Are you sick?' He tried to control his breath, but he was stumbling over his words.

'Sick?' I asked surprised.

'Yeah! I mean, you haven't visited me for a generation, so I guessed you had disappeared. Got lost.' His breathing was now almost normal.

'Got lost?'

'Yeah. When you don't hear from an old friend you assume he's strayed off. Or do you just need a written invitation before you pop in?'

Now I remembered what Jóanes' teasing was like. In the old days he'd been a pro at pulling people's legs, and clearly nothing had changed.

'Ah, shut up, Jóanes,' I said, laughing. 'You could always come and drink Highland Park at mine.'

'If it wasn't a Monday I'd be over there in an instant, but

you know, early to school tomorrow and homework to mark tonight. When you phoned I was out in the garden looking for snails in this damp weather. I was planning to take them into my classes tomorrow. You probably know that the sex life of a snail is of a very particular nature…'

'Hang on a minute with the snails, Jóanes.' I knew he entered into his work with heart and soul and could easily talk for hours about, say, the exciting sex lives of snails. Once he got going it certainly wasn't easy to stop him again. 'Can't we save snail sex until there's a bottle of whisky between us? Just now there's something else I want to ask you about.'

'Fire away! Fire away!' came an eager voice from the receiver.

'There are some environmental authors I don't know, but maybe you know who they are?' I read the names off the newspaper page: Aldo Leopold, John Lovelock, Arne Næss, Hans Jonas and Michel Serres.

'That's quite a group there!' laughed Jóanes. 'Yep, I know all those guys. Most of them are dangerous bastards!'

'Dangerous?'

'They want to move people from the centre to the periphery. In future people won't have any special rights, but will be equal to animals and trees. If you have to choose whether to end the life of either a tree or a human, it's not a foregone conclusion that the human will win.'

'Now you're exaggerating,' I chipped in.

'Nope, not at all. Let's just consider the least extreme of the ones you named, the Norwegian philosopher Arne Næss. He reckons that the Earth's population needs to decrease by about one hundred million. Others say five hundred million. One, a William Aiken, says it's our duty to eliminate about ninety per cent of human life… To protect the environment.'

'He sounds disturbed.'

'Maybe you and many other people here might think that, but in the big wide world he's highly respected. He also says that we need to work together to decimate humanity ourselves. He doesn't say how, but maybe the Nazi extermination camps gave him ideas. No one went on about

240

nature as much as the Nazis. No country today comes close to them in terms of animal protection laws. But human life on the other hand was of little value.'

Jóanes was silent for a moment.

'People like Aldo Leopold, Hans Jonas and Michel Serres are dangerous to humanity. They have philosophised themselves away from love for one's neighbour and think exclusively of nature as a unit. A dog, a tree or a human are all the same. We're used to thinking of the world in a certain way, with humanity as the subject and the rest of the world the object, but that's not what these guys think. They'd rather turn it all upside down, with the result that humanism disappears.'

'If I understand you correctly,' I said slowly, 'humanity isn't particularly important for these authors.'

'No, there's no difference between a human being and, for example, a bush. There are so many more plants than people, and if we include animals and insects too, the relationship is even more skewed. And why should humanity have any particular right to do whatever it wants when it's just one of many species on earth? No, if people hurt animals or plants, off with their heads!'

We were both silent and I reflected on how this worldview seemed to match what had been happening in the Faroes over the past few weeks.

'Why do you want to know about these environmentalists? Has it got something to do with the attacks on the Faroes?'

'Yes,' I answered. 'It's probably these authors' thoughts that are behind what's been going on.'

'Well then, God help us!' said Jóanes Winther seriously.

There was silence again for a moment, and then he said hesitatingly:

'The Dutchman that they found dead in the concrete house above Boðanes – is he also involved in this?'

'Yes, there's no doubt about that.' I didn't tell him that I was the one who had found Joost Boidin.

'That house, or should I say that ruin of a house, is used for smoking weed, and a guitar-playing Scot is often part of the party.'

'How do you know that?'

'My pupils told me. And I've tried to tell them to stay away. But who listens to an ancient teacher?'

This had my undivided attention. 'You say that some of your pupils hang out in that concrete box and that one of the ringleaders is a Scot?'

'Yes.'

'And they sit smoking weed?'

'Yes, definitely. And stronger stuff. But they don't tell me that. I assumed the Scot might have something to do with cannabis smuggling.'

'That's not impossible,' I answered evasively. 'But for now it's the environmental pressure I'm thinking about.'

'Yes, of course. And that's completely right,' said Jóanes Winther, slightly confused. 'I just thought…'

'And thank you,' I interrupted him. 'You have given me something to think about. Go back to the snails in the garden and I'll try to have a rethink.'

'You mean like a division of labour?' he laughed. 'You ponder the environment, I'll collect snails and we'll combine our efforts.'

'I don't know whether that's exactly what I was thinking of, but let's meet up in the not-too-distant future and we'll talk about it.'

Once I'd put the receiver down, I lit a cigarette and tried to summarise what I'd learned. Alan McLeod was using the yellow house for something. Jóanes thought it had something to do with drugs, but I thought he was wrong on that. There was no doubt that drugs were involved, but probably only as a cover. That Joost Boidin had been killed in the same house, but not moved elsewhere, was obviously a problem. If Alan had killed Joost, something must have prevented him from hiding the body.

If, if, if. This was all moving very slowly. But at least I knew now that Alan McLeod had the same extreme thoughts as these environmentalists and that, as a former member of the SAS, he was dangerous.

I sat there trying to make head or tail of all the confusion when the telephone rang.

Fifty-One

We sailed up the Nólsoy Fjord in thick fog. We had a GPS system on board, so Haraldur reckoned we'd easily be able to find our way to Gøtuvík. It was just the two of us on Haraldur's fibreglass boat and we were on our way to a whale hunt.

Haraldur had called me to let me know that a hunt was on and had asked whether I'd like to head north with him. A few boats from Gøta were by a pod of whales right out in the northern part of the bay and they were wanting some help to drive them in to land. As I understood it, the main objective was to stop the people from Klaksvík leading the pod in that direction. I protested a little, saying that we wouldn't be able to see anything in the fog. Haraldur dismissed my protestations and stated that the meteorologists had promised that the wind would later move to the west and that the fog would therefore ease up a little. When I said it was a long way to sail, Haraldur laughed and said that *Rani II* went at about 15-16 nautical miles and the current was with us, so it wouldn't take us more than three quarters of an hour to cover the distance.

I had given in and hurried to leave, but remembered to take my mobile phone with me. As we sailed out of the Tórshavn harbour I called Duruta, who had invited me for dinner that evening and told her that I'd probably be back in Tórshavn quite late. She said that as long as it wasn't too late, I'd be welcome any time. That was nice to hear.

As we passed around Mjóvanes the fog eased a little and we were able to see the cluster of boats in the north by Gøtunes. There were thirty at most, so they had managed to keep it fairly quiet.

'Do you know how many whales there are?' I asked Haraldur.

'My cousin in Syðrugøta said they reckoned there were between eighty and a hundred whales. If no more of us turn up than those we can see now, we'll get a lot each.'

I thought to myself that Haraldur might as well have my share too, if he gave me some dry-salted blubber in return. I didn't care for fresh or dried whale meat, but I kept quiet for now.

'Take the controls, Hannis, and I'll find something we can use to throw so that we can be of some use.' Haraldur moved from his seat just inside the wheelhouse and I took hold of the little steering wheel.

The whales, which were now close to land, seemed to be completely calm. Water bubbling up from their blowholes could be seen now and again, but otherwise they were just small black marks in the sea. The boats sailed slowly back and forth outside the pod, waiting for their chance.

As I sailed across the bay, I looked down into the room in front of the wheelhouse and could see that Haraldur's girlfriend hadn't been here. There were bunks to sleep on and a table to eat at, but the whole room was such a mess of bins, cod rods and all possible fishing tools, that you couldn't get in. On board *Rani II* it looked just like it had done previously at the owner's house. In some way I found that encouraging.

As we approached the boats we made sure we kept back a little so that we wouldn't be in the way. I was mostly thinking of myself, but Haraldur said that he was also unsure of how the group would proceed, as he had never taken a boat to a whale hunt in Gøta.

Screeching seagulls hung in the air above the pod of whales, as if they knew that a lavish mealtime was on the cards. You could hear snorting from the whales' breathing holes and screeching sounds as the whales rubbed against each other. Some were rising and sinking in the water, so that every now and again their heads came into view and then disappeared.

'Once I've tied ropes to some plummets, we can help them

245

if necessary.' With a look of satisfaction Haraldur poked his ruddy face into the wheelhouse.

'Should I take over?'

'By all means,' I said, before stepping outside. I didn't much feel like handling another man's boat in the confusion that was about to ensue.

The sun was about to break through and the sea was completely still. There was no better weather for driving a pod of whales to land. Only now did I catch sight of the leader's boat, which with a Faroese flag on the rear was sailing between the whales and the boats. Most engines were idle, so the sounds from the whales could be clearly heard. Then there was a call from the leader's boat:

'Drive the whales!'

In a flash the engines were put into gear and the sound of the boats covered all other sounds. The mass of boats moved towards the pilot whales and rocks were thrown into the water to drive them towards land. It nevertheless took some time before the whales understood that it wasn't a good idea to stay where they were any longer. Slowly they moved towards the shore, while the men and boats made as much noise as possible. Then the pod started to move faster and the boats followed them so that they wouldn't have an opportunity to stop and realise what was happening to them.

We stayed near the group of boats and headed slightly northwards with some of them so that the whales would head for Syðrugøta. As the hunt was well organised and no one was sailing in front of the pod, it all went very quickly. But as the whales neared the beach and the water became shallower, they stopped, as if they suspected danger. A whaling spear was sent into the tail of one of the whales at the back and blood spurted out. The wounded whale shot forwards and within a second all of them darted towards the shore. The pod created a foaming wave before them and before they realised it, they had swum ashore.

Whalers teemed forwards from all sides, throwing themselves into battle with shiny knives. The whales' throats were cut at violent speed and before long the sea was red with blood. It was noisy, with the air filled with calls and shouts. Beyond the beach boats sailed back and forth to stop the few whales that hadn't yet beached from escaping.

We were in the midst of the action and even I felt the primal instincts of a hunter; an intoxicating feeling of the joy of life amid the slaughter. Suddenly I caught side of Alan McLeod. He was on board one of the larger boats, the sort we used to call Greenland boats. I saw him nudge the guy who was steering and point over to us.

What on earth was he thinking?

The driver turned the boat and they slowly approached us. Alan was in blue overalls, so he was hardly here as a tourist. I told Haraldur that a boat was heading for us, but he was so excited by the hunt that it didn't register.

I took hold of a rope with a plummet, in case we needed to defend ourselves, but Alan McLeod was laughing heartily, pointing at himself and then at us.

What did he want?

From the movements of his mouth, I could see that he was saying something, but there was such a noise that you couldn't hear anything. The Greenland boat was next to us now and the Scot indicated that I should come closer. I moved over to the low railing and asked as loudly as I could what he wanted.

He put his hand behind his ear to indicate that he didn't understand what I was saying. I put the rope and plummet down and leaned over the railing. Alan McLeod did the same, so I was looking straight into the smiling, blue eyes in that fair, bearded face.

He stretched out his right arm as if he were going to shake my hand. Slightly confused I offered my hand and in the next moment I was thrown overboard.

Fifty-Two

The first thing I noticed was the cold. The water was freezing. And I couldn't see anything. Everything was murky and there was a violent noise from the motors and screeching whales. I touched the sandy ground, so I realised which way was up and which was down, but I didn't dare go to the surface. Without a doubt Alan was ready up there with something to hammer into my head as soon as it came into view.

I heard a boat passing above me, but couldn't see anything. I had to get away, while making sure that the propellers didn't hack me to pieces, which is probably what the Scot had been planning.

Which way was away? I twisted and turned on the seabed as I took off my duffle coat and kicked off my boots. I headed in the direction where there was least noise. I counted my strokes as I swam. When I got to ten, my lungs were close to exploding and I made for the surface.

Being able to take a breath was like a gift from God, but about fifteen metres ahead against the sunlight I could see Alan McLeod's back. He was bent over, looking down into the water.

'Bastard,' I thought. I dived down again and swam further out. If the two of them on the Greenland boat discovered me, they'd no doubt sail me down. It was a maximum of two hundred metres over to the quayside, but it was the coldest swim I had ever experienced. And even though I tried to swim faster and faster and didn't go below the surface, I was frozen stiff when I reached the boat ramp. I staggered ashore and shook like a dog.

I needed to let Haraldur know that I was alive, but first I had to get warm. I knew some people in the village and knocked on the door of one house, which was highest on the hill above the quayside. My friend's wife opened the door.

'Good gracious!' She put her hand over her mouth. 'Is that Hannis? Did you fall overboard? You poor thing.' She was about seventy, a little shorter than average, thin and animated with curly hair. 'Don't just stand there – come in and get some dry clothes on.'

She took me by the arm and pulled me into the entrance hall.

'But I'm dripping…'

'So what? That can be dried. It's not every day we have a hunt here.' She opened the door to a bathroom and pushed me inside.

'Take your clothes off and get under the shower. You'll warm up. I'll find some of my husband's clothes for you to put on.' She closed the door.

As I took my clothes off, my teeth were chattering from the cold. I got into the shower and made the water as hot as I could stand. And today that was quite a lot.

For the first five minutes I continued to shake, but then it eased, and once I'd been under the flow of hot water for a quarter of an hour, I started to feel like a person again. In the meantime, the lady had fetched some clothes and given me underwear, socks and overalls.

Half an hour later I was wearing clogs and far too large, green overalls on my way down to the beach. I had eaten homemade rolls, drunk coffee and felt good again. At the same time anger was boiling. How could I have let myself be tricked by that arsehole? I'd pay him back. With interest.

Down on the beach they were already tying ropes to the whales and dragging them to the large ramp by the quay. Most people had disappeared back into the village and you could already hear the singing that accompanies Faroese dancing in the distance. On the other hand, the place was teeming with children, who were poking the dead whales with knives and daggers. One brave boy tried to cut himself a piece of blubber from the head of a whale, but the adults were furious and chased him away. The girls stood back, watching and giggling. Individual boats sailed back and forth out on the sea, but other than the ones that had hauled the whales, most of the boats were now side-by-side between the jetties.

Haraldur was there tying up one whale that was mostly on the beach. When he caught sight of me, he straightened himself up and laughed. There was a trail of blood from the shaft of his knife running down to his inner thigh.

'108 whales! The two of us will do well out of that!' Haraldur had got his share all right.

'You disappeared?' he continued. 'For a moment I wondered whether you'd gone over, but a nice Scot from one of the other boats told me he'd seen you jump on to another boat. What did you do that for? And why are you wearing overalls?' he asked in surprise.

'That Scot is a lying bastard,' I burst out. 'He pulled me overboard, hoping the propellers would tear me to shreds.'

Haraldur stood there with his mouth wide open and his blood-soaked hands hanging lifelessly.

'Fortunately I got away from the boats and managed to swim to the boat ramp. I went to a friend's house and they gave me all this.' I pulled at the overalls. 'The man of the house weighs at least fifty kilos more than me.'

'That Scottish swine!' said Haraldur emphatically. 'I'll personally...'

'Do you know where he is?' I asked.

'No, I don't remember seeing him after I spoke to him.' Haraldur looked around. 'I don't think he's here. Maybe up in the village.'

'I doubt it. No doubt he sneaked off once he thought he'd done away with me. No, he'll be heading to Tórshavn. Which is exactly what I plan to do,' I added.

'What about your share? You can't miss out on that. I've registered two of us and a boat.' Haraldur looked at me in amazement.

'No, there's no reason why my share should go to waste. If you're happy enough to take it home, you can have it.'

'Don't you worry about that,' said Haraldur, pleased. 'I'll

probably stay here tonight. I'm sure there'll be a big party. But tomorrow I'll come to Tórshavn with your share and mine and we can talk then about what will happen to yours. Don't you think Duruta would like some fresh whale meat?'

I ignored the fact that now Haraldur had also started to tease me about my relationship with Duruta. Right now I couldn't care less about whale meat and the party here tonight. I just wanted to get to Tórshavn and catch up with Alan McLeod.

'If that Scot is bothering you so much, phone Karl and ask him to arrest him,' said Haraldur seriously.

'On what grounds? That he pulled me overboard? It's his word against mine. You didn't see anything and probably don't know what boat he was on either.'

'No, I didn't pay any attention to that.'

'Then we have nothing on him. I need to go to Tórshavn myself to sort this out. And that can't happen soon enough.'

Fifty-Three

Darkness was starting to fall by the time the lorry set me down on Jóannes Paturssonargøta. It was on its way to the old people's home and to Lágargarður with a whale for each. Fortunately I had kept my keys in my trouser pocket out of habit, so I wasn't forced in break into my own house. On the other hand, my mobile phone was somewhere on the beach in Gøta. It was hardly going to work now anyway.

I went into the living room, phoned Duruta and explained to her that unfortunately I had other things I needed to do that evening, but that I would go round tomorrow.

'You're always welcome, Hannis.' That rang around my head once I'd put the receiver down. Who knew whether the two of us might one day…? And her daughter was really lovely.

I pushed all thoughts of Duruta, her daughter and cosy nights in to one side and dialled Karl's number.

'Have you found another body?' Karl asked sarcastically, once Katrin had dragged him away from a Danish crime series on the television.

'No, I haven't,' I answered drily. 'But I have seen more than enough death for one day.'

'What do you mean?' Now he was curious.

'I've been to a whale hunt in Gøta with Haraldur.'

'Ah, screw you. I thought something was wrong.' You could hear the relief in his voice. 'How come you're in Tórshavn already?'

'Haraldur's taking care of the whale meat and blubber and will sail back tomorrow. I had some things to take care of, and that brings me to what I needed to ask you.'

'Yes?' His tone was inquisitive yet sceptical.

'Did you ever find out who owns the yellow house above Boðanes?'

'It wasn't hard to find out who owns the house and the land around it. It's the company that's going to be putting up the new townhouses. But they say that they don't know anything about anyone living in or using the house. They say it's stood empty for several years and if anyone has been there, they've broken in.'

'Then how can it be that there's water in the taps? In a house that's supposed to be empty?'

'Now you're asking more than I can tell you. Presumably someone or other from the council has forgotten to turn off the water. What do I know? Why are you asking?'

'I was just curious to find out who's been hanging out there recently. Whether they had permission or not.'

'According to the owner, no one has rented it,' said Karl a little distantly. 'That crime series…'.

'You go back to your made-up crime stories.' As I put the receiver down I heard Karl call: 'Don't you go interfering in…!'

I went upstairs and got out some clothes. I was glad to be out of those tent-like overalls. Then I went up into the attic with a torch to find my gun.

Shortly afterwards I was sitting in the kitchen greasing my Remington. I took another glass of whisky. The gun had been well put away, so that wasn't a problem, but I was a little more doubtful about the cartridges that were about ten years old. They would have to do. Five calibre 12 cartridges were loaded into the chamber and I was ready.

Fifty-Four

Upstairs at Heljareyga, nothing seemed to be out of the ordinary. There was no one around. It was about ten o'clock on a Monday night, so you'd expect someone to be home, but there was no answer from Alan McLeod or Robin Nimier. I put my gun down and opened the door into the attic with my pocket knife. Here things had changed. A large black suitcase on wheels was standing in the middle of the room and on the bed were the clothes that had been in the wardrobe. On top of the clothes was Alan McLeod's guitar in a bag. But the man himself wasn't to be found.

Where on earth could he be? He'd clearly been planning to leave, but where was he now?

I went into the corridor and closed the door behind me. I put my gun under my wind jacket, which was the only coat I still owned. The whole shaft was sticking out, but I tried to hold it down by my thigh so that it wasn't so obvious.

Once I had got outside, I turned down Dr Jakobsensgøta and slowly walked down to the Káta Hornið junction, holding the gun tightly all the while. The weather was beautiful and calm and the stars could clearly be seen. The moon looked like a thin sail in the sky. Nevertheless, the streets were almost empty.

I continued down to the harbour and made sure the gun was on the side away from the road. But the whole way down to Café Natúr I only met two people and neither of them suspected anything. I put the weapon in the bushes below the Danish Governor's residence and went into the pub along Kongabrúgvin.

It was rammed full with people and the smoke billowed

back and forth under the ceiling. Most were men, a number of them were known bums, but there were some women too. The music was playing loudly, but although it was in English, I couldn't understand a word. I went over to the bar and asked a busy young man with long, blond hair whether he had seen Alan McLeod.

'Yeah, he was here not long ago.' He looked around the room. 'No, he's gone.'

'You don't know where he's gone?'

'You never know where Alan is.' The blond man smiled as he spoke. 'But he's probably off somewhere or other with one of his girlfriends.'

'What do you mean?'

'You don't look old enough to have forgotten what to do with women,' the young man said impertinently.

I leaned over the bar, grabbed the man by his hair and pulled him down to the counter.

'A couple of hours ago someone tried to kill me, so I'm not really in the mood for insolent morons,' I whispered into his ear.

'Let go, dickhead!' he almost howled.

'I'll let go of you when you tell me where Alan hangs out.'

'I don't know.' He tried to grab hold of my hand, but I pulled his head over the edge of the counter so that he couldn't get out of it.

'Ow, ow, for God's sake!' Now people had started to notice that not everything was as it should be over by the bar. 'Try the house at Yviri við Strond,' he finally said in a choked voice.

I felt a hand on my shoulder, so I let go of the blond man and turned around. It was a barmaid in her twenties. She had a dark complexion and black curly hair.

'What are you doing?' she asked. I looked into her brown eyes, which reminded me a little of Duruta's.

'Just messing around,' I said, before walking to the door and leaving. I could feel everyone in the pub looking at me.

With my gun under my jacket again, I walked up through Krókabrekka, along Krákusteinur and down onto the main road. So the house by Lágargarður was Alan McLeod's lovenest. Among other things. Who knew whether he'd dared go back there again? Not a week had passed since the Dutchman had been found there, but the police wouldn't still be keeping an eye on the place.

Twenty minutes later I was close to the yellow house. The line of windows that faced south were dark, but at a little window above there was light between the frame and the lowered blinds. This time I had a little pocket torch with me. I had gone into a kiosk at the bottom of Jónas Broncksgøta and bought one the size of a fountain pen.

I walked up the concrete stairs and shone the light on the front door. On the handle there were the remains of some red and white plastic tape. Someone had ripped through it. I opened the door and in the beam of light I could see that the place had been tidied. The junk had gone. That was presumably the work of the building company. Then I heard a woman's silvery voice laughing upstairs. I cautiously climbed the stairs. Once I was on the landing I turned the torch off and listened.

You could hear groaning from the room that I had turned the light on in, the room that had a mattress on the floor. I let the two of them carry on with their game, turned my torch back on and walked to the large room. The door was ajar and I pushed it open. The hinges squeaked and I held my breath. But the love-hungry pair carried on with their play and had evidently not heard anything.

The stove was still in the middle of the room, but there was no heat now. Otherwise the room was exactly as it had been. With the exception of Joost Boidin. I put my torch in my pocket and with my gun ready slowly walked back to the other room. It was quiet inside. Then I heard Alan McLeod's voice.

'You like that, my darlin' ?'

I had pushed the handle down and chose now to kick the door open.

On the mattress on the floor were the Scot and the girl from the Prime Minister's Office, the one with the various colours in her hair. Alan was in a white shirt and the girl was only wearing the black velvet choker with the silver medallion. She was pretty.

'If you move as much as an inch, I'll shoot you!' I said in English, taking aim at Alan McLeod's chest.

The girl started to squeal and shook her arms with clenched fists.

'Shut up and get lost!'

She stopped immediately and started to gather her clothes together. All the while I kept my eyes on the Scot, who sat on the floor, smiling.

'So you're not dead,' he said, matter-of-factly.

'Shut it!'

I could see that he was still grinning. It would take more than this to scare a former member of the SAS.

The light in the room was coming from a paraffin lamp that was hanging on the wall. The yellowish light suggested a cosy night in, but there was still something eerie about the long shadows it cast.

The girl had started to sob.

'I need to talk to Alan,' I said. 'If you get out of here now and keep your mouth shut, I won't tell anyone down at the office about this.'

I didn't dare take my attention away from the man on the mattress, but I heard the girl's barefoot footsteps disappearing down the stairs.

'Alone at last,' smiled the half-naked man.

Fifty-Five

Most of all I wanted to blow the bastard to smithereens as he sat there smiling ironically at me. But I didn't think that would be a good idea. The result would just be me having to do time.

'Put your underwear on, but slowly.' With the gun I pointed to a pair of black boxers that were lying on the floor.

Alan cautiously stretched his right arm across the floor. He took hold of the underwear and asked:

'Was that slow enough or do you want me to take my time?'

'Shut up!' was the only thing I could think of to respond.

Once he'd put his boxer shorts on, I told him to get up, take down the paraffin lamp and come with me.

I backed out of the door and into the larger room. Alan McLeod followed me with the lamp in his hand. He was ready to pounce on me at any time, but I had my finger on the trigger, so it wouldn't take much for a shot to go off.

'Put the lamp on the table and sit down on the floor with your back to the sofa.'

Once he'd put the lamp down, Alan walked the few steps over to the sofa, but remained standing in front of it, facing it.

'If you're thinking of trying anything, you're a dead man,' I said, stressing every word.

Alan turned around and smiled.

'It's annoying that you didn't end up in the boat propellers in Gøta.' He sat on the floor and crossed his legs.

'How did you know I was in Gøta?' I asked.

'I saw you and that fat guy board his boat and at that same time we heard about the pod of whales. I guessed you were on your way there. And I thought that a whale hunt was the best place to do away with someone who's going around causing problems.'

'No, you environmentalists don't have much respect for human life,' I said mockingly.

'Why should we?'

'Well, because human life is sacred, for Christ's sake!' I myself could hear how hollow that sounded when it didn't come from a lectern.

'Ha!' Alan laughed. 'You haven't been where I've been and seen what I've seen. Respect for human life. Respect for human life in large parts of Africa is zilch. And in the Middle East and the Balkans. And here among us too when it comes down to it. As long as we're happy, have enough to eat and something to warm ourselves with, everything's hunky-dory. As soon as there are real problems, all so-called humanity disappears and people are simply animals like the rest.'

The former SAS man had clearly lost all illusions as regards humanity.

'I choose the animals every time. They don't hurt anyone.' His eyes were glowing.

'They tear each other to pieces,' I protested.

'Yes, because they need to. People destroy and kill everything that gets in their way. And not least on these windswept islands. You have all you need and more, but you still kill whales. A completely innocent animal that does nothing to you and that you don't need to kill.'

There was no point trying to discuss anything with this man. His attitude towards the whales was absolutely clear: they were not to be killed.

I changed the subject. 'Why did you kill Jenny McEwan and Stewart Peters?'

'Who says it was me?' He gave me a sarcastic look.

'There's no doubt that you killed Joost Boidin and presumably the same person killed the two Scots. Why kill two of your own?'

Alan McLeod suddenly looked very tired. He rubbed his hand across his forehead.

'They weren't Scots. They were from northern England, just educated in Scotland. Well, it's all the same. I liked them, but their consciences were starting to get the better of them. Spreading ISA across the whole country was a terrible burden for them and they were planning to tell the authorities. Fortunately I work at the Prime Minister's Office, so I knew they'd requested a meeting. Then it was just a case of getting them out of the way before the meeting. Luckily the whale hunt gave me an opportunity to do away with them and make life tough for the Faroese.' He smiled in self-satisfaction.

'Mark Robbins didn't agree with you.'

'Mark Robbins!' he said mockingly. 'That weakling! As soon as someone dies, GOS send that office boy up here to poke about. And then he gets in touch with you and asks you to investigate the murders.' Alan McLeod snorted with contempt. 'There was nothing to do but finish him off.'

'Did you place the bomb on his plane yourself?' I asked.

'No, I'm not really up on explosives. A friend came up on a flight from Copenhagen and headed back that evening. You know, old boys' network and all that.'

'What about Jenny's pocket diary? You didn't find that?'

'What diary? I don't know anything about that.' There was no reason to believe that he wasn't telling the truth. Presumably Sonni Christiansen had turned the whole place over looking for the diary.

I took a packet of cigarettes out of my pocket, still making sure that the gun was aimed at the Scot on the floor.

'Want a cigarette?' I showed him the packet.

'No, I've given up. It's much too dangerous.' He laughed out loud, but suddenly stopped and looked up at me again. It was obvious that he was off his head.

I lit a cigarette and something suddenly came to me. 'Who helped you with the two youngsters? You weren't alone when you put them among the whales.'

'No, I forced the salmon boss to help me. He was dead scared, but I told him he'd end up like the others if he didn't help. Afterwards he was so afraid and unreliable that he had to be taken out of the equation too.'

Alan MacLeod laughed loudly. 'You should have seen his face when I cut his throat.' He indicated with a finger from one ear to the other across his throat. 'Don't you think it was a good idea to throw him in the fishing ring?'

I didn't answer, but asked instead: 'Where were Jenny and Stewart killed?'

'Here.' The big man on the floor indicated the room we were in with his hand. 'And Joost Boidin, as you already know.' He smiled. 'But it was a little unfortunate.'

'What was unfortunate?'

'That I had to go to Iceland the day after I killed the Dutch guy. He'd seen me with the salmon boss and started to have his suspicions. He'd also found something out over at Sound Salmon. He followed me out here and then phoned you, if I'm not mistaken?' He looked questioningly at me.

'Yes, he phoned me. But what's this about Iceland?'

'On Sunday morning they phoned from the Prime Minister's Office and said that I had to go to a committee meeting about whale hunting that same day in Reykjavik. The upshot of it was that I didn't get to move the body and when I came back late on Wednesday evening, you'd been here.' He shrugged his shoulders.

'How could you leave a dead man in the room?'

'None of the young ones who hang out up here would go into a room I'd locked. I can guarantee that.' He spoke emphatically.

I was happy to believe him.

Then it dawned on me. 'You were in Iceland from Sunday to Wednesday evening?'

'Yes,' he answered.

'So you're not the one who shot at me west of Tvøroyri?'

'I've never been to the southern islands,' Alan answered.

'So you're not the one who shot at me in Sund either?'

'No, I've never shot at you. I prefer to use knives. It's more natural.' Even though a gun was pointed straight at him and he was sitting on the floor, he looked pleased with himself.

'So who has been shooting at me this whole time?'

'That was me,' said a female voice in English behind me. I turned around and saw Robin Nimier in the doorway with a rifle in her hands. The barrel was aimed at me.

Fifty-Six

'You took your time,' said Alan McLeod as he got up. 'I've been sitting here entertaining your friend for a good long while now. He came along and wrecked my goodbye screw.'

'I don't care what you and your tarts get up to.' The blonde-haired woman's voice was firm. 'Put some clothes on instead of walking round like a moron.'

'Well, well,' Alan teased. 'Who's rattled your cage this evening? You know that we Scots don't wear anything under our kilts.' Nevertheless, he walked out the door and into the other room, where you could hear him cursing over how dark it was.

'So you're the one who's been shooting at me all these times?' I looked at the elegant woman with the rifle. She was in the same light blue coat that she'd been wearing earlier today and brown leather boots.

'Yes, that's right.' Now she smiled and the whole room lit up. 'But it's not something I'm going to boast about. Twice I've tried to get you and twice you've got away.'

'Maybe I should have guessed it was you when you called him Alan McLean. I couldn't quite get that to fit with how meticulous you were otherwise.'

'I know.' Her look became serious. 'As soon as I'd said it, I cursed myself and hoped you hadn't noticed it. But you did.'

'Yeah, but it didn't mean anything to me. I thought you'd maybe had an affair with him and had got over it now. I never guessed you were the sniper. I just assumed it was a man.'

'That's this world for you. Women aren't considered equal to men. But sometimes that's an advantage.' She took two steps towards me. 'Sit down!' She pointed at one of the chairs by the dining table with the rifle.

I sat down. I still had my gun in my hand, but it didn't seem to bother the white woman from Africa.

'Put your gun on the floor.'

I did as she said.

'There's one thing I don't get,' I said. 'At Sund, why didn't you shoot me before I got into the car?'

'I didn't want to shoot you in the back.' She laughed to herself. 'I've been doing this for almost ten years.' She clapped the rifle with her right hand. 'But I've never shot anyone in the back. It's pride, I suppose. It's a cowardly thing to do. Maybe that's a little stupid, but that's how it is.'

Alan McLeod came in. He wasn't wearing a kilt, but dark blue trousers. But he looked just as Scottish as he had at Café Natúr. His jacket had silver buttons and his waistcoat was tartan.

'So do you both work for Guardians of the Sea?'

'Hell, no!' laughed Alan. 'They're a bunch of wusses. Talk big and do nothing. You saw how good they were with the two they sent up here. As soon as it really mattered, they lost their bottle. And their babysitter wasn't much better.'

'Babysitter?' I asked curiously.

'Yep, that snazzy Mark Robbins.'

'How about tying up Hannis Martinsson?' Robin Nimier chipped in.

So she knew what I was called. I reckoned I had told her at some point, but still.

'Why not just cut his throat now?' Alan lifted up one trouser leg and took out a dagger. The blade was about three inches long.

'This is my sgian-dubh. Sharp as anything.' He ran his thumb along the edge.

'No,' said Robin Nimier curtly. 'Tie him up first and then we'll worry about the rest later.'

The knife disappeared back under Alan's trouser leg and the Scot started to look for something to tie me up with.

'What organisation do you work for?' I asked, trying to keep this going as long as possible.

'We don't work for the same organisation,' Robin answered. 'Alan's involved with one of the more extreme environmental organisations. One that fights cases on behalf of trees and ants.'

'And if we didn't, who would?' asked Alan, who had found a washing line in a drawer. 'Trees and ants can't do it themselves, so obviously others have to take it upon themselves. We can't allow people, who are all arseholes, to behave as they see fit.'

He pulled my arms behind my back and tied my hands together. Then he tied my ankles tightly.

'The package is ready to be sent to hell,' he smiled.

'Put him on the sofa,' said the woman with the rifle.

'Why?' asked the Scot.

'Just do what I tell you to do!' she replied.

'OK.' He picked me up under my arms and threw me onto the sofa, so that I was lying on my right side, looking into the room.

'That's that,' he said, before sitting down on the chair I had been sitting on.

Robin Nimier walked over to Alan McLeod, pointed the rifle at his ear and fired.

Fifty-Seven

Alan McLeod fell sideways on to the dining table, which meant that he remained seated. A trail of blood flowed on to the table top.

'Why did you do that?' I asked, astonished.

'It's my job. That's what I get paid for.' She placed two fingers on the Scot's throat to feel whether there was a pulse.

'And am I going to meet the same fate?' I could hear that my voice was shaking. Who's brave when he's about to be executed?

'Why's that?' She looked genuinely surprised.

'Well…'

'Ah, because I tried to kill you before and now I have the chance?' She laughed to herself. 'No, that's not how I roll. There's no reason to kill you any more, so I won't. I've done my job and I'll get my money. I don't go around killing random people.'

'Why did you try to kill me on Suðuroy then?'

'Because you didn't take my warning shot seriously, but carried on snooping around. And when I wasn't lucky there, I tried again later. Fortunately for you, I didn't do any better there. In the meantime, Alan rocked the boat more than necessary.' She looked down at the fair-haired Scot, who sat there with his mouth open and eyes staring into thin air.

Robin Nimier left the room and I heard her go down the stairs. Shortly afterwards she was back with a shiny little metal case. She placed it on the table and opened it, before starting to take her rifle apart. She was fast – she'd done this before.

Once she'd closed the lid again, she said, 'And then there's you.' She looked down at me.

'It won't do for you to rush over to the police and tell them everything that's happened. So you'll have to stay lying there until I'm well and truly away from here. There's a flight to Copenhagen early tomorrow morning at eight. At some point in the afternoon I'll phone someone so that you don't end up a skeleton.'

'Did you break into my house and take the postcard?'

'Yes, you have to have some fun.' She smiled. 'And I'm the one who paid a visit to your office, but I didn't find Mark Robbins' envelope.'

'How did you know that he gave me an envelope?'

'When I saw him go into your office, I went to the other side of the harbour and into a storehouse. That's where I later shot you from. With my telescope I could observe what went on between you two.'

She paused and then asked: 'Where did you hide the envelope? I don't imagine you'd have it on you?'

'On the floor below my office there's an old electricity meter in a black plastic box. I taped the envelope to the inside of the box.'

Robin Nimier looked at me with respect. 'It's always hardest to see through amateurs.'

She turned to leave. I called after her.

'If you don't work for the same people as Alan McLeod, who do you work for?'

She half turned back. 'Who asked me to make sure that things here change according to their agenda? It doesn't matter. But I can tell you that the Faroese economy is weaker than ever before and new drilling permits are to be issued.'

Robin Nimier walked through the door with the metal case in her hand. She lifted her left hand and waved with her fingers without turning around. Then she was gone.

Oil! That had never occurred to me. I had always wondered how the environmental organisations seemed to have such an easy time of it on the Faroes. But if there were oil interests behind it all, that was a different story. Countries went to war over oil, so why not take a little country to the verge of bankruptcy just to get drilling rights?

Those bastards! First they get GOS to spread ISA and the psychopath Alan McLeod to stoke the fire. With him nearby, they knew there would be trouble. Then they send a professional sniper to clear up the mess if necessary.

Ein finna tú ert í talvinum, har pengarnir fólkið flyta, I hummed. You're just a pawn in a game of chess when money is moving the pieces.

The paraffin lamp illuminated the table that the dead man was sitting at, as if turned to stone. Through the window I saw the stars and the waning moon.

I lay there, waiting.

Epilogue

If they find a proper elephant, that is, a large oil field, then many people will move to the Faroe Islands and maybe we'll get a proper football team.

Faroese businessman

Robin Nimier, or whatever her real name was, kept her word. At about five o'clock the next day I heard footsteps downstairs and before long Karl walked into the room I was in. I got the usual snide remarks about death and me, but he loosened the ropes that bound me. Other than being thirsty and half-frozen, I was fine. My pride was hurt, but I was alive.

Down at the station it was a relief that Piddi had left. Karl and one other guy heard my explanation and weren't any more sarcastic than usual. Several times they said I was exaggerating or imagining things, but bit by bit, as I put the individual puzzle pieces together, they had to admit that there could well be something in what I was telling them. They acknowledged that the ISA virus had been deliberately spread across the various Faroese fisheries and that there was a conspiracy behind the attacks on the Faroes. The extent to which the two English youngsters had been killed to stoke the fire, they doubted, but they had to admit that it wasn't impossible. They didn't protest either against both of those things being blamed on the dead Scot.

As far as Robin Nimier was concerned, they didn't know what to think. They knew that she had been on the morning flight to Copenhagen that morning, but that no one at

Kastrup was in a position to tell them where she'd gone after that. I tried to tell them that it wasn't that strange, because it was highly unlikely that she was called Robin Nimier and thousands of people passed through the Danish airport every day. When I asked them how they'd found out where I was, they said that a woman had phoned the station. I pressed them and discovered that the call had come from London and that the woman had spoken English. They maintained that that did not prove that it was the same person who had lived in Heljareyga and according to me – they stressed that bit – had killed Alan McLeod. Who else it could have been, they didn't say.

It was almost ten o'clock as I walked up Jónas Broncksgøta on my way to Duruta's house. At the police station we had also spoken about how the attacks on the Faroes would probably stop now that the culprits were either dead or had disappeared. Maybe the evidence against the Scot and Jenny McEwan's pocket diary could be used against the environmental organisations. But we doubted that. That there might be oil interests behind the aggression – that it was directly financed by them – didn't interest them at all. On the contrary, they asked me to keep quiet about that kind of thing as it might cause immeasurable damage to the Faroes if it got into the newspapers. Then maybe no one would drill for oil after all!

But what was going around my head more than anything was what Karl said to me just as I was leaving.

'Stop finding dead bodies now. Go up to your girlfriend and your daughter instead and have a break.'

I asked what he meant.

'Are you so bloody blind that you can't see that Turið is the spitting image of you?'

'I'm not Turið's father,' I objected.

'Work out how long it's been since you left the Faroes and how old Turið is. It's almost eight years since you left and Turið is seven. And I can guarantee that Duruta wasn't fooling around with anyone else around that time.'

'Why hasn't she said anything?' I stuttered.

'Because she's proud and wants you to work it out for yourself. The rest of us worked it out ages ago.'

As I turned into Hoyvíksvegur, I felt a mixture of warmth and fear in my chest. I had to admit that Leonard Cohen was onto something when he said that you don't know what it is to be scared until you're a father.

Translator's Note

In recent years Scandinavian crime fiction has ridden something of a wave of popularity in the United Kingdom. Fans of this 'Nordic Noir' may be surprised to learn that the Faroe Islands, the smallest Scandinavian nation with just 50,000 people, have their own crime fiction writers. The most prominent by far is Jógvan Isaksen, with the best known of his books focusing on 'consultant' Hannis Martinsson. With nine titles in the series at present, the books have proved very popular on the islands. Yet the reach of these stories has already expanded beyond the Faroes' rocky shores and translations of various parts of the series have appeared in Danish, German and Icelandic. It is exciting that Isaksen's stories about this exotic, little-known yet so not-so-distant island nation will be brought to an even larger international audience through their translation into English.

For this translation I have essentially had the rare but fortunate opportunity to have two original texts to work from. The Danish version of *Walpurgis Tide*, *Korsmesse* (Torgard, 2009), was translated by Jógvan Isaksen himself. Although my English translation is, of course, heavily based upon the Faroese original, Isaksen's Danish text proved useful as an insight into how he felt certain aspects of Faroese culture could best be framed for a non-Faroese audience. As one would expect, Isaksen also made other slight and infrequent alterations to his narrative the second time around and these are largely reflected in the English translation.

My heartfelt thanks go to the entire Norvik Press team for the considerable effort they have put into making the publication of *Walpurgis Tide* a reality. Individual mention must be made of Marita Fraser and Elettra Carbone, but particular thanks must be extended to Janet Garton for her excellent editorial work.

John Keithsson

DAN TURÈLL

Murder in the Dark

(translated by Mark Mussari)

Murder in the Dark sports a winning combination of engaging crime narrative and cool, unsentimental appraisal of Scandinavian society (as seen through the eyes of its shabby, unconventional anti-hero). There are elements of the book which now seem quite as relevant as when they were written, and like all the most accomplished writing in the Nordic Noir field, there is an acute and well-observed sense of place throughout the novel. The descriptions of Copenhagen channel the poetic sensibility which is the author's own: "Copenhagen is at its most beautiful when seen out of a taxi at midnight, right at that magical moment when one day dies and another is born, and the printing presses are buzzing with the morning newspapers".

Murder in the Dark
ISBN 9781870041980
UK £11.95
(Paperback, 282 pages)

BENNY ANDERSEN

The Contract Killer

(translated by Paul Russell Garrett)

Karlsen is a down-on-his-luck private investigator looking for work. When the only job on offer is a contract killing, Karlsen agrees despite his lack of experience. Things don't go to plan and it seems the contract is open to negotiation. The play follows the twists and turns of an inexperienced contract killer with a weakness for turquoise dresses and wide-eyed women. This absurdist comedy by one of Denmark's best-loved writers sees the fates of the eponymous contract killer, his target, the employer and his wife, twist, turn and hang in the balance. What is a life worth? Who will survive? And will the hair dye ever make it to Pakistan?

The Contract Killer
ISBN 9781870041782
UK £5.95
(Paperback, 50 pages)

JØRGEN-FRANZ JACOBSEN

Barbara

(translated by George Johnston)

Originally written in Danish, *Barbara* was the only novel by the
Faroese author Jørgen-Frantz Jacobsen (1900-38), yet it quickly
achieved international best-seller status and is still one of the best-
loved classics of Danish and Faroese literature. On the face of it,
Barbara is a straightforward historical romance. It contains a story
of passion in an exotic setting with overtones of semi-piracy; there
is a powerful erotic element, an outsider who breaks up a marriage,
and a built-in inevitability resulting from Barbara's own psychological
make-up. She stands as one of the most complex female characters
in modern Scandinavian literature: beautiful, passionate, devoted,
amoral and uncomprehending of her own tragedy. Jørgen-Frantz
Jacobsen portrays her with fascinated devotion.

Barbara
ISBN 9781909408074
UK £11.95
(Paperback, 306 pages)

AUGUST STRINDBERG

The People of Hemsö

(translated by Peter Graves)

The People of Hemsö (1887) will come as a surprise to most English-language readers, used as they are to seeing the bitter controversialist of plays like *The Father* and *Miss Julie* or the seeker for cosmic meaning and reconciliation of those mysterious later dream plays *To Damascus* and *A Dream Play*. This novel, a tragicomic story of lust, love and death among the fishermen and farmers of the islands of the Stockholm archipelago, reveals a very different Strindberg. The vigour and humour of the narration, as well as its cinematic qualities, are such that we witness a great series of peopled panoramas in which place and time and character are somehow simultaneously specific and archetypical, and we leave the novel with memories of grand landscapes and spirited scenes.

In a recent essay Ludvig Rasmusson wrote: 'For me, *The People of Hemsö* is the Great Swedish Novel, just as ... *The Adventures of Huckleberry Finn* [is] the Great American Novel'. His comparison is an apt one: if the Mississippi becomes the quintessence of America, the island of Hemsö and the archipelago become the quintessence of Sweden.

The People of Hemsö
ISBN 9781870041959
UK £11.95
(Paperback, 164 pages)

Printed in December 2022
by Rotomail Italia S.p.A., Vignate (MI) - Italy